Never Hurt Me

Never Hurt Me

SHAWN McGUIRE

Shawn McGuire 2015

This book is a work of fiction. Names, characters, places, and events are products of the author's imagination or are used fictitiously. Any resemblance to actual events, locales, or persons, living or dead, is entirely coincidental.

ISBN 978-0-9961035-4-1
ISBN 978-0-9961035-5-8 (ebook)

Published by Brown Bag Books

www.Shawn-McGuire.com
www.Facebook.com/ShawnMcGuireAuthor

Cover Design by Karri Klawiter
www.artbykarri.com

Other Titles by Shawn McGuire

THE WISH MAKERS Series:

Sticks and Stones
Break My Bones
Never Hurt Me

For Eli

Because you said hippies are cool. Just like you.
I love you!

Chapter One

I'd never gotten close to any of my charges. Not that I hadn't cared about them, I had. It's just that I was put on their life path to do a job, not to become attached to them. We were never meant to have long-lasting relationships. Then came Mandy and Crissy.

In a little more than three months, those girls had become a permanent part of *my* life path. I'd do anything for them. That's why instinct took over when Crissy was being attacked. I hadn't thought, I'd just reacted. The call afterward to appear before Kaf, my boss, didn't surprise me. The fact that he'd waited so long did. Crissy's wish had ended days ago. Maybe the delay was a timeout, of sorts, so I could think about what I'd done.

I found King Kaf at the very back of his cave seated on a throne. An actual one this time, made of gold and emerald instead of the cloud formation he usually perched upon. Very formal. That couldn't be good. Orange and green smoke swirled behind him like an acid trip through a kaleidoscope. He had his big book, his compendium of wishes, out and opened to a specific page. One that had been bookmarked by a strip of tie-dyed fabric.

"Is that from my shirt?" I asked.

Like a kid caught stealing a second dessert, he hesitated before answering, "It is."

I'd been wearing that shirt the day we entered into our arrangement. I had jumped from the car I'd been riding in a split-second before it went over the edge of the road. Still, I tumbled a good seventy-five yards down the embankment before coming to a stop. I was broken and bloodied, barely conscious when Kaf appeared, my clothes little more than shreds.

"I don't know if that's a sweet souvenir or a twisted stalker-thing," I said of the saved shirt strip.

As I stood before him my hands started to sweat, my heart to race. I tried to cross my arms, but they wouldn't stay where I placed them so I let them hang limply at my sides instead.

"Just tell me," I finally blurted.

"Tell you what?" he asked.

"What my punishment is," I said.

"Why would I punish you?"

"Because I broke the one rule I had agreed to."

"What rule, Desiree?" He asked this like a teacher would ask a student what she had learned when a lesson finally sunk in.

During Crissy's wish I'd started to suspect my long-held belief that I couldn't interfere with a wish was all in my mind. I now realized that I'd always been allowed to make decisions for my charges. The fact that I interacted with them at all was interfering. I could have simply sent a message that said "your wish has been granted" and moved on. Instead, I stood face-to-face with them and chose the details that would ensure their wish would be completely fulfilled.

"You understand now," he said. I nodded. "Do you also remember where this self-imposed prohibition came from?"

I tried to think back to the beginning. Had I done something wrong with one of the wishes?

"Do you not remember what happened with your friend in the commune?" Kaf prompted.

Friend? What friend? My boyfriend, Glenn, had been there. My only other friend… "Do you mean Marsha?"

He gave a single nod.

"What about her?"

He waved his hand in the air next to him, as if removing fog from a window, and a small cloud formed. His version of a crystal ball.

An image slowly started to emerge inside the cloud. The answer was coming. As the image became clearer, my foggy brain also cleared. While we lived in the commune, Marsha had gotten heavy into pot and acid and heroin and I didn't even know what else. She was stoned more often than she wasn't and it was literally killing her.

Kaf's cloud revealed a movie, or more accurately a playback from my memories, of the two of us. Marsha was lying on a blanket beneath a tarp that someone had strung between a tree and a VW bus. She was completely baked and when I begged her to stop using, she told me to quit interfering in her life.

Call it interference if you want, I'd said, *but I call it love and I will never stop loving you.*

The thing about Marsha was that the more you pushed her one direction, the more she ran the opposite way. I knew that. I should have left her alone. Because I kept pushing, she kept using. My best friend died from a heroin overdose and it may well have been my fault.

"Ah," Kaf said. "You remember, do you not?"

"I wasn't prohibited," I said, speaking the truth out loud. "All this time, I could've been helping my charges."

"This is what you still do not understand," Kaf said,

dismissing the cloud with another wave of his hand. "You did help. For nearly five decades you helped make the lives of hundreds of people better. That is what we are here to do. We help people. We make lives better."

For that moment, he sounded like Glenn. Passionate about making a difference in the world.

"Why didn't you ever tell me?" I asked. "Why did you let me go on thinking I had to remain at a distance?"

He stepped down from the platform his throne sat on and stood inches away from me. I expected to see anger or irritation there. Instead there was a glint of amusement in his emerald eyes.

"You are very much like your friend, Desiree," he said. "Anytime I have asked you to not do something, you have asked why? Anytime I have told you that you were free to help in any way you saw fit, you have said I cannot interfere." He paused to let me think about that. "You said that. Not me. From the beginning, I gave you full power to do whatever was necessary for a wish."

"Then why did you stop me from helping Crissy the night Brad was raping her?" Tears stung my eyes at the memory. My heart shattered for her as I stood in her backyard, remembering how the men in my commune had done basically the same thing to Marsha. They were never violent with her, but like Crissy, Marsha never thought she could say no because she had already said yes in the past.

"If you had helped her that night," Kaf said, pain of the memory clear on his face as well, "what do you think would have happened to her?"

"She never would've found the strength to say no to Brad and stand up for herself." I'd been so mad at Kaf for holding me back. "That was the night I decided to stop standing by."

"That was the night you decided to return to your true self," Kaf said. "The girl who stands up for others rather than standing back and letting them suffer alone."

Wow. Kaf understood me. I hadn't realized he was capable of that.

"You see," he said, a look of caring on his face that I'd never seen before. "Two birds, one stone. By not letting you help her, I also helped you."

As we stood there in the damp, chilly cave, warmth radiated from him. It was just the two of us and I felt exposed. Not endangered, Kaf would never hurt me, but defenseless. By pointing out how he had helped me, it seemed like Kaf was now done with me. All of a sudden I felt alone in the world and needed assurance that all would be fine. Glenn had been able to do that for me. He could make things right with a simple hug when I was upset. I wanted Kaf to do that. I wanted him to put his arms around me and make me feel okay with wherever my life path was about to lead me.

"If I didn't break any rules," I asked, looking down at my feet, "what am I doing here?"

He took my hands—I startled at the contact—and positioned them with my palms flat, facing the floor. Then he placed his palms beneath mine. He closed his eyes and as our hands touched, the magic I'd carried inside me for forty-five years drained away.

"You took my powers?" Every nerve in my body went on high alert. What did this mean? "I haven't fulfilled my contract. It's only been forty-five years. I agreed to fifty."

"Indeed you did."

"But when we made the agreement, you told me if I didn't complete my indenture you would return me to the condition in which you originally found me." Broken, bloodied, and barely conscious.

He placed a finger under my chin and tilted my face up to his. "Have you forgotten your wish?"

"My—?" Oh. I had forgotten.

It had been near the end of Mandy's wish. She was going to get the chance to right all her wrongs. She was going to confess to her mom the things that she had done wrong, or thought she'd done wrong. Her mom would forgive her. Mandy's wish had brought up my own bad memories. I was bitter because she was going to fix her mistakes, something I'd never be able to do.

What is your wish, Desiree? Kaf had asked.

I wish I was done with you, I'd told him.

"That's not what I meant," I told Kaf now. "I was angry at the time."

"Desiree," Kaf said gently and moved even closer to me. One more step and we'd be pressed against each other. "You have served me well. Despite our arguments,"—he let out a small chuckle—"our many arguments, every wish you were assigned, you completed successfully. None of my other Guides have a record of lasting success like yours."

Touch me, I thought at him. *Put your arms around me and tell me that I don't have to leave. I can stay and be yours. Not just one of your Guides, but yours.*

He looked into my eyes and slid his tongue across his lips. His massive chest heaved with every breath he took and I swear I could hear his heart beat, beat, beating.

"I know you were upset that night," he said gently. "That is not the wish I am referring to."

"The only other wish I made was to not die in that gully."

He shook his head. "No. You wished to receive a second chance at life. That is the wish I granted so long ago." He paused, tilted his head, and studied me. "You really have no idea that you have been on your own journey this entire time, have you?"

"I…what?" My knees became weak and the room went off-kilter. If I dropped, would he catch me? "These last forty-five years have been *my* wish?"

He lifted a bulky shoulder. "Some wishes require more time than others."

"Forty-five years?" How had I never realized this? I

thought that being a Wish Mistress was my second chance.

"Before you could move on to a second life, you first needed to leave your past in the past. Mandy's wish helped with that. It brought almost everything to light."

"I've been stuck at eighteen years old for *forty-five years*. You couldn't have assigned me a few leave-my-past-in-the-past wishes a couple of decades ago? When my parents were still alive?"

They never knew what happened to me. Kaf had placed two conditions on saving my life. First, I was to work for him as a genie for fifty years. Second, I wasn't allowed to interact with my friends or family during that time. That rule, not being allowed to contact them, I did try, many times, to break. I tried to transport myself to their living room. I tried to walk through their front door. I even tried to jump in front of their car once. It was physically impossible for me to place myself anywhere that they could see me. I couldn't call them. I couldn't send a letter. No contact, ever.

"As you have told your charges, we all choose our own paths, Desiree. You could have moved things along. You chose to hang on to the righteous indignation that sent you on that road trip with your friends so long ago."

Bite me.

"With Crissy's wish," Kaf said, "your true self reemerged. You decided what you would and would not accept and you acted upon that decision. Now you must choose the path that will lead to the end of your wish and the beginning of that second chance at life."

"How am I—?"

"Only you can know when you are where you want to be."

Holy carp, as Crissy would say. Is that how I sounded to my charges? No wonder they got so annoyed with me.

"Your indenture with me is complete," Kaf said. "I anticipated you would need fifty years to come to this understanding. It appears I miscalculated."

Relief flooded my body, but a second later, panic set in. What was I supposed to do? Where was I supposed to go? I'd said I wanted to be done with him, but that wasn't true. As infuriating and chauvinistic as he could be, the thought of never seeing him again tore at my heart.

"I will give you two options," Kaf said, reading my mind. And I was pretty sure he could literally do that.

I barely heard his words. He was still so close to me. If I raised up on my toes, our lips would press together. He must have realized this because he backed away then, just a step. A mile-wide chasm couldn't have felt bigger.

"Options?" I repeated dully and turned away from him. I didn't want him to see the heartbreak that had to be clear on my face.

"Yes," he said as he returned to his throne. King Kaf again in place. "You once told me that like Mandy, you wished you could go back and right your wrongs." He cleared his throat and wouldn't look me in the eye anymore. "If you choose, I can arrange that."

What was he saying? That I could go back to 1969? Because that was when the worst of my regrets had started. In particular, the day Glenn, Marsha, Stan, and I left on that road trip. We never said goodbye to anyone. Well, I hadn't. Maybe the rest of them had.

"That means everyone would still be alive?" I asked, not believing it possible. "My parents and Craig? Marsha?"

"Correct."

"But you said we can't bring people back from the dead."

He glanced quickly at me and away again. "A fabrication to save us from a lot of work. Nearly everyone who has lost a loved one wishes for their return."

"What are you saying?"

"I'm saying that under certain circumstances we can bring people back, but it is very difficult. It would be less difficult to send you back."

If I went back, I'd make sure we didn't go on that trip because if we hadn't, Marsha wouldn't have died. If I went back, maybe I could convince my brother Craig to not go to Vietnam. Maybe I could convince him to go to Canada or Mexico, anywhere that the military couldn't find him. I could prevent the pain my parents suffered by first losing him and then never knowing what happened to me.

The thing was, this was Kaf presenting me with this option and I knew him very well. "What's the catch?"

"Is it not obvious?" he asked, one eyebrow arched in question. "If you go back, you will not go on the trip with your friends. Correct?"

I nodded.

"If you go back and do not go on the trip," he said in that infuriatingly methodical way of his, "you will not be in the car accident. You will not almost die. You and I will never meet because you will not need me to save you." He paused and swallowed. "You will not become a Guide."

I waited for the conclusion to the story. But he wouldn't say more.

"So?" I finally demanded.

"Again, is it not obvious?" He waited for me to fill in the blank. When I didn't, he sighed. "If you do not become a Guide, none of the wishes that have been assigned to you will be granted."

Chapter Two

My knees gave out and I dropped to the cave floor. How was I supposed to choose? My parents, Craig, and Marsha or Mandy, Crissy, and all my other charges? If I went back I'd still be with Glenn, but I'd never meet Kaf. How could I go back and let three people live if it meant hundreds would not get the lives they wished for?

"If I go back, other guides would take my wishes." Even as I said the words, I knew it wouldn't be the same.

"But they are not you," Kaf said, adding a touch of warmth to his logic. "None of the others take the time to so intimately learn about each charge the way you have." He paused. "They would not know to produce Lexi and Lance. You really have been remarkably astute with your analysis and conclusions."

Lexi and Lance. If Lexi never came, Mandy would go on believing she had been responsible for her sister's death. She would never find the courage to tell her mother about the unforgivable words her father said to her the night he left because Lexi was the only other one who knew about them. If Lance never came to boost Crissy's self-confidence and teach her self-defense, she might not survive Brad's abuse.

"Would I remember them?" I asked. "My charges and their wishes?"

I may have only gotten close to Mandy and Crissy, but I did remember all of the others.

After a moment's thought Kaf said, "I could allow you to forget. That would be the decent thing."

If I twisted that logic around enough, he was right, it did seem decent.

How could I do it though? None of my wishes had ended badly. A few didn't go smoothly along the way, but all of them resulted in the charge being happy or at least satisfied with their new life path at the end. How could I risk handing them over to a Guide who might not get it right?

"What's my other option?" I asked. The ripping sensation in my chest was me being torn away from my family and friends again.

"You simply move forward from this moment," he said. "Your life will once again be yours and you will be able to do with it as you choose.

"How will I survive?" I asked him.

"Your wish has not completed, only your indenture to me. I will provide you with what you need to bring your wish to a satisfying conclusion."

Ouch. Those were the exact words I told Crissy when she pleaded with me to help her because she was sure Brad was going to kill her. Had I really come across as that uncaring?

Kaf jotted notes furiously in his compendium, his feather quill looked like it was trying to take flight it jerked about so much. Probably reassigning wishes to the other Guides that were supposed to go to me. Straight to work. He really was ready to be rid of me. The quill stilled and he asked, "Do you choose to remain here or go back?" As if he'd come to the point where he needed to note my decision in his compendium.

That book contained the details of every wish Kaf had ever allowed to be granted. Not just the ones I acted as Guide for but every wish. Every one of them was unique but each had followed one common rule: the wish wouldn't complete until the wisher's soul was satisfied. I was no different than any other charge listed in that book. My journey—with Kaf as my Guide—wouldn't end until I achieved what my soul longed for. I had wished for a second chance at life, so the question was, what sort of do-over did my soul want?

"As I see it," I said, adopting Kaf's business-like manner, "I have two choices. First, I could stay with Mandy and Crissy. They've become like family to me and I think they would do what they could to help me." I paused to steady my voice. "Or I can go find the one family member I have left."

"Carol?" he asked.

The fact that he knew my sister's name took me off guard. It was the kind of personal detail that Kaf usually couldn't be bothered with.

"Last I checked she was still living in San Antonio," I said. That had been quite a while ago though. For the first few months after becoming a Wish Mistress, I checked in with my sister daily. Then weekly…monthly…on special days. I stopped watching altogether after ten years because she was such a drag. She was doing well—by which I mean she had plenty of money—but she was a remarkably unhappy, bitter person.

"You have chosen to move forward?" he asked.

He seemed genuinely curious, as if invested in my decision. What difference would one or the other make to him?

I turned away from Kaf and directed my consciousness to the cosmos. With my eyes closed, I listened to water dripping somewhere in the cave. To wind blowing through a narrow passageway. To my heart and my soul. *What do you want?* I asked.

I envisioned a scale with my options sitting balanced on each platform. *What do you want?* As I watched, my heart and soul open to either option as long as it was the right one, the scale tipped.

"I understand what you told me," I said, "but I don't believe destiny can truly be altered. Sidetracked for a while perhaps but not altered. I don't want a second chance at what might bring me right back to where I am now. I'm going to San Antonio. I'm going to find my sister and try to move forward with her."

If the microscopic slump of his massive shoulders meant anything, he was pleased with this choice. Or relieved. Or something. But his words were typical Kaf.

"No need to adopt the role of martyr, Desiree. I have offered you a choice."

Yeah, a choice between not so good and not so great.

"I'm dropping back into the real world. You'll give me money, I assume, since I no longer have the power to manifest any."

My powers were gone.

The fact finally hit me with a force that nearly made me fall to my knees again. I felt incomplete, like I'd lost a limb. My eyes started to fill with tears before I could even ask the next question. They spilled when I finally did. Damn it. "Can I keep my bus?"

It's like there was an invisible, un-severable bond connecting me and my bus. It had become a part of me over the years, the one constant in my world that made me feel normal. I couldn't imagine living anywhere else. Or living without it.

When I first became indentured to Kaf, he had told me I would live across the valley from his cave with the other Guides. There stood a castle with ornate, tapestry curtains and hand-embroidered carpets in every bedroom. Every bathroom was dominated by huge bathtubs carved from emerald and adorned with gold fixtures.

Beautiful. If you liked that kind of thing.

"The tower room is currently unoccupied," he had told me.

I would live in a castle with all the other Guides in a room in a tower with a view of mountain peaks and an expanse of the Sahara Desert? That could be fun. Like a never-ending slumber party. I had met the other Guides though. They were all subservient and oh-so willing to please The Master, as they called Kaf.

"Oh, I'd be like a damsel in distress," I had said, clasping my hands and batting my lashes at him. He held his head high and puffed out his already-bulging chest. "Thanks, but I'm nobody's damsel."

The mountain range had been chosen because the people who lived in the area claimed it was cursed, evil, haunted. I believed the locals from long ago made up a story of a curse to save face. The mountain was unclimbable with sheer rock walls and not a hand or foothold to be found. Anyone who had ever been brave, drunk, or stupid enough to even attempt to scale it had fallen to their death.

The curse kept people away but even though no one ever attempted to explore the mountain itself, people drove past it every day. Traveling across the desert is hard on cars, they tend to overheat, and on that day a bus had broken down alongside the road.

"I want that bus," I'd told Kaf, pointing down the mountain to the yellow speck next to the road.

"You want to live in a school bus?" he asked.

"Sure. Wouldn't that be a gas?" I said. "That way I'll be available for wishes and can still see the country. I won't be trapped in a castle on a mountain."

"I am sorry, Desiree, but I cannot allow that," he said.

"Can't allow what?"

"All of my girls are presumed to have died or are in hiding because they do not want to be found. You cannot be seen by anyone but your charges. If a charge refuses the wish after you have offered it and explained the conditions, their memory of you will be cleared. Think of it as a sort of witness protection program."

"Your 'girls'?" I got stuck on the possessive for a moment. "You mean the women you've tricked, it seems, into doing your bidding?"

We had known each other for approximately two hours at that point. I could tell, he had already started to question the intelligence of bringing me on staff. Good. I didn't go anywhere quietly.

"You never said anything about having to stay out of the public eye," I said. "You can't force me to live where you say."

"I could," he had said and gave me a ten-second zap of the unbearable pain I'd felt while lying broken in the gully after the car accident. "You do not have to accept my offer. Not everyone does. There is always another choice. Yours is death."

"Okay, peace, man," I'd called out. The pain stopped. "Can we compromise?"

He had said something about me probably disrupting the harmony in the castle anyway and had agreed to let me live in my bus as long as I stayed out of sight. That's why it was currently parked in a valley in the middle of the Rocky Mountains in Colorado.

"You may keep your bus," Kaf said.

I nearly collapsed with relief. Whatever lay ahead was going to be a challenge, but as long as I had my bus, I could make it.

"Is that it?" Kaf asked. "Are you ready to begin this final leg of your journey?"

"Well…"

His head dropped forward. "What is it now, Desiree?"

"The last time I started on a road trip I didn't say goodbye to anyone. I need to say goodbye."

Chapter Three

I stood in front of the familiar, faded-red barn for a good five minutes, trying to summon the courage to go inside. Things were different now. I wasn't magical anymore. What if they weren't interested in the simple-human me?

Shit or get off the pot, my father would've told me. He was cuddly that way.

My sandals crunched on the gravel drive as I took slow steps toward the barn. Through the open doors. Past Mandy's green car. Over to the ladder. Mandy was in the loft. Music—part-pop, part-classical—was playing up there. She must have been practicing what she'd been learning in dance class.

I grabbed a ladder rung and froze. *She's busy, you'll be bothering her.* I let go.

You'll be gone soon, this could be your last chance. I put both hands on a rung and started to climb before the voices in my head started messing with me even more.

"Hey, little sister," I said as I peeked over the edge of the floor into the loft.

Mandy let out a shriek, just like she had the first time we met.

"Desiree? You're back. What's wrong?"

For a few seconds, the look on her face was also the same as the one she'd given me the first time we met. I was an intruder, invading her space.

"Nothing. Sorry, I didn't mean to bother you. I'll go." I took a step back down the ladder.

"Don't be dumb. You startled me. You were just here two days ago, I'm surprised to see you again so soon." She gave me a confused look as she turned down the music. "Something's different. You're climbing the ladder."

"How else am I supposed to come up?" I asked, hoisting myself into the loft.

"I don't know. Usually you,"—she did explosion hands—"poof."

"I do not poof." I took a seat in my favorite hanging hammock chair and instantly relaxed, like my entire body exhaled. Being with Mandy, in her world, made me feel normal.

"You know what I mean. Why didn't you poof?"

"Here's the thing," I said and dug around in my bag for my granny glasses. I took my time, acted like I couldn't find them, because I didn't trust that my voice wouldn't betray me. 'Be sure of what you wish for' was what I always told my charges. I thought I had been sure. "I can't anymore."

"You can't what?"

"I lost my powers." My hands shook as I plugged my glasses onto my face and the world tinted moody through the blue lenses.

"Because you interfered with Crissy's wish?" Mandy asked.

I nodded. Shrugged. Shook my head. "There's a little more to it than that."

"Wow. I figured there might be a punishment but not

that you'd get stripped of your powers." She sat for a moment, letting it all sink in. "So you're human again."

"I don't have magical powers anymore, no. I've always been human."

She was making this complicated. I'd just come to say goodbye.

"Why the attitude?" she asked. "Isn't this what you wanted?"

"I thought so," I said. My brain was scattered—happy, sad, excited, terrified—and wouldn't settle on a thought. "No. I mean, yes, this is what I wanted."

Mandy pulled a T-shirt on over her tie-dyed leotard, took a seat on the futon beneath a six-foot wide window, and tucked her legs beneath her. I knew that look on her face. She wanted me to explore my feelings. What was there to explore? I got what I asked for. Couldn't change my mind now, even if I wanted to. Not that I did.

"How's Crissy?" I asked.

"Better every day." Her voice caught. She sat taller and cleared her throat. "Physically she's healing remarkably fast."

"Yeah," I said, "I put in a request..."

Kaf refused to heal her completely, but did agree to speed the process up. He said the pain was part of her journey, so she'd remember and never let something like that happen again. Jackass.

"Thanks," Mandy said, as if the act was a personal favor to her, but then she frowned. "She has nightmares some nights. And she can't get past the feeling that she did something to cause this no matter how often Mama and I tell her she didn't." She shrugged. "She'll be okay. She's one of the toughest girls I know."

"And she's got the greatest friend in the world," I said.

She looked at me like she might cry, touched her hand to her heart, and bowed her head in thanks.

Really, I'd never met anyone as caring and giving as

Mandy. I was going to miss her so, so, so bad it already hurt.

"She's still here." Mandy pointed toward Crissy's camera set up on a tripod in the corner of The Haven, as she called her loft. "She says she needs to practice taking movement shots. I'm her subject. She's getting the backup battery for her camera from the house. She'll be happy to see you."

"Are you sure?" Crissy was having nightmares and I wasn't sleeping at all due to guilt. It was my fault her wish went the way it did. I had to let her learn a lesson. Just like I had to force Mandy to learn a lesson before getting her wish. When had I become so bitter that I couldn't just let people be happy without the strings attached?

"I'm sure," Mandy said. "She doesn't blame you."

I laughed, skeptical.

"Desiree," Mandy waited until I turned my eyes to her. "She would have told me. Crissy doesn't hold back on her feelings. You know that."

"I don't hear music." Crissy called from the barn below. "You're supposed to be practicing for a recital."

"We have company," Mandy said.

If any good had come from the way Crissy's wish had ended, other than Crissy finding her new life path, it was that Mandy and Crissy were now as tight as two people could be.

"Who?" Crissy asked.

There was a lot of grunting as Crissy climbed the ladder. Her ankle should've been nearly healed. It was most likely her wrist that was giving her a hard time. Her casted arm appeared first and clunked on the loft floor.

"Desiree," she said in a soft, breathy exhale. Her left eye was ringed in a soft purple-green-yellow bruise. The last one Brad would ever put on her.

I burst into tears at the site of her. First Crissy and then Mandy were at my side. They didn't say anything, just let me cry. One of them held my hand while the other stroked my hair. Their immediate display of sisterhood made me cry all the harder. What if I never saw them again? What would I do without them?

"What's going on?" Crissy asked Mandy.

"She lost her powers."

"Because of me?" Crissy asked.

"No!" I insisted and composed myself. "You didn't do anything wrong."

Mandy took Crissy by the elbow and led her to the futon. They settled in and Crissy propped her left foot on Mandy's leg. It was still wrapped and the bandage made me cringe.

"Spill it," Mandy said.

"Spill what?" I asked.

"Whatever the deal with your powers is," Mandy said. "And your story. You told me at the end of my wish that you'd tell me your story sometime. I think that time is now. I assume you don't have anything else going on."

"I have a few minutes," I told her. "I have to report to Kaf soon."

"Okay, that for example," Mandy said. "Who is Kaf?"

"Kaf is my boss. Was my boss."

"He's magical?" Crissy asked.

"Yeah, he's like the head of all of us. He decides which wishes are worthy of granting and then assigns one of us from the group to be the guide for that wish. You two got me. Aren't you lucky?"

"How is he magical?" Mandy asked, ignoring my self-pity. "I mean, is he like the genie from *Aladdin* or more like Jeannie from *I Dream of Jeannie*?"

Seriously. Forty-five years and those are the only two comparisons anyone ever has for me.

"Kaf rarely talks about how he got his powers," I said. "From what I've pieced together it was a lot like what happened to me. He was either about to die or needed to get out of whatever situation he was in. I don't know where the magic comes from. The universe maybe. Anyway, Kaf has full powers. The rest of us only have what we need for our wishes. Kaf's way of keeping us in line."

"So there are more Wish Mistresses?" Mandy asked.

"I'm the only Wish Mistress," I said. "Self-imposed title, remember? The rest are called Guides. There are a couple dozen of us in his harem."

"Harem?" Crissy asked.

"Yeah," I shook my head, disgusted. "Kaf is a total chauvinist. He believes women are beneath him. That we're his servants."

They looked at each other, nodded, and then turned back to me.

"But you like him," Mandy said.

"I…um, sure. I guess. What?"

"You're smiling," Mandy said. "You're tone is all negative, but the whole time you've been talking about him you've got this sappy smile on your face and your eyes are all sparkly."

"You're totally flustered," Crissy said with a nod.

"I don't know what you're talking about." I focused my gaze out the window at a cloud. Immediately I thought of how Kaf's throne was usually made from a cloud that he floated on. Sometimes pillow-shaped, other times more like a lounge chair.

"So is he hot?" Crissy asked with this annoying little sister grin on her face.

I shrugged. "I guess. He's Japanese and has these muscles." I held my hands out six inches from my arms and shoulders to demonstrate how massive he was. "He's got long black hair that he wears in a ponytail. And three tattoos of Japanese symbols." I tapped three places on my shoulder. "Strength. Truth. Love."

Crissy blinked at me.

"What?" I asked.

"It was a yes or no question," she said, again with the annoying little sister vibe. She gave Mandy a shoulder bump. "She likes him."

"Agreed," Mandy said. A second later she sang out, "You like him. You like him. Desiree's got a boyfriend."

"He's my boss."

"Was your boss. He's nothing to you now." Mandy grinned. "So you can date him if you want."

"I…I thought you wanted to know my story," I said. "Why are we talking about Kaf?"

"I only asked if he was hot," Crissy said.

"You know that I was a hippie in 1969," I started with my story like the topic of Kaf hadn't even come up.

Mandy's cat Brulée jumped up next to them. He started in with the turning in circles multiple times and kneading routine so Mandy waved her hand at me in a *go on* motion.

"I grew up in San Antonio as Gloria Calhoun."

"Gloria?" Crissy asked.

"You mean your name isn't Desiree?" Mandy looked affronted, like everything I'd ever told them had been a lie.

"It is now," I said. "And I've been Desiree for way longer than I was Gloria."

Mandy scowled.

"See," I said, "I split with some friends during the summer of 1969. First we road tripped to Woodstock. You know what Woodstock is, right?"

They shook their heads. Really? I figured everyone knew about Woodstock.

"It was this three day concert at this farmer's field in New York. It's a cultural phenomenon." I could go on for hours talking about Woodstock.

"We'll Google it later," Crissy said. "Continue."

"After the concert," I said, "a group of us decided we wanted to live in a commune and went to San Francisco. That didn't turn out the way I thought it would. It was more of society's same misogynistic directives but on a smaller level. The men worked, the woman took care of the household. Anyway, the day I decided I'd had enough and was ready to go home, I got in a car accident and almost died. Kaf appeared and offered to save me if I agreed to work for him for the next fifty years. I've been stuck at eighteen, because that's how old I was when I almost died, and have been granting wishes for the last forty-five years."

Mandy checked her watch. Well, pretended to. She wasn't wearing a watch.

"That took ten seconds. I did not settle in with my kitty-cat here and Crissy's foot in my face for a ten-second life story."

"You want me to move?" Crissy asked.

"Nope, you're fine," Mandy said. "What I want is more details."

"Got any food?" I asked, knowing the answer. Chef Mandy always had something wonderful in her kitchen. Or the ability to whip up something wonderful. "I'm starving. And I can't, you know,"—I wiggled my fingers—"*poof* a meal anymore."

Crissy moved her foot, Mandy got up from the futon, and Brulée complained because two seconds earlier he'd decided on an acceptable spot.

"Let's go to the kitchen," Mandy said.

"I just climbed that damn ladder," Crissy grumbled.

"I'll make us something while you talk. What do you want, Desiree? Or should I call you Gloria."

I made a face at her. "A chicken salad sandwich." My mouth started to water. I loved chicken salad. My mother used to make great chicken salad. I had little to no cooking abilities though and never could replicate her recipe. I couldn't even manifest it. Guess there was some secret mom magic that couldn't be duplicated. "I've been in search of a decent chicken salad sandwich for decades."

"Why didn't you ask me before?" Mandy asked as we all climbed down. "I would've made you one."

"Wasn't supposed to fraternize with my charges."

"Glad we don't have to worry about that anymore."

For the next two hours we sat in Mandy's red and white

kitchen as I told them all about my life.

"I grew up in middle class, suburban, San Antonio, Texas. I had every opportunity in the world, which I didn't realize until it was too late," I said. "I wanted to go to college and get a degree in sociology. I wanted to fight for the rights of women and minorities."

"I can see you doing that," Crissy said. She was sitting at Mandy's kitchen table with her foot now propped on a pillow on a chair. "You never went to college?"

"Never finished high school," I said. "I ran off to Woodstock before my senior year and never made it back."

"And then you went to the commune?" Mandy asked while chopping celery for the chicken salad.

I nodded and folded and unfolded a kitchen towel on the table in front of me. "That's my biggest regret."

"I'm guessing not just because of the car accident," Crissy said.

"No," I said. "The accident was like the exclamation point at the end of a really bad decision."

I told them about Marsha, her spiral into drugs, and how she died from the overdose. As I did, Mandy and Crissy kept glancing at each other. They knew exactly what it was like to fight to get a friend out of a deadly situation. It's just that the threat of death was external for Crissy instead of internal like it had been for Marsha. Then I gave them more details about the car accident and how I became a Wish Mistress.

"Wow," Mandy said as she set plates with sandwiches and fresh fruit in front of us. "I knew you had a story to tell, but I had no idea."

"We all do stupid things when we're teenagers," I said.

"Um, we still are teenagers, thanks," Crissy said, pointing at herself and Mandy. "And technically you're only eighteen."

"So I guess I still have stupid left to do," I said. As if I hadn't already done enough awful, stupid things. Maybe I'd hit my limit. I took a huge bite of my sandwich. Creamy dressing balanced by the crunch of celery and pecans. "This is so good. Maybe even better than my mom's."

Mandy gave a nod of thanks.

"I want to apologize," I said.

Mandy cocked her head to the side. "For?"

"Lexi. I chose to bring her to you, you know. I decided that the way for you to figure things out was to bring around your dark side. And for you that was probably the cruelest thing possible."

"Yeah, pretty bitchy of you," Crissy said. "And you got me beat up."

My heart stopped. She didn't laugh or shrug and say it was okay. Guess she hadn't told Mandy all of her feelings.

"I see now how wrong I was," I said. "If that matters. And for the record, I would've died myself before I let you die."

She gave me a blank stare. "Big words from an immortal."

"I'm not immortal."

"You were at the time." She shook her head. "Look, it's done and in the past. I'm not mad at you anymore."

Anymore.

"I'm sorry," I said. "In my defense though, Brad was getting ready to explode before I came around."

Crissy considered this. "True. Like I said, it's all good now."

"I understand why you did what you did," Mandy said.

"Why did I do it?" Honestly, I wanted to know.

"Life didn't turn out the way you expected. You lost everyone important to you. I get how that can turn you into someone you're not."

I'd messed up on a lot of things. Looked like karma had finally caught up with me.

"So if you didn't lose your powers because of me," Crissy said, "why did you?"

I laughed, not that this was funny. "Turns out I've been

on my own wish journey this entire time."

"You mean since you died?" Mandy asked. "Well, since you almost died."

"Yep. I wished for a second chance at my life. Another shot at getting it right."

"Whoa," Crissy said, "a wish within a wish."

I turned to Crissy and tears started to sting my eyes before I even started to speak. "When I stood up for you, it was like I was standing up for Marsha."

"What do you mean?" Mandy asked and popped a grape in her mouth.

The words wouldn't come easily.

"I should have been able to save her," I said. "I saw what was happening. I didn't do enough."

"You can't fix everything." Crissy gave Mandy a grateful smile. "The other person has to meet you halfway."

"I know." Many things, like my brother going to Vietnam, I knew I couldn't fix. Not saving Marsha was the one thing I couldn't let go of. "Anyway, standing up for Crissy helped me leave my past in the past, as Kaf put it. Now I can move forward and find the path I need to be on."

We spent the next two hours talking about anything but me. Normal friend stuff. When the conversation lulled into comfortable silence, my chest tightened. I had to say goodbye. Kaf was going to summon me any second. I couldn't believe he hadn't already.

"You're leaving, aren't you?" Mandy asked, her chin quivering slightly.

I couldn't speak so I just nodded.

"But you'll be back." Crissy said. It wasn't a question.

"I don't know. And it's not that I don't want to. I'm going to San Antonio to find my sister, but past that I literally have no clue what will happen to me." I took a deep breath and crossed my arms in front of my chest. Mandy was moving closer to me, she was going to try to give me a hug. A hug just might undo me.

"You'll be fine," Mandy said as if reading my thoughts.

I couldn't stand it anymore. I took a step toward her and held my arms out. Without missing a beat, she wrapped hers around me. Crissy was there a half-second later.

"I hope so," I whispered and didn't try to hold back the tears any longer. "I don't want to go. What a trip it would be to spend some normal time with you two." I choked out a laugh. "You're like the dorky little sisters I never wanted and now you've kind of grown on me."

"Desiree." This voice was a deep baritone.

I pulled out of the hug. Mandy and Crissy both stood there with eyes wide and jaws dropped.

"Japanese?" I asked without turning to look.

Mandy nodded.

"Big muscles?" I asked.

Crissy nodded and asked, "Kaf?"

My turn to nod.

"Daaaa-mn, girl," Crissy said. "You have got to go for that."

Finally I turned. Sure enough. A shirtless Kaf stood there with his huge arms crossed over that rippling chest. Fortunately he hadn't bothered with the puff of smoke around his legs that usually accompanied his entrances. Because really, that was all for show and over the top.

"You couldn't put a shirt on?" I asked.

"No-no," Mandy said quickly at the same time Crissy said, "We're good."

"It is time to go, Desiree," Kaf said. And I swear he purposely flexed. I don't know how many of the charges he'd come face-to-face with over the years, the number was small, but he was blatantly strutting his stuff for Mandy and Crissy.

"I know," I said.

"We'll see each other again," Mandy said and actually shot Kaf the Evil Eye. Which made for an interesting expression considering she was still drooling over his shirtlessness. "Soon."

“Ever the optimist,” I said and hugged each of them one last time. I held on extra-long to Crissy. She’d said all was forgiven, but I still felt like I had making up to do.

I took a few steps back to stand next to Kaf. He placed a hand on my shoulder and the only two friends I had in the world disappeared from my view.

Chapter Four

Transporting was always a wild experience. The world around me faded to black and it felt like I was being sucked through a tube just big enough for me to fit through. It didn't hurt. The whole process happened so quickly I barely had time to register it. This time, when my surroundings became clear again, I found myself at the base of the Rockies next to my bus which Kaf had moved to a two-lane dirt road heading east.

Since the day Kaf had given me my powers, I had the ability to transport myself and my bus anywhere I wanted or needed to go. I'd been all over the world during my indenture. All seven continents—Antarctica was sort of a drag with all that white, white, white so we only stayed a couple of days—and nearly every country. I found that I liked mountains and island beaches best. Deserts did nothing for me.

There was a problem though. Because I'd had the power

to transport, I had never once driven the bus. And now, I no longer had powers.

"I don't know how to drive," I told Kaf. "Are you going to transport us to San Antonio?"

"Like your charges before you," he said, "you are on your own to figure out your wish. I have already allowed you your bus."

"So you're okay with me crashing in the next twenty minutes and dying on the roadside again?"

He considered that and then placed his palms together in Namaste and lowered his head. Just that fast my brain filled and I knew how to drive.

Without a word, he stepped inside.

"What are you doing?" I asked and followed him.

"You are no longer a Guide. This means your ties to the magical world are severed." He began touching items in the bus—my computer and monitors, items of clothing, my food. As he did, they disappeared.

"Hey! What the hell are you doing?"

"These are all items you have manifested over the years. You are no longer entitled to them."

"I didn't manifest everything," I protested. "I found a lot of it. Some things my charges gave to me."

"I am aware of which items were manifested." He touched my desk chair and it vanished. "They have a magical aura around them."

When he reached for the potted flower on my desk, a little Texas bluebonnet, I grabbed it before he could touch it.

"Oh come on," I protested. "Not Bonnie. She's like a pet."

Kaf closed his eyes and shook his head but backed away from my plant.

"Admit it," I said with a coy smile, "you're going to miss me."

He responded by holding the bus keys out to me.

"How do I get to San Antonio?"

"I thought," Kaf said, "that you were an independent woman. One who could make her own way in the world?"

I snatched the keys out of his hand. "I am. I'll find it."

He stood there, arms at his sides, muscles in his chest flexing at random. I wasn't quite sure what to say to him. We'd been together, so to speak, for forty-five years. And for much of that time I'd wondered what it would be like to run my hands over that chest. What would happen if I threw myself into his arms right now and kissed him?

"Thank you, Kaf." It felt like we were breaking up. "For saving me and letting me have a second chance."

He blinked once. And once more. His jaw clenched. "Good luck, Desiree."

And he left. I mean one second he was standing two feet from me. Close enough for me to reach out and discover what those arms felt like. And then he was gone. For the first time since the day he saved me in February of 1970, I was truly alone.

I climbed the ladder on the back of my bus and went onto the roof. Sitting there, looking at the mountains surrounding me, listening to the immense silence, I'd never felt so small. I'd never felt more vulnerable. Never in my life had I set off on my own. I'd gone on plenty of vacations with my family. Glenn and Marsha were with me on the Woodstock to San Francisco road trip. Kaf watched over me after that. Now I was on my own. Now was my chance to prove that I really was the independent woman I claimed to be. If it wasn't for the sudden, burning ache in my chest, I'd have been excited.

Was he really gone? Would I really never see him again? Was this how my charges felt when they'd made it to the end of their journey and I left them?

Independent woman? More like a scared toddler who wanted to hide behind her mother's skirts.

Then again, he said I was still completing my wish journey. That meant Kaf was my Guide. That also meant he could monitor everything I did.

"I don't want you watching me," I called out. My voice bounced off the mountains and back at me.

When Mandy got to the end of her wish, she practically overflowed with self-confidence and certainty over where she was headed. Crissy, though physically and a bit emotionally broken, had a full spirit and was ready to charge through life and become the kind woman she wanted to be. Until that moment I hadn't realized that I had gotten as much from them as they had from me. If my wish ended the same way theirs had, with my confidence restored and path clear, I couldn't ask for more. I just needed to find that path.

Right now though, the sun was closing in on the mountain peaks. How long had I been sitting there? Regardless, it would be dark in no time. No sense starting the drive now. One last night in the mountains and I'd start my new life with a new morning.

The sky was cloudless and full of stars, stars, stars. The night crisp but not too cold. I climbed down the ladder and shoved a few blankets and pillows up through the skylight in the roof over my bed. Back on top of my bus, snuggled in my blankets, I fell asleep watching meteors shoot across the sky.

☮☮☮

I woke to the perfect peace of nature—a brook babbling in the distance and the call of a few birds. For a few minutes I forgot. The mountains surrounded me like they had every morning for years so I couldn't reconcile where I was with the memory of saying goodbye to Mandy and Crissy. A failed attempt to manifest a mug of tea brought me back into reality.

"Not a dream, my dear," I told myself with a croaky morning voice. "You got what you wished for."

I ran my hands over my face and sat up. Considering I'd slept on the roof of a bus, I should've been achy and stiff.

The bus had a way of comforting me no matter the situation though. It was my shelter from whatever came my way. I dropped the blankets and pillows back down through the skylight and took one last deep breath of the clear, pine-scented mountain air.

The point of the wishes we'd granted was to make things end well. *That is what we do*, Kaf had said. *We help. We make life better.* It was my turn at a better life. Everything would be fine. All I had to do was find the end of my wish.

Inside on the driver's seat I found a small zippered pouch of white wool with a peace sign on it. Inside the pouch was a driver's license, with an unflattering picture of me, and a small stack of bills. The pouch felt very personal with that peace sign. I wanted to think that Kaf had chosen it especially for me and clutched it to my heart.

"You're being stupid, Desiree," I scolded myself. "You mean nothing to him. You were simply a charge. A vulnerable, broken soul he found lying in a ditch." I swiped angrily at a hot tear that slid down my face. When had I become so pathetic?

The sun visor was tilted down, so I studied my face in the mirror there. There was a bit of fear in my eyes but still the same set to my jaw my mother always accused me of having.

"So determined to make your own way in the world," she had said once after one of our many one-sided discussions about my views on life and what I planned to do with mine. "Even if you have to use a bulldozer to get there. I can see it in the set of your jaw."

She'd been proud, not patronizing. Though at the time I hadn't realized that.

I squared my shoulders, wiped my hands across my face, and stared into the eyes of the girl in the mirror.

"He means nothing. You will be fine. No doubt about that."

Before starting off in search of my path, I went to my

little refrigerator. Kaf had left me three cheese sticks and some grapes. Normally I'd simply manifest more food. Now I'd need to find a grocery store and buy some supplies.

For the first time I took hold of the wheel. It felt foreign and my hand trembled slightly as I put the key in the ignition. The words Craig had whispered in my ear the day he left to report for active duty came back to me. *What if I made the wrong choice?*

What if *I* had?

"Can't change it now," I told the girl in the mirror. "And you don't want to. You're getting what you asked for."

I flipped the visor up and opened the glove box to put the money pouch inside. Except for the day I moved into the bus when I checked over every nook and cranny, I couldn't remember ever opening the glove box. There, in the very center, lay a picture. I recognized it before I even touched it. The last time I'd seen it, it had been taped to the mirror in my bedroom at my parents' house. The four of us. Marsha and I with our arms around each other as we stood behind the other two girls who were my very good friends: Janice and Gail.

We had all gotten together the first day of junior high school. None of us knew anyone in our particular lunch period so we shared a table. That's how it started, the simple act of sharing. Over the years, Marsha and I gravitated toward each other, Janice toward Gail. We were all so different—Marsha the wild child, me the outspoken one, Janice the poster girl for never rock the boat, and Gail the eternal peacekeeper.

Except for not saving Marsha, my biggest regret was not saying goodbye to Janice and Gail before leaving on that trip.

"Why are you giving me this?" I called out to Kaf, holding the picture up. "To torture me? To let me know I made the wrong choice?"

Once a wish has started, there's no stopping it. No matter what happens, no matter what path things head down, I cannot stop it.

That was the warning I'd given every one of my charges before they accepted their wishes. I'd already accepted mine. The only option I had was to move forward. I put on my granny glasses and shoved the bus into drive.

☮☮☮

I had to stop for gas in a little town in northeastern New Mexico. The thousand dollars Kaf gave me seemed like a fortune when I first saw it. However, standing there, watching the numbers on the gas pump spin faster than I could focus, I knew I'd blast through the bills in my little pouch quickly. In 1970 gas was something like thirty-five cents a gallon. It was more than ten times that now. The bus used a lot of gas. It was approximately one thousand miles from the valley in the Rockies to my sister's house in San Antonio, which meant it would cost nearly six hundred bucks to drive there. If I pinched pennies the way my father used to, the remaining four hundred should last a while. But I'd only be buying necessities.

"Where you headed?"

I turned to see a guy, a year or so younger than me, who stopped me in my tracks. He wore a bandana over the dreadlocks that hung half-way down his back and he had a full beard. A three-foot-tall canvas rucksack covered his back. His jeans hung loose and low on his hips, well-worn Birkenstock sandals, like mine, peeked out beneath the shredded cuffs. He was so thin his T-shirt and threadbare flannel shirt appeared draped over a hanger instead of his shoulders. He seriously could have been Glenn. Except for the dreads. Glenn wore his hair in a normal ponytail.

"Excuse me?" I stammered. One of his two scruffy but otherwise healthy-looking dogs licked my hand.

"Fritz," he softly tapped the dog's nose. "Sorry. He has no manners. I asked where you were headed."

"Why? You looking for a ride?"

"That would be my guess," a voice from my other side said.

I turned again and found a police officer.

"Picking up hitchhikers is not a recommended activity," he said to me. And to the boy, "Move along, buddy. Leave the little lady alone."

"Little lady?" I asked and shot him a look that, I hoped, said he was a chauvinist pig.

"I meant it as a term of respect," Officer Block, according to his badge, said.

"Officer," I said, "shouldn't I be the one to decide if I want to give a fellow traveler a ride?"

Officer Block let his gaze drift first over me and then to my bus where it lingered for a long moment.

It was the paint job. The day I had claimed the bus as mine I'd found half a dozen cans of paint inside and had started painting. It ended up mostly blue, my favorite color, with multi-colored peace signs and flowers and words of love not war all over it. It was fun, a way for me to express myself, and something to keep me busy while sitting in the middle of a mountain valley all by myself.

As I drove from Colorado to this little New Mexico town, the bus had attracted a lot of attention. I got a lot of honks and V-signs and stares from little kids. At first it was fun. I'd honk and V back. Then it got annoying. Yes, my bus was unique, but I didn't like everyone staring, invading my space that way. It brought me back to the stares and glares we used to get in the Woodstock days. Especially from people our parents' age and older, they'd sometimes look at us like we were no better than animals in the zoo. A drain on society. "Get a job," was the favored verbal lob.

That was how Officer Block was looking at me now.

"If I didn't know better," he said, "I'd swear I just slid back in time forty years."

"Forty-five," I said, the old feelings of being vilified and misunderstood cloaking me like a prisoner's uniform on an innocent woman.

He lowered his sunglasses and gave me a look that said I was being unnecessarily contrary. I wanted to proclaim justifiable contrariness, but bit my tongue instead. Guess I'd grown up a little since the 60s.

"Like I said," the officer repeated, "it's not a good idea to pick up hitchhikers. Especially for a gal travelin' alone. So I suggest that you two head in separate directions."

I held my hand out to the Glenn-boy. His blue eyes sparkled from beneath all that hair and layers of dust. "Pleasure to have met you. I'm Desiree. Sorry I can't give you a lift."

"I'm Ritchie." He took my hand and placed a gallant kiss on it. "The pleasure is all mine. Peace-out, Desiree."

Once he and his dogs were a couple hundred yards away, Officer Block faced me with his shoulders pushed back and his chest puffed up.

"I'm gonna give you a little friendly tip. You have a big attitude, but you're a little spit of a thing." He jabbed a thumb over his shoulder at my bus. "You got any other *fellow travelers* in there."

"No, sir, I do not," I said, proud of being on my own.

He didn't speak again until I looked at him. "Be careful. Attitude will only get ya so far."

My chest clenched for a second or two. He'd meant it as a caution from an officer of the law, but the shadow playing across his face was more paternal than professional. Suddenly I missed my dad more than I had in decades.

The gas pump clunked to a stop at one hundred eighty-nine dollars and fifty-three cents. "Thank you, Officer Block. My tank is full. Am I free to leave?"

He laughed that chuckling kind of laugh that said I was a stupid child. "I'm simply offering a little free advice. You remind me of the kids I used to hang around with back in the 60s and 70s. We thought we were going to rule the world."

This guy was a hippie? Either he didn't remember things

correctly or he was trying to make a point of some kind.

"Is that what we wanted?" I asked. "Or did we just want to change it for the better?"

He narrowed his eyes—considering either me or my words or both—and handed me his business card. "I hope you won't need it, but if you find yourself in trouble, call me."

As he hitched up his pants and walked away, I thought of my dad again and my heart clenched a little. And then things took a funky twist because I realized Officer Block and I were, chronologically, the same age.

I went in the store to pay for the gas and get a few necessities. TaB soda pop wasn't available anymore. At least not at this store. I had no idea since I'd been manifesting cans for forty-five years. I chose Diet Dr. Pepper instead. It was two dollars for a bottle. Two dollars! My memory might have been off but I remembered soda pop being fifteen cents a can in 1970. A bag of grapes, a package of cheese sticks, a loaf of bread, and a jar of peanut butter was going to set me back ten dollars.

"What, have you been under a rock for twenty years?" the gas station attendant asked when I complained about the price of the food.

"Forty-five," I said.

"What?"

"Never mind," I said. "Does food cost this much everywhere?"

"This is a convenience store," he said like I was a ditz. "It costs more here because it's a convenience. It's cheaper at the grocery store."

"Where's that?" I immediately defended the question with, "I don't live here. I'm just passing through."

He pointed left. "About six blocks down on the right."

I put the food back but did buy a road atlas. That cost twenty of my precious dollars. I found the grocery store and stocked up. The guy was right, the prices were a little better, not a lot, but I needed to save pennies where I could. When I came out of the store with my bags, I discovered a group of people clustered around my bus.

"What's going on?" I asked, worried that something was wrong with it.

"You gotta check out this bus," a man in baggy sweatpants and a holey T-shirt said as he took pictures of it with his phone. "I'd love to meet whoever—" He stopped talking when he saw me and scanned me from head to toe. "Dude! It's got to be yours."

"Yeah. So?"

He nodded at the bus. "The paint job." He nodded at my clothes. "The hippie wear. You in a play or something?"

Bell bottom jeans, cropped T-shirt, love beads… Not exactly the current clothing trends, but I was comfortable. And this was all I had. I suppose I did look a little like I was in a play.

"You've got to see it inside," some guy a little older than me, mid-twenties, wearing cowboy boots and tight jeans said as he stepped out of my bus.

"What are you doing?" I barged in front of him and stood with my back to the bus door, blocking anyone else's entrance, like a mother shielding her child from a stranger. "What the hell were you doing in my home?"

"Your home?" the guy asked.

The man with the camera started taking pictures of me. What was wrong with these people? What I wouldn't have given to have my powers back for one minute. Camera guy's phone would stop working, maybe even fly out into the road where it would be crushed under the wheels of a passing semi.

"You live in a bus?" The guy who'd been inside looked moderately impressed. "Never seen a bus like that before."

"Is anyone else in there?" I asked, looking over my shoulder. I couldn't believe he'd just walked right into my bus. I'd never felt more violated.

"No. I'm sorry," the intruder said and extended his hand as a peace offering but realized my hands were full of grocery bags so dropped it again. "I'm Cam and really, I'm sorry. It's just so,"—he swept his hand at the bus from front to back—"different. It's like some kind of Victorian gypsy wonderland in there. My little girl would love it. We all figured it was a promo vehicle of some kind."

"Well, it's not," I told him. The bags of food were getting heavy. "It's my home."

He lowered his eyes to the ground, sufficiently chastised. "You really should lock it."

Lock my bus? I had never once locked my bus. It had never occurred to me. There hadn't been a reason for me to since the day I moved into it. I parked it in places where no one could see it let alone try to enter it. If this was the kind of attention I was going to get, I understood why Kaf never wanted me to drive around.

"It doesn't have a lock," I told Cam.

"Usually the driver locks the sliding doors from the inside and leaves through the back because that door should have a keyed lock."

"You were inside," I said. A quick wave of nauseous violation hit me again. "It doesn't have a back door. My bed is where the door used to be."

Cam nodded. "I take it you've been off the grid for a while."

"What does that mean?" I asked.

"That you've been living where there aren't many people."

"I've been living where there aren't *any* people."

That caught him off guard.

"So you've come out from the back of beyond and are trying to join society again?"

Society. The Man. The thing we wanted to get away from. Well, I'd successfully dropped out. And now it was time for me to drop back in. Really though, how hard could that be?

“I’m on my way to San Antonio. My sister lives there.”

Cam ran his hand through his blonde hair and let out a sigh. “So you’re heading into a metropolitan area in a bus that is your home and doesn’t have a lock. You sleep in there and don’t think anything of the fact that anyone could just walk on in.”

“Well, I hadn’t until now,” I told him. “Look, I’m not stupid. I get the whole stranger danger concept and all that. I’ve just…yes, I’ve been off the grid for a long time and a lock wasn’t something I thought about.”

He nodded and once again looked scolded. “I’m sorry. I don’t think you’re stupid.”

I set the bags on the ground and shook out my now-numb arms. “How about you help me get a lock installed?”

“Me?”

“Yes, you. It was your idea. And you entered my home without permission. I think it’s the least you can do.”

He sighed, but didn’t argue, and pulled out his phone. After a few calls he’d found a service station that could do the job.

“What’s it going to cost?” I asked.

“Not sure yet. I’ll come with you to make sure he doesn’t gouge you.” He grinned at me. “It’s the least I can do after the breaking-and-entering thing.”

Cam was a nice guy. I could tell he hadn’t meant any harm. “Guess it’s not really breaking if there wasn’t a lock. Just entering. I appreciate your help.”

The guy he found to install the lock needed about an hour to go pick it up and get back to his shop. Cam and I passed the time by me telling him more about me—which was tricky considering I had to be creatively vague about my life up to that moment—and him telling me about his little girl and life in this dinky town.

“Boring as hell most of the time and gossip like you wouldn’t believe,” Cam said. “People will be talkin’ about you and your bus for days. They'll also be talkin' about the fact that you and I spent all this time together. They'll have us engaged in about three conversations."

He was joking, but still my cheeks flamed with heat.

I followed Cam to the station and he stayed with me, which was a good thing. Nick, the station owner, did try to overcharge me.

"You're not taking a hundred from her," Cam said. "The lock cost like twenty-five bucks."

"There's my labor," Nick said.

"Your labor ain't worth seventy-five bucks. Fifty for both."

Nick scowled. "I had to drive all the way to the school bus place and back. That's time I coulda been workin' here. Seventy-five for both."

"Sixty. Ten dollars for gas and driving time," I said, cringing at the fact that ten dollars would've filled a car's tank twice in 1970.

Nick studied me while sucking his teeth. "Fine. Sixty bucks."

An hour later, Gypsy V—I had decided to give the bus a name after Cam's Victorian gypsy comment—had a nice, secure lock on her door. Nick handed me the key and I handed him sixty bucks. After buying the atlas, food, and the lock I only had two hundred and sixty necessities dollars left.

"Do you know where you're going?" Cam asked, hands in his back pockets.

"San Antonio," I said, trying to sound like I knew exactly where I was going.

"But do you know how to get to San Antonio?" Cam asked.

I pointed vaguely southeast. "I have a map."

He gave a little sigh. "You need Highway 87 first. In about five hundred miles or so you'll want to switch over to Highway 10. That'll take you into San Antonio."

Sounded easy enough. Good thing I bought the atlas

though.

"Don't push this old bus too hard," Cam cautioned. "With everything you've got in there, it'll be working pretty hard. Take it easy and stop for the night somewhere populated in case you have problems."

I could only nod. My confidence had taken a bit of a beating since I pulled away from the mountains.

He scribbled something on a little scrap of paper.

"My phone number. Call me if you have problems. May not be able to do much depending on where you are but I'll help if I can. Don't let anyone take advantage of you."

Everything seemed expensive to me now, so it would take me a little bit to figure out which prices were fair and which weren't. Many things were different, but overall the world hadn't changed that much. Something my mom always said was for sure the same, people were mostly good. Cam was proof of that.

"I'm kind of glad you broke into my bus," I told him.

He smirked at me. "I didn't break in. It wasn't locked."

"Thanks for the help." I held up the paper scrap. "And the phone number."

His head bobbed up and down, up and down. "Take care of yourself, Desiree. I hope you find whatever it is you're searching for."

Chapter Five

Cam was right about not pushing Gypsy V. I couldn't get her to go much above fifty-five without a lot of chugging and pinging in protest from the engine. That was fine on four-lane highways because people could get past me in the left lane. Motorists on the two-lane roads, however, honked and flashed hand signals of a non-peaceful variety.

After thirty or so miles, I saw a figure alongside the road. As I got closer, I saw that the figure had a rucksack on his back, a walking stick in one hand, and two dogs on leashes in the other. Ritchie.

I started to slow down but remembered Officer Block's warning and sped up. Then I thought of how nice Cam had been to me and how we had never hesitated to pick up a traveler along the way from Woodstock to San Francisco. There was always room for one more. So I pulled to the side and stopped.

Ritchie kept walking at the same leisurely pace. When

he caught up to the bus he stopped by the open door.

"Desiree," he said like an exhausted man who'd just found the world's most comfortable chair. It sent a hot thrill through my body.

"Ritchie," I greeted back. "You don't walk very fast. How'd you get this far down the road?"

"Farmer let us jump in the back of his pickup. Gave us a ride 'til he had to turn off."

"You still looking for a ride?" I asked.

"You still headed,"—he pointed down the road—"that way?"

I waved him in and he sat in the one chair Kaf hadn't taken. It was an oversized wingback that my very first charge had given to me. She insisted on thanking me for reuniting her with her runaway son. The velvet fabric was practically worn through and the thing wobbled a little, but over the years it had formed perfectly to the shape of my body. Ritchie settled into it and his dogs curled up on the floor, one on each side of him.

I asked where he'd been ("Everywhere.") and where he was headed ("Wherever the road leads.") He asked where I'd been ("Everywhere.") and if I was heading for something in particular in San Antonio. ("My sister.") Talking to Ritchie was easy. Like coming home to an old friend after having been away for a long while.

"Do you have any food?" he asked.

I hadn't gotten a lot at the store but it was enough to last me about a week. At Woodstock and the commune, we all shared what we had freely with each other. Rarely did anyone take more than their fair portion.

"I've got some, not a lot though," I said. "I didn't think I'd need to feed anyone other than myself."

"I'll buy more," Ritchie said. "I pick up jobs whenever I come across one that pays cash. Mostly farm and construction work so I've got money. Don't worry, I'm no freeloader."

I looked him in the eye in the mirror hanging from the sun visor. He seemed sincere. And hungry. I pictured a bony, sunken face beneath that beard.

"There are cheese sticks in the refrigerator. There's some grapes, bread, and peanut butter, too. Help yourself."

"You're an angel, Desiree." He blew a kiss to the mirror.

After five or six hours, both Gypsy V and I were getting tired. I wanted to go farther, but I didn't want to risk falling asleep while I drove or pushing the bus too hard and damaging it. I couldn't afford repairs. I filled the gas tank (one hundred ninety-two dollars sixteen cents) so we'd be ready for the next day and then we stopped at a little campground somewhere between Lubbock and Abilene, Texas. A camping pad would cost forty dollars for the night. To me that sounded ridiculous, but I heard a man telling his wife, "See? Told you camping was way cheaper than hotels."

I flipped through the bills in my little money pouch, hoping more had manifested or I'd counted wrong. After one day on the road I had spent over half of my gas money and a third of my necessities fund. It was a good thing I had picked up Ritchie.

"How about you pay for the camp site?" I said, zipping the pouch shut again. It was only fair since I was doing all the driving and he'd eaten half my cheese sticks and drank almost all of my Diet Dr. Pepper.

"Sure," he said and pulled two twenties out of his pocket. "No problem. I'll get more food tomorrow, too."

A group of people were gathered around a campfire a couple of pads down from us. One of them came over to Ritchie and me.

"Join us," the guy said. "We've got plenty of food and more people always makes a party better."

"Can't argue with that," Ritchie said.

I locked Gypsy V. Not that I really needed to. We'd only be fifty yards away. But it had a lock, might as well use it.

Ritchie took my hand and I froze, taken off-guard by the

contact. Actual skin-to-skin contact. He glanced down at me, a questioning look on his face. I smiled and shook my head a little—*nothing's wrong, everything's fine.*

"You look tired," Ritchie said as we walked.

"My day started fourteen hours ago," I said and yawned. "Yeah, I'm beat."

Ritchie found a blanket from somewhere and spread it out by the fire for me.

"Sit. Relax," he said. "Are you hungry?"

"Starved," I said and lowered my body to the ground. Sitting upright took too much effort so I lay down. It felt good to just chill. Even better because we'd joined up with a group of people that felt distantly familiar. The sound of people laughing and talking, the smell of the fire, the smell of the food cooking over the fire, it all brought me back to the times on the road with Glenn, Marsha, and Stan. There was one day we came across a group of travelers. They'd been cooking hot dogs over a fire pit when we stumbled upon their campsite.

"Are you asleep?"

I opened my eyes and for a few seconds I was sure it was Glenn standing there, hot dogs and a roasting stick in one hand, a couple of beers in the other. And then Glenn turned into Ritchie.

"Just resting my eyes," I said. Disappointment made my momentarily light and fluttery heart deflate and turn to stone. I missed Glenn more than I had in a long time. "Suppose I need to cook that, huh?"

"They're better that way," Ritchie said.

"Yeah. That would require me to sit up though."

He set two beers on the ground by me. "One of those is mine. I'll make dinner."

Just like Glenn would sometimes do for me.

Ritchie cooked the hot dogs—the smell made me crazy with hunger—and then he made me one more. I really was starving. Later he made me a double-decker S'more. The marshmallow oozed all over my fingers and I ended up with melted chocolate on my chin. Ritchie rubbed the chocolate off with his thumb and then licked the chocolate off his thumb. When we were both full and content, he sat behind me on the blanket and wrapped his arms around me while I leaned against him.

Someone took out a guitar and played quietly. Ritchie and a few others sang along. Ritchie's voice, deep and smooth, vibrated in his chest and relaxed me even further. Little sparks from the fire shot up into the huge, star-dotted sky. Ritchie's dogs joined up with the other campers' dogs. It was one big, happy-mellow party. Peaceful memories of the road trip and Woodstock and good days in the commune filled my head.

"Hey, man," some guy asked Ritchie at one point, "you got a few bucks to help with food cost."

"Sure. I've got something else, too," Ritchie said and held his hand out in front of me. "Keys?"

"What?" I asked.

"Keys to the bus?"

"What do you need?" I moved like I was going to get up and he held me down.

"You stay. You're all settled in here. Just give me the keys."

Give him the keys to Gypsy V? That felt a little like a mother handing her child over to a stranger.

He must've sensed my hesitation. "I'll be right back. I gotta get my sack."

I leaned to the side so I could look him in the face. When I did, he placed a quick kiss on my mouth. I leaned further back so I could get the keys from my shorts pocket. He kissed me again, deeper this time, and put a gentle hand on my face.

"Okay," I said, breathless, touching the spot on my cheek where his fingers had been. "If you're not back in like three minutes I'm sending him after you."

I pointed at the guy who'd asked for money. He was huge, huge, huge. Well over six-feet and probably three hundred pounds of muscle.

"Scouts honor," Ritchie said but held up a peace V instead of the Boy Scout sign. A couple minutes later he was back with his rucksack. "Time to really get this party started."

He dropped to the ground next to me, pulled a small tin from his sack, and rolled a couple joints. About half of the group gathered around and waited patiently for him to finish.

"I've got these, too." He produced a bag of pot candies and held it out to the crowd.

"Thanks for taking me in," he said to me once everyone had taken what they wanted. "And my dogs. It's a lot nicer being with you than in the back of a pickup."

He held his joint out to me. I stared at it, thinking of Mandy and Crissy. They'd thought I was high when they first met me. And at various stages throughout their wishes. The truth was that until their wishes came along, I hadn't lit up in more than three decades. Thought it best that I remained fully alert for any incoming wishes since my job involved messing with people's lives. Wishes were not my problem anymore though. I wasn't responsible for anyone but myself so I took the joint from Ritchie.

Must've been low quality stuff because I wasn't feeling anything. So I took another long hit.

"Whoa, angel," Ritchie said, trying to take it from me. "Slow down, little lady."

"Little lady?" I asked, shooting death rays from my eyes, and took another long hit.

Ritchie stared at me with this strange expression. He shrugged and quietly said, "Suit yourself."

A feeling of happiness and peace with myself and my decision to move forward instead of going back settled over me. Ritchie took what was left of the joint from me and handed it to someone else. He lay down next to me and kissed me, slowly and gently, just the way Glenn used to. With my eyes closed and his beard tickling my face, it was easy to pretend he was Glenn.

I fell asleep and must have been out for quite a while. When I woke up, dying for another hot dog or s'more or anything edible, the party was over, everyone had gone back to their respective campsites. Someone had put a blanket over me and there was still a small fire burning in the pit. The flames swirled together, hypnotizing me as they twisted and turned on each other in oranges and greens. Wait. That couldn't be right. Flames weren't green.

I blinked, long and slow, and when I looked again I saw a face in the flames. A face with narrow eyes and dark hair. I blinked again and Kaf was there. Not in the fire but right next to me.

"Desiree," he said, kneeling down, looking me in the eye. "Desiree, you need to wake up. Ritchie is—"

But I didn't hear the rest. I pulled the blanket over my head. I didn't care what Kaf had to say. He left me. He told me I was on my own. So he didn't get to tell me anything anymore. He didn't get to have any say in my life.

The next time I opened my eyes it was morning. Or mid-day. I had no idea what time it was. My brain felt fuzzy and I couldn't get thoughts to fully come together. Had Kaf really come to me in the night? The weed Ritchie gave me had packed a slow but super-powerful punch. Not at all like the mellow buzz I used to get. Yet another thing that was different now. I should've stopped when Ritchie warned me.

It took a minute for me to realize I was still on the blanket Ritchie had placed by the fire for me last night. The smoke from the fire seemed to have permeated everything—my hair, my clothes, the blankets over and under me, and the air around me. As I became more lucid, I started to feel nauseous from the smell of smoke but hungry at the same time. And I had to pee wicked bad.

I pushed myself up to sitting, then standing, and shuffled

to the toilet shack a few yards away. When I came back out, I realized I was alone. As in the campground was empty except for a few tents and campers in the distance. Everyone had packed up and taken off to the next stop on their journeys.

"Wait," I said to…no one. "Something's wrong."

I turned very slowly in a circle. Three tents and two campers in the distance. There was nothing but empty camping pads near me. Everyone was gone. Including Gypsy V.

Disbelief hit first. My bus couldn't be gone. That wasn't possible. I went back to the campfire site, sat back down on the blanket, and tried to remember what had happened last night.

Slowly, very slowly, images started to come together. I remembered joining the group of people. Ritchie cooking a hot dog for me.

"Shit!" I jumped to my feet and paced back and forth. My heart raced and I didn't know if I should scream or cry. "I gave him my goddamn keys!"

My vision started to go black. I needed to sit down or I'd fall over. My bus. The one constant in my life, the single place where I felt like the world couldn't touch me, was gone.

"No. No," I said and started pacing again. "No, he's coming back. He went to get food or something."

There was a picnic table near where Gypsy V had been parked. I sat on the table, facing the campground entrance. It was flat for miles. I'd see my bus as soon as it got close.

I sat there for a long, long time. Cars and campers pulled in and claimed sites. Animals scurried past me. Birds flew overhead. The sun beat down, slowly burning my exposed skin. Hours later there was no sign of Ritchie or my bus, but I did see a police car. It pulled to a stop a few yards away and the officer walked over to me.

"Ma'am?" the female officer asked in a strong southern

accent. “Are you okay?”

She was pretty with bobbed, blonde hair. I shook my head but couldn’t speak.

“I’m Officer McElroy. Do you need medical attention? You look like you’ve got a pretty good sunburn goin’ there.”

I held my arms out in front of me, they were lobster red. I had jeans on so my legs were fine, but the skin on my face, arms, and the bits of my back and stomach not covered by my cropped T-shirt felt tight and hot. A good burn indeed.

“Are you waitin’ for a ride? Help me out here, sugar.” She pointed across the campground. “Some of the campers over there say you’ve been sittin’ alone here a long time.”

“He,” I started but my voice came out dry as the dirt around me. I cleared my throat and tried again. “He took my bus.”

“Who did?”

“Ritchie.” How could he have done this to me? How could I have been so stupid?

“Who’s Ritchie? Honey, if you give me some details we can figure this out a whole lot faster.”

I thought of the look on his face as I sucked on that joint. He knew what it was going to do to me.

“I was giving Ritchie a ride to San Antonio. Or wherever he wanted to go to.” Officer McElroy bristled and Officer Block’s warning about hitchhikers rang in my ears. “I fell asleep by the fire last night and when I woke up, he was gone. And so was my bus.”

I couldn’t figure out if I felt like a little girl who’d lost her parent or a mom who’d lost her kid. That’s when the tears started, hot little rivulets on my dusty, burnt cheeks. What was I going to do?

Officer McElroy bent down to look in my eyes where she surely saw the remnants of that joint. “You fell asleep? Were you drugged?”

I tried to focus on her but my still-fuzzy brain wouldn’t let me.

She sighed. "I mean against your knowledge."

I shook my head. I had watched Ritchie roll. The joint he gave me came from the stash he'd handed out to everyone. It's just that I used a lot more of it than anyone else did. Ritchie knew. That's why he told me to slow down. But did nothing to really stop me.

With tenderness she asked, "Have you been assaulted?"

Flash of Crissy after Brad had forced himself on her that night.

"No," I said, bile rising in my throat, "I don't think so."

"Good. All right. Come with me, darlin'. We'll get this taken care of."

She drove me to a small, square, single-story building that was the same color as the dirt that surrounded it. 'Police Station' had been hand-painted in black letters on the stucco over the door. Inside the walls were generic tan, covered with the standard informational posters and plaques.

Officer McElroy pointed to one of the two old steel desks and gave me a plastic cup of water. And another. And then some cream for my sunburn. As I gave my statement, she filled out a report on a computer that even I could tell was ancient.

"You picked up a hitchhiker," she verified. When I nodded, she hooked her hair around her right ear and frowned. "Honey, you know that's not safe, don't you?"

"Yes, ma'am," I said, too devastated to even think about being unnecessarily contrary.

"We all want to believe that nothing bad will happen to us." Her compassionate ways faltered some, incredulousness at my idiocy elbowing its way in. She scribbled a few more things on her paper then set her pen down and locked her gaze on me. "Be grateful that he only took your bus and not your life."

This wasn't just advice from an officer of the law. She wasn't old enough to be my mother, too old to be a sister. A caring, street-smart aunt seemed the best classification. That was nice, I'd take it.

"Do you think you'll be able to find my bus?"

"Well," she tugged at her collar, it was another hot day. "It's unique which helps. It'll be hard to blend in driving something like that. I'll put the word out right away. You're welcome to stay here with me for a while."

I didn't have anywhere else to go. Mandy and Crissy were too far away to help me. Cam had given me his number, I could call him. I'm sure he only gave it to me to be friendly though. He wouldn't really want to come six hours to help a stranger. Besides, after all that work to protect me with that lock, it would be humiliating to admit to him that I'd basically given my bus and all my belongings to some street punk.

"Thanks," I said. "How long is a while?"

"Let's get the word out about your bus," she said, patting my hand. "We'll figure something out after that."

"Would you happen to have any food?" I asked. Bloodshot eyes weren't the only aftershocks from that joint. I still had wicked bad munchies.

She peered over her glasses at me and made a disappointed face that told me she knew exactly what my condition was. "Follow me."

After an hour of sitting in the break room that smelled like burnt coffee, watching the second hand tick around the clock hanging on a tan, cinderblock wall—225 blocks made up each long wall, 192 for the short ones—I was going a little stir crazy.

Making it worse were the thoughts of Kaf that wouldn't leave me alone. He had been there last night. He tried to rouse me from my haze and alert me to the fact that Ritchie was about to steal Gypsy V. That was nice. He cared. Except he did nothing to stop it once he realized he couldn't wake me up. What kind of a jerk stands there while someone's getting ripped off?

I found Officer McElroy at her desk, staring at her

computer screen.

"Did you get enough to eat?"

A box filled with candy bars, chips, and nuts sat on one side of a table in the break room. A little refrigerator filled with juices and soda pop at the other. A taped-shut box with a slot for money and a "Be Honest" sign sat between the two. Officer McElroy had told me to take what I wanted. She'd cover the cost. I ate all the chips and nuts and drank all of the juice—sitting in the Texas sun for three hours really dehydrated a person. I stopped myself from tearing in to the candy bars.

"Yeah. Thanks. I'm going for a little walk," I told her.

"The town's only five blocks long and three wide. Doubt you'll get lost but I'll come look for you if you're not back soon. It's a scorcher out there."

Scorching didn't come close to describing it. After only fifteen minutes of walking down the empty streets in the mid-day early-July Texas sun and humidity, I was dripping and desperate to be back in the air conditioning.

"Desiree!" Officer McElroy poked her head out of the police station door when I was about fifty yards away. "They found your bus."

Chapter Six

I sat in Officer McElroy's squad car, staring at Gypsy V. At one point during my short, sweaty walk I'd given up hope that I'd see her again. Now I almost wished that was true.

"There's no sign of this Ritchie person," Officer McElroy informed me. With cautious optimism she added, "The other officer says it's still drivable. The keys are in the ignition."

Ritchie had only gone twenty-five miles from the campground. At that point he ran off the road and into a fifty-foot tall juniper tree. Gypsy V's left front corner and fender were crunched in, the headlight smashed. Ritchie, or someone, had sprayed graffiti all over her. Big black blobs now resided where my beloved peace signs had been. Cross-out circles of garish red imprisoned my words of non-violence.

"Why would he do that?" I asked, my voice unsteady.

"Well," Officer McElroy said in her no-nonsense auntie

way, “recreational drugs make people do all sorts of stupid things.”

As bad as the graffiti was, I could fix it. It wouldn’t be the same but maybe Gypsy V was entitled to a makeover for our new journey. She’d been the hippie-mobile for four decades. Maybe it was time for her to be something else and me to be someone else. A bright side to the storm cloud.

I climbed the stairs and stopped dead at the landing. The inside had been stripped almost bare. The lace curtains, the tin ceiling tiles, the crystal chandeliers, every little piece of memorabilia. Gone.

My bed and bathtub were still there, probably because he couldn’t get them out. They’d been the first things I’d installed. Everything else—the shelving that served as my closet, the refrigerator, the kitchen cabinet—went in after. He’d taken my bedding though. The satin-and-lace skirt, the velvet spread, all of the hand-stitched pillows I’d collected from around the world. Gone.

He took my towels, the rugs on the floor by the tub, and the little crystal chandelier that had hung over it. The refrigerator was cleaned out as was the cabinet. I couldn’t believe he left the fridge. Either he forgot about it or got interrupted before he could take it.

My bluebonnet lay on its side on the floor. One of the stems had bent so the flower hung to the side instead of standing tall and proud. I swept the dirt back into the pot and set Bonnie on the counter.

The money pouch Kaf had given me lay on the driver’s seat, the embroidered peace sign taunting me. I picked it up. The money, of course, was gone. The driver’s license surprisingly still there. Basically anything Ritchie could use or sell, he’d taken. He’d left my clothes. How kind. Guess I should thank him for that if I ever ran into him again. That is, if I didn’t run him over first.

My hand shook a little as I reached for the sun visor. When I tilted the visor down, the picture of me, Marsha,

Janice, and Gail fluttered down and came to a rest on the seat. I had my broken and bruised bus, my clothes, and my best friends to keep an eye on me. What more did I need?

"I'm sorry, Desiree," Office McElroy said.

The words were genuine, but her demeanor had shifted to by-the-book police woman. Maybe because other officers could hear her. Maybe because we'd landed on each other's paths and now we were about to continue down separate forks again.

"There are two sets of tire prints outside the bus here." She showed me the prints. One set on the side by the door, the other near the back. "Probably trucks or delivery vans. Something big to haul everything away."

"He had partners?" I asked, numb. "He set me up?"

"Hard lesson," Officer McElroy said, "but learn from it. All right? I don't want to hear over the scanner that something worse has happened to you."

Once all the police business was done, I was free to go. I wanted to say goodbye and thank her for her kindness. But Officer McElroy gave me a simple nod and got back in her squad car. So I did the same and took my place in the driver's seat of my bus. I tried to start Gypsy V, but she refused to turn over.

"I'm sorry, okay," I said and rested my forehead on the steering wheel as tears stung my eyes. "I get it. I can't trust everyone. It won't happen again. I promise."

It started right up after that and we limped down the highway toward San Antonio.

There were still more than three hundred miles to go before I got to my sister's house. At least the gas tank was full so I could get that much closer. After that I had no money to fill her up.

When we were down to little more than fumes, I pulled into a truck stop. I considered filling and running but three things stopped me. First, I'd pushed my luck with the law as much as I cared to. Second, Gypsy V wasn't exactly a getaway vehicle. We'd get stopped before we made it back to the highway. Third, the gas pump said I had to pay first.

As I stood there trying to figure out what to do, an old man with buzz cut hair and a big belly pulled in to fill his car.

"Sir," I said, "could you help me?"

He narrowed his eyes and looked from me to my bus. "Wha'd'ya want?"

"My bus," I started, but my voice broke. I pointed and swallowed. "It was stolen and I just got it back. The thief took all my money and I'm out of gas."

"How's that my problem?"

"I'm just wondering, could you spare a few dollars?"

"You need money? Get a job."

So, so, so many times when those of us living in the commune were out bartering our services for necessities, we'd been told to get jobs. My indignation flared. I wanted to tell this guy that kind of attitude made the world an ugly place.

Then Glenn, ever calm and always together Glenn, entered my thoughts. He had negotiated situations like this with respect and politeness. If he was with me right now, he'd place a hand on my shoulder, the signal for me to let him try, and he'd calmly talk to the man until either a deal or an impasse was reached. If an impasse, he'd extend his hand to the man, thank him for his time, and wish him a beautiful day.

I looked down, invoked my best Glenn attitude, and turned empathetic eyes to the man.

"I'm not asking for much, sir. I obviously don't know your situation, but mine is desperate. Just a few dollars will help if you can spare them." I glanced inside his car. Messy didn't begin to describe it. "If you'd like, I'd be happy to clean up your car for you in exchange."

That was risky. I may have just offended him, but what other choice did I have?

He looked sideways at me, picked something out of his

tooth and wiped it on his chinos.

"Tell you what," he said. "I was gonna go inside and grab a bite. You clean 'er up, I'll give ya five bucks."

I had a feeling this job was worth more than five bucks, but again, I had little choice.

That's how I spent the afternoon. First, explain my situation and ask for a donation and if that didn't work, offer to do a little job for them. Some people wanted their cars vacuumed and the windows washed. Some had dogs that needed walking while they went inside. A few gave me money outright, like the elderly couple that said I reminded them of their granddaughter. They handed me a fifty and refused to take it back when I said that was too much. Many others gave me that disgusted get-a-job sneer.

The sun was going down by the time I'd earned enough to fill Gypsy V's tank. I was grimier, stickier, sweatier, and smellier than I'd ever been. I had enough for gas, a small bag of mixed nuts, and two apples though. I had worked up a huge appetite so that little bit would hardly satisfy my hunger, but it was better than nothing.

"Quite a show you been puttin' on out there," the attendant inside said when I went to pay for everything. He was a scrawny little dude, not a whole lot bigger than me. He was also about as dirty as I was.

"Desperate times," I said with a tired smile. I was dying of thirst too but would have to settle with water from the drinking fountain.

"How desperate are ya?" He gave me a lecherous grin that nearly made me spew.

With my face screwed into the best *you are worse than the scum now caked under my fingernails* look I could conjure, I calmly said, "Never, no way, could I ever be desperate enough to do what you're implying."

The grin didn't fade. "You clearly ain't far enough down yet." He grabbed his privates as though making me an offer I shouldn't refuse.

One minute, even thirty seconds of my powers back…

I shoved all of my money across the counter at him and walked out. I managed to pump the gas but was too upset from the run-in to drive so pulled into a secluded picnic area five miles down the road. I turned off the engine and locked the door. Walking up and down the aisle of my stripped bus, I tried to pull myself together. I ended up collapsing onto the bare mattress and bursting into tears.

How much worse could things get? I had nothing to my name but an empty bus, a few changes of clothes, and a broken bluebonnet.

"You've been hungry before," I reminded myself. The road trip from Woodstock to the commune in San Francisco included minimal food. "You've been dirty before." At Woodstock when the rain came and turned the farmer's field to mud. "You've never been alone before though. Not like this."

As I lay on my back, staring at the spot where my chandelier had been, the tears started again, flowing down my temples and into my hair. I sat up cross-legged and wiped my face. I closed my eyes and took in four or five deep breaths, slowing both my spastic breaths and my too-fast heart.

"This is what you wanted." Breath. "The universe agreed to give you what you asked for." Breath. "You can do this." Breath. "The universe will provide."

At some point during my motivational meditation, I fell deeply asleep. It was early morning when I woke to the sound of rain falling softly, then hard, then softly again on the roof of my bus. When I realized Gypsy V was getting washed, I stripped down to nothing but my tunic, grabbed the little sliver of soap from the holder in my tub, and went outside to take part in the cleansing.

The rain had turned soft, not much more than a thick mist.

"Harder," I begged the universe. "Let me wash away all

that happened yesterday. Allow me to prepare for this new day of my new journey."

In answer to my plea, the rain came down hard enough to drench me in a matter of seconds. When I looked around and saw that there was no one else at the little tucked-away picnic site, I pulled off my tunic and lathered my body, twice, from face to feet. There wasn't enough soap to wash my hair, too, so I made due by scrubbing the rain through and through and through. I rinsed away Ritchie and the disgusting truck stop attendant. Soon I was clean outside and refreshed inside.

The rain slowed and then stopped, confirming that I'd done enough. The clouds parted and offered me a peek of blue on the other side.

My color. A sign from the universe. All would be well.

Chapter Seven

Today I would make it to San Antonio. I thought of that as I sat on my bed, nibbling a handful of nuts and appreciating every crunchy bite of one of my apples. One problem though.

"I don't have Carol's address," I called out to Kaf. I knew he was watching me. Probably really enjoyed the cleansing.

The piece of paper Cam had written his phone number on appeared next to me on my bed. Carol's information was written there now, Cam's number gone. And not like it had simply been erased, but as if it had never been there at all. Guess Kaf didn't like me having another guy's number.

Now I had her address, but what was I supposed to do when I got to her house? I assumed she'd recognize me, but then what? Should I tell her the truth and wait for her to accept that I was the same person, physically at least, I'd been when I left home on August 1, 1969? Should I just chat with her until she figured it out? Should I pretend to be my own daughter? No, granddaughter? That would get confusing.

Truth was best, but I needed a memory or a fact, something that only Carol's sister could know. When we were kids, Carol was the prissiest, most do-nothing-wrong person I knew. Well, except for Janice. There was one time, however, when Carol stepped out of her box. It had been during her sophomore year, my freshman, and she had just started dating Roger and thought he was totally boss.

"Carol's got a boyfriend," I sang at her. She didn't roll her eyes at me which meant I was spot on.

"I'm sneaking out," she whispered to me one night after shutting our bedroom door.

"You're what?" I asked and put my hand to her forehead to check for fever. "It's Wednesday. We're not allowed to leave the house on a school night." Not that the day of the week was even close to the point. It was the *Carol* sneaking out bit that was the shocking part.

"I know, I know," Carol said with this dreamy look on her face. "Roger and I are going out Friday night, but we can't wait that long. I'm going to meet him at the park down the street. Just for an hour." She actually clasped her hands and begged. "I'll owe you forever."

To my knowledge, that was the only time Carol had broken a rule. And even while doing so, she followed her self-imposed rule to the letter. She said one hour. She was back in our room, window closing, as the clock ticked over from fifty-nine minutes to sixty. There's no way she would have ever told anyone else about that. The only reason she told me was because we shared a bedroom. Otherwise she would've claimed she had cramps and was going to bed early. No, that was the excuse I used. Carol never would have mentioned anything as personal as cramps to our parents. She'd claim a headache.

With less than two hours until I finally made it to San

Antonio, my nerves started to kick in. When I was two miles from her house, I pulled into a local park and made sure I looked as good as I could. Carol had always been impeccable when it came to her appearance so I put on my nice shorts, a cropped peasant blouse, and my knee-high moccasin boots. I was clean after my rain bath. My body was at least. My hair was a mess. All I could do was secure it place with a headband.

As I inspected myself in the mirror—Marsha, Gail, and Janice joining the scrutiny from the picture tucked behind it—I suddenly felt out of place. I wished I would have asked Indira for a makeover before leaving Kaf's harem. She'd done an amazing job with Crissy's hair. What would I look like as something other than my hippie self? Was there another me waiting to get out? I'd been born Gloria Calhoun. Desiree was my Wish Mistress self. Should I change my name again to fit whomever I'd become on this new journey?

I parked Gypsy V on the street outside of Carol's house. It was a tan and red brick monster with a perfectly landscaped yard. My sister had done well. Or rather, Roger had. My sister had never held a paying job a day in her life. At least she hadn't during the time when I checked in on her.

As I stepped out of the bus, two perfectly made-up women walking teeny-tiny dogs strolled by. They looked first at me and then scowled at Gypsy V.

"Wasn't I just talking about this?" the woman in bright yellow workout clothes told the woman in baby pink. "If we all pitched in we could install a guarded gate and this kind of thing wouldn't happen."

She meant my bus, of course. Maybe she meant me, too. This was exactly what I'd wanted to get away from when I was a kid. People with more than they knew what to do with trying to control those who didn't have enough. Nothing had changed. For as different as the world was in some ways, it was still exactly the same in others.

"May I help you?"

I knew that voice. It had deepened a little over the years, but the slightly snobbish emphasis on the word *help* identified her like a fingerprint.

I turned to see Carol dressed in a pair of khaki capris and a sleeveless polo shirt. She was standing on her front steps staring at Gypsy V like it was a mobile drug den. Then she looked at me. Her eyebrows scrunched together and the color drained from her face. She knew who I was. For about five seconds she was a teenager again, sitting across our bedroom trying to figure out why I dressed the way I did and why I couldn't just follow the rules like the respectable girls.

"Who…?" she started, her voice weaker now. "What…? May I help you with something?"

I didn't know what to say. It had been almost forty-five years, to the day, since I'd last seen her. She was in her mid-sixties now and still wore her hair in a proper bob. She was still thin and athletic in appearance. I pictured her playing tennis or golf—maybe both—at the country club twice a week. Her face was still wrinkle-free. She must've gotten a facelift or two. Carol had always been a sun worshipper. Her deeply-tanned skin told me she still was. It was her but at the same time it wasn't. My sister was a complete stranger.

"Who are you?" she asked more gently this time, like maybe I was a little thick in the head and needed kid-glove handling.

"Who do I look like?"

At the sound of my voice she startled. Did I still sound the same or was she just surprised that this strange girl before her could speak?

"You look," she began and shook her head. "That's not possible."

"Carol—?"

"Excuse me," she said, straightening her shoulders. "That's Mrs. Stratton to you."

"I know exactly how strange this is," I said. "Trust me, my life has been nothing but one strange day after another for forty-five years."

Carol laughed, like this was the most insane thing she'd ever heard. It probably was.

"Forty-five years? You can't be more than seventeen."

"Eighteen."

She shook her head, clearing away the crazy. "What do you want? I have things to attend to."

Charity functions. Mint juleps with the girls. Maybe organizing a collection for that gate they wanted to install to keep the unsavory sort out.

"I came to see you."

"How could you come to see me?" She looked side-to-side, on defense, like maybe the neighbors might be listening or worse, gathering. "You don't even know me. And I have no idea who you are."

"But I do know who you are. You know me, too. I've been away for a long time, I know, but I need help."

"Now look here, Gloria—"

As my birth name came out of her mouth, she paled and had to brace herself against the pillar of her doorway.

"You know it's me," I said softly. "And if you let me in, I'll explain where I've been."

☮☮☮

Carol sat in an overstuffed flower-print chair in her sunroom off a pristine white, gourmet kitchen that smelled like lemons. A glass of sweet tea clutched in a death grip rested on one thigh. She hadn't moved in nearly half an hour. The sweat from the glass had run down the sides and formed a baseball-size wet mark on her khakis.

I had just finished explaining how when I left with Glenn, Marsha, and Stan it was only supposed to be for two weeks. She was following along, numbly, as I explained about Woodstock and the commune. I lost her though when I started to talk about Kaf.

"Glenn put you up to this, didn't he?" Carol asked.

"Glenn?" Did she know where he was? I had checked in on him a few times as I had with her and the rest of my family. Like everyone else, he had assumed I'd died in the accident and after a year or so started dating someone new. Even though I was happy that he was happy, it was too painful to watch, so I stopped checking in.

"He somehow found you and put you up to this," Carol said. She noticed the water mark on her knee, frowned, and set the glass next to the plate of lavender sugar cookies on a silver tray perched on the ottoman between us. "I admit you look remarkably like her. If I brought out a picture it would be hard to tell the two of you apart."

She had pictures of me? That was sweet. I didn't have pictures of anyone. Well, except the one of me and my friends.

"This has been very entertaining," Carol continued. Her southern drawl had turned soft and saccharine. A sign as obvious as blinking neon that I was in trouble. "You tell Glenn, good job. He pulled off a top notch gag. But it's time for you to leave now."

She got up from her chair, picked up the tray, and turned toward the kitchen.

"You snuck out the window," I blurted.

She stopped with her back to me and cocked an ear slightly my direction. "What?"

"Your sophomore year in high school," I said. My hands shook. This was my last shot. I had no other way to convince her I really was me. "It was a Wednesday night. You were going to go on your first date with Roger on Friday." The glassware on the tray in her hands clinked together as a crack formed in her composure. "You snuck out for precisely one hour to meet him at the park."

The tray fell to the ground. I jumped up to guide her back to a chair and then I cleaned up the broken glass, tea, and cookies.

"Be careful," she mumbled and gestured vaguely toward the kitchen. "There's a broom and dustpan in the pantry. Don't cut yourself."

After I'd cleaned up the mess, I returned to the sunroom to find Carol crying.

"How can you still be alive? How can you still be eighteen?"

"I told you," I said. "I know it's hard to believe. I should have died that day alongside the road—"

"That's right," she said, rising to her feet, her shoulders back. "You should have died. Or, after all this time, you should have let me go on believing you did. What right do you have to come and upset my world again?"

What was she saying? I understood this was all a shock to her, but was she really not even a little happy to see me? "Carol—"

"You left and I had to take care of everything." Rattler venom laced her words. "Craig died. Did you know that? Did you know that our brother *died* in Vietnam?"

"Yes, I—"

"He died and I had to be the one to hold Mama and Daddy together. As if you running away hadn't upset them enough already." While she paced, she shredded the tissues she had been using to wipe her tears a couple minutes earlier, the pieces floated down and littered her tile floor. A vision as unlikely as snow in San Antonio. "I was the one who had to listen to them rant and rage about how you left. And then there was their agony believing you were dead. But there was no body so we never knew for sure."

"I'm sorry," I said lamely. She'd never understand that Kaf had made it first possible for me to live and then impossible for me to contact them.

"Too little, too late," she said. "You have no idea the pain you put us through. Craig was understandable. He was serving our country. But you,"—her face twisted in disgust "you were just a selfish hippie, determined to do what you wanted, when you wanted."

"Carol, that's not true," I said. "I was coming home. I was on the way to call Marsha's parents and—"

"Marsha's parents!" Carol said as though this was the final straw. "Do you have any idea what Marsha's parents went through?"

No. I had no idea what had happened to anyone else's family. I never checked. I'd told myself it was too painful.

"Marsha's mama," Carol said, "had a nervous breakdown. Her daddy became an alcoholic."

A chill shocked me at the mention of Marsha's father. Cold dread. Something really bad regarding him...

"Thank you for stopping by," Carol said, dismissing me.

"Carol," I said pathetically, "I came to you because I need help. I know after all this time—"

"What, exactly, do you know?" Carol spun on me.

I couldn't even look at her. "I have no job. This guy stole all my money."

"Ah," she said. A full range of emotions—clarity, hurt, and disappointment—all came through in that one word. "Money. I should have known. I don't know how you still look eighteen, but a lifetime has passed. It's not my fault that you're a sixty-three-year-old hippie with nothing to your name. If you need help, go talk to Kaf, or whatever his name is. He's your savior, right?"

"I can't," I said quietly. "He won't do any more for me."

"So you show up on my doorstep?" She walked to the front door, clearly expecting me to follow. I did. "Sorry, Gloria. You don't get to disappear, put us all through hell, and think you can just waltz back in. I adjusted to being an only child long ago."

"But you're not an only child," I said desperately. "I'm still here, we can try to repair things."

"I'm not giving you any of the inheritance."

All the air whooshed out of me as surely as if she'd punched me in the gut. "What?"

"As the only living heir," she lifted her chin regally, "I got everything from Mama and Daddy when they passed. Rightfully so as I was the only one here to support them in the end."

"You think I want inheritance?" Of everything she'd said to me, this was one thing I wasn't prepared for.

"Obviously," she said, opening the front door wide. "I'm glad to know that you are alive and somewhat well. But you do not get to come back into my life and turn it upside down. I wish you well, but I have nothing for you."

She reached out and for a split second I thought she was going to hug me. Instead she placed a hand on my shoulder and guided me out her door.

"I'll give you fifteen minutes," Carol said, her face set in a look colder than I ever dreamed my own sister capable of. "Then you and that bus need to be out of my neighborhood or I will call the police."

Chapter Eight

What would I have done? If the situation had been reversed, would I have welcomed Carol back or would I be as bitter as she was? These and about a thousand other questions went through my mind as I sat in the driver's seat, waiting for the shock to wear off.

"The universe was supposed to provide," I told Gypsy V or Bonnie the bluebonnet or whoever was listening. Maybe that rain shower this morning wasn't the universe providing. Maybe it was the universe crying over my sad story.

I pulled away from Carol's house. Slowly. Hoping until the last second that she'd come running out and invite me back in, say that we needed to try. That we were the only family the other had left so we needed to reconcile. She didn't though and I had no doubt about her fifteen minute time limit. So I drove away.

I'd actually circled the entirety of San Antonio before it occurred to me that I was using up what little gas I had left.

Besides, I was numb and distracted, not paying attention to where I was or what I was doing, endangering the lives of all the travelers around me.

According to the road sign, the next exit led to downtown San Antonio. Downtown didn't seem like a good place to me, crowded and busy and all, but Gypsy V had other plans. I tried to muscle the wheel left, but she insisted on going right and taking that exit. After the initial surprise, I didn't fight it and let her choose the way. After all, what did it matter where I went? I was happy, grateful even, to let choices be made for me.

I found a fairly deserted street, probably because it was so late in the day and people had gone home for the night, so I pulled over, taking up almost three parking spots. I needed a plan of some kind. Any kind. I had no money and a quarter of a bag of nuts. I'd eaten my last apple before going to Carol's. My stomach rumbled, so I took a very small handful of the nuts, lay down on my bed, and hoped the point of all that had happened in the last three days would come to me. I finally understood what Mandy and Crissy and all of my other charges had felt when I tossed them into the middle of a wish and let them sink or swim on their own.

A strange sound woke me. It took me a minute to realize that someone was knocking on my door. Kaf had never knocked. He just appeared without notice so it couldn't be him.

I opened the door to find a police officer standing outside. This made officer number three since I'd pulled away from the mountains. I was starting to think Kaf had charmed me to attract the fuzz.

"Good evening," he said.

"Hi," I said. "What time is it?"

I had fallen asleep while trying to grasp even the tiniest hint of where my journey was leading me. I didn't feel at all rested so probably hadn't been asleep for that long.

"It's nearly nine o'clock, miss," the officer said.

"You've been parked here for a number of hours. It's a two-hour zone."

"Sorry, sir. I didn't think it would be a problem since the street was clear and all. I've been driving for three days and just got into town." To my surprise, I kept talking. "I thought my sister would help me but she won't. I don't have any money because some guy stole it." I motioned to the inside of my bus. "He took everything but my clothes. I'm down to probably a gallon of gas. So I pulled over—"

He held up a hand for me to stop. He peeked inside my bus and easily verified my story. It was as barren as the desert surrounding Kaf's cave and had obviously been stripped clean.

"I'm sorry for your situation," he said. "But you cannot leave your bus parked on the city streets."

"Even if no one is here?" I asked. "No disrespect, but it's not like I'm bothering anyone here."

He considered that. "Driving for three days?"

I nodded and blinked a few times. I would not let myself be one of those women who cried to get out of things. My rambling, hysterical monologue was embarrassing enough.

"Okay, look," he said and let out a sigh, "I'll let you stay here for the night because it's dark and, I assume, you don't know your way around. Get a good night's sleep. You look like one of the walking dead."

"Thank you, officer."

"You need to move out of here first thing in the morning though."

"Where am I supposed to go?" I sounded whiney, needy. But I truly had no idea. "I don't have any money to go anywhere else."

He nodded. At least he was sympathetic to my situation.

"You're going to need to find employment. Plenty of places are looking for help. Restaurants need servers. The hotels always need housekeeping staff."

Far from the sociologist I'd always envisioned myself

becoming, but it would pay the rent, so to speak.

"There's a parking lot for buses,"—he pointed—"a few blocks that way. But you'll need a permit and it's only a short-term lot. There are some campgrounds east and south of here. You could leave your bus at one of those and try to find a job near the campground. I'll grant you, there won't be as many opportunities as there will be here. And you have to pay more to stay at a campground."

"What am I supposed to do then? Abandon my bus somewhere?"

"I wouldn't suggest that," the officer said. "You'll get towed and have to pay a small fortune to get it out of the impound lot."

My chest tightened as the desperation of my situation became more clear.

"There's a great free place not far from here," the officer said and pointed the opposite direction from the parking lot. "It's called Rita's Kitchen."

"As in free food?" That was the best news I'd heard since Cam helped me with the lock on my bus.

"Yep. I hear its good food, too," the officer said. "She also has contact names of places that can help you out. Your best option may be to let the bus get impounded, find a shelter to stay at, and get yourself a job."

He made it sound so easy. Finding work shouldn't be that hard. Letting my bus get impounded, however, felt like letting my child become ward of the state.

"I'll be patrolling the area all night so no one else will bother you," he said. "But you do need to be gone before the start of the business day tomorrow."

"Yes, sir. Thank you, sir."

I closed and locked the door and dropped onto the floor. Now what? It made the most sense to stay downtown if this was where the jobs were. But what was I supposed to do with the bus? I covered my face with my hands and sent a silent plea into the universe for help. A puff of cold air hit me a second later. And there was this faint smell of smoke. Not the something-was-on fire smoke. The sweet-and-spicy, bitter-and-sour smoke that always hovered around Kaf.

I peeked through my fingers, expecting to see him standing there and prepared to go ape on his ass for letting me suffer the way I had for the last few days. He wasn't there though and because I had no control over my emotions, I switched from angry to disappointed.

He had delivered two pieces of paper and set them in my lap. One was a one-week permit to park in the bus lot the officer had told me about and the other a map that showed that the lot was about six blocks away.

There was also a Zen stone. The same type of emerald-green stone with the slightly-opened circle etched on it that I'd given each of my charges. This one the size and shape of a Ping-Pong ball except flat.

"What does it do?" Mandy had asked when I'd handed a flat, egg-shaped stone to her two months earlier.

"First, it starts the wish," I'd told her. "After that, think of it as a mystical paging device. If you really need to, you can call me with it."

If this stone worked the same way as those I'd handed out, Kaf would have to appear the moment I touched the circle. My heart fluttered at the thought of seeing him and I actually reached out for the circle but pulled back. I knew very well that a wish's path didn't always go smoothly, but overall I was safe. Yes, I was hungry, but I had a place to get breakfast in the morning. I had a parking permit. I was getting by on my own, living like the independent woman I professed to be.

I also knew that, as I had for my charges, Kaf had provided me with what I needed for my wish to end successfully. That meant everything that had happened was leading to that end. What purpose nearly losing my bus could serve, I couldn't guess. I needed to be patient and remember the rules. Because no matter how much I wanted to be, I wasn't special. My wish, and presumably Kaf, knew where my new path was and all these events had to be guiding me there.

So why bring me to downtown San Antonio? What could possibly be waiting for me here?

☮☮☮

Turned out that Rita's Kitchen was only three blocks from where I'd parked for the night. I had already pushed the kindness of the San Antonio PD as far as I dared so moved the bus to the lot and walked back nine or ten blocks.

I'd never been to a soup kitchen before so didn't know what to expect. From the outside, Rita's appeared nice and homey. It was on a corner, windows made up the front wall, navy and white awnings kept the intense Texas sun out. From the sidewalk, I saw a few people moving about inside. The sign on the door said breakfast was served from six until eight o'clock. Hopefully I hadn't missed it.

The first thing I noticed was the aroma, something spicy. My stomach roared and my mouth watered. The next thing was a set of three sinks to my right by the front door with the instruction to 'Wash Up!' in hand-painted letters on the wall over them. Then came the dining room. It was big but simple with ten, ten-foot long tables, and five round tables, each surrounded by ten chairs.

In the far corner, straight across from the entry, was a little sitting area with two old couches and two stuffed chairs. On the wall were the words 'Sit. Read. Relax.' A man and woman sat on one of the couches with books in their hands. Two kids filled the chairs. They'd pulled a coffee table up close and were playing a board game.

The walls especially captured my attention. They were covered with murals and drawings in various stages of completion. I instantly thought of Gypsy V with her paint job that made sense only to me.

A man wearing grungy, loose-fitting workpants was sitting on the floor to my left and working on one of the murals. He was painting a life-sized dog, a shaggy mutt, next to an already painted life-sized park bench. He was good. The images were so crisp and clear, I'd swear the mural was a photograph from a distance.

"That's Hank." A woman in a navy apron was wiping down the table closest to the door. 'Rita' was embroidered in white over her heart. On the right side was a steaming bowl of soup on a blue-and-white checked tablecloth and 'Rita's Kitchen' below it. "Hank's the dog by the way. Henry is the artist."

"He's really good," I said. "Henry, I mean."

The woman chuckled softly. She still hadn't looked up from the table. When she did, she froze and the color drained from her face. She swayed and held onto the edge of the table.

"Are you okay?" I rushed to her side and took her by the arm.

She shrugged away my hand but never took her eyes off of me.

"I'm okay," Rita said. "Sorry. You just...you look almost exactly like someone I knew." She laughed, embarrassed. "Ever had that happen?"

"Sure. Happens to everyone."

"I'm Rita Morales," she said. "I run this place."

Rita was a little taller than me, probably in her forties, average build. Her light-brown hair tied up in a messy bun gave her a slightly disheveled appearance, like a busy mom with too many kids. Nice. Who wouldn't want to eat a meal cooked by Mom? Then I remembered that this wasn't a restaurant. The food was free. If you had nowhere else to get a meal and a free one was offered, you wouldn't care if it was made by Mom, Dad, or the crazy uncle everyone whispered about.

"Would you like something to eat?" Rita asked.

Despite how hungry I was, I suddenly felt embarrassed to be there.

"You're not hungry enough if you're hesitating," Rita said. "Or are you here for some other reason?"

"Breakfast would be great." My voice shook a little. I wasn't quite sure why. "Am I too late? Looks like you're cleaning up."

"You're just catching the end of it," Rita said and went to the serving line, diagonal from the front door. She waved me over, her eyes still on me like I was someone come back from the dead. "We had breakfast burritos with scrambled eggs, chorizo, and Monterey jack cheese this morning. There are a couple left. Just so you know, you get here before the food runs out and you can eat. Otherwise you'll have to wait 'til lunch. Breakfast starts at six and closes at eight. Later if we have a lot of people left to serve and haven't run out of food yet. Earlier if the food runs out."

A quick glance at the clock centered on the wall behind the food line told me it was eight-twenty.

"Wash your hands, please," Rita said and pointed at the hand washing station by the front door. "I'll get you some breakfast. And before you ask, I don't take orders and I don't make more once the batch is gone."

If Rita was a mom, she was nothing like mine. My mother would make whatever you wanted, whenever you wanted. Of course she only had five of us. Rita probably had fifty times that many mouths to feed.

She handed me a plate with a burrito and home fries.

"Have a seat anywhere. Forks and such are on that table over there." She pointed at the condiment table. "There's milk and juice down there, too. Help yourself. Just so you know, I encourage everyone to leave after they've eaten. If guests have nowhere else to go or nothing to do, they can stay. I just don't think it's good for people to sit in here all day."

Go out and play. Get some fresh air and sunshine. It's

good for you. My mom used to tell us that all the time.

I nodded and took a seat at a table across from Henry. He was slow and detailed with his work.

"Was that your dog?" I asked.

Henry jumped and made a grumbling noise at the smudge that had happened as a result.

"Sorry," I said. "Didn't mean to startle you."

Henry returned to his painting without answering my question.

"He doesn't talk," Rita said, wiping down another table now. "Not sure why. He came in for breakfast one day, pulled a pencil out of his pocket, and started drawing on my wall."

Henry paused in his work and turned slightly toward Rita as she spoke.

"I yelled at you at first, remember?" she asked him. "Until I realized you were sketching what turned out to be my logo and not just graffiti-ing up my place."

She pointed to the 'Sit. Read. Relax.' corner. I turned and saw the logo I hadn't noticed before—'Rita's Kitchen' in two-foot tall letters and the same soup bowl on a tablecloth that were on her apron.

"Henry used to be in marketing," Rita said.

"If he doesn't speak," I asked, "how—"

"He wrote a few details down for me one day," she supplied.

I looked at Henry, the way he held himself—mostly tall and confident despite the grubby clothes and beaten down by The Man demeanor—and wondered what had happened in his life to change his path from professional to soup kitchen guest.

The burrito was a simple concoction—eggs, chorizo, red peppers, cheese. Maybe it was just that I'd had nothing but nuts, apples, and water for two days, but it was really good. The milk was super cold, just the way I liked it. And while the dining room was sparse and reminded me of a school cafeteria, it also had a warm, homey feel that made me want to stay. I think it was the artwork. It was easy to tell that many people had added to the walls. Some of the drawings were detailed and precise like Henry's. Others were more of the stick-figure influence. Decorating at will must make the guests feel like it was their place. I had the urge to pick up a paint brush and add a peace sign.

I finished my breakfast and brought my dishes to the cart near the serving line.

"Are you new around here?" Rita asked from the far side of the food line she was wiping down. "I haven't seen you before. And I remember all the faces that come in my door."

"I'm passing through." I could tell by her reaction, a simple nodding of her head, she heard that all the time. "I came to find my sister. We had a falling out a long time ago. She decided I don't fit in her world now."

Why was I telling all of this to a perfect stranger? Must be that mom vibe she had going on.

"I'm sorry to hear that," Rita said in a caring but business-like way. "If you need someplace to stay—"

"Oh, no," I said. "I'm not homeless. I just don't have any money. I need to find a job."

"Plenty of places looking," Rita said.

She kept glancing at me. It made me uncomfortable.

"Is something wrong?" I asked. "You keep looking at me. Have I stayed too long? I can leave."

"No," Rita said, "you're not in the way or anything like that. Sorry to stare. Like I said, you remind me of someone. It's uncanny really."

I wanted to ask who the person was. Had they parted on bad terms? No, Rita's reaction was more sorrow than bitterness. Had the person run away? Had she died? It was almost like Rita could sense my questions because before I could ask, she moved on to a different topic.

"I'm wondering about your story," she said. "I've heard practically every situation you can think of over the last five years. I'm just trying to tag one on you."

"Okay," I said, "any guesses?"

She studied me a bit longer, smiling a little as she did, and then shook her head. "Nope. I can't get a reading on you. What's your name, sweetheart?"

"It's Desiree," I said. "Thank you for breakfast. It was really good." I jerked a thumb over my shoulder. "I should go look for a job now."

"You goin' dressed like that?" She asked the question in that casual *it's up to you but you might want to reconsider* way a mom would.

I looked down at my bell bottom jeans, tie-dyed tank top, and fringed vest. I'd even added my favorite strand of love beads to complete the look.

"What's wrong with my threads?" I asked. "I've got shoes on."

I double checked. I did. That was saying something. My feet preferred to be free.

She gave me that squinty-eyed look again. Analyzing. Trying to figure me out. Have at it, sister. Let me know what you come up with.

"It's not exactly an interview outfit," she said, again in that mom way.

Ordinarily a stranger critiquing me this way would irritate me. Rita seemed to have a genuine interest in my success though.

"This is all I've got. Well, there's a long dress back in my bus. It's kind of hot for that today though."

"Bus?"

"That's where I live," I said.

Her left eyebrow arched and for the first time I wondered if there was something wrong with living in a bus. No. She didn't understand about Gypsy V.

"You should at least wash your hair," Rita said. "And I'm not saying that to be mean. I'm trying to help you present the best you that you can."

Now I'd been scolded. By someone else's mom. She was right though. It had been days since shampoo had touched my hair and honestly, it was nice that she cared enough to say something.

"Do you know of someplace I can take a shower?" I asked.

"In fact, I do," she said and held up a finger, indicating I should hang on a moment. She slipped into the back room and came out a minute later with a towel, a little bar of soap, a little bottle of shampoo, and a key. She placed the bundle in my hands and pointed at a doorway near the reading corner. "Through the door and up the stairs you'll find a bathroom. Clean yourself up and clean up the bathroom when you're finished. If I go up there and find it a mess I won't let you use it again."

"There's seriously a shower I can use? That's so bitchin'."

"Our guests need all the help they can get getting back on their feet," Rita said with total sincerity. "They come for breakfast, clean up for the day, and go in search of employment."

"Thanks, Rita." How great to be able to help people in need this way.

"There are a few items of clothing up there. You find anything a little more,"—she checked out my outfit again—"current, feel free to borrow it. Then I suggest you head on down to the Riverwalk. There are tons of places there. Good luck. Stop back if you need another meal. We serve lunch noon to two and dinner five to seven-thirty."

It was amazing the effect a full stomach and a shower had. I felt energized, ready to get a job, and truly start on my new journey.

☮☮☮

It had gotten hotter and more humid outside while I was

inside Rita's. Or maybe it was just that Rita's Kitchen was air conditioned. Either way, sweat was trickling down my spine after walking only a few blocks.

The first sign I came to announcing the Riverwalk had an arrow pointing down a flight of stairs. What kind of restaurants would be below street level? Usually people did their best to stay away from hidden places. Still, Rita said that was a good place to find a job so down I went. By the bottom of the staircase I felt like I'd stepped into a secret world. Easily one of the grooviest places I'd ever seen, and I had been to a lot of groovy places.

The Riverwalk was like an oasis below the streets of San Antonio. While the street level was like any other big city, all concrete and tall buildings, the Riverwalk was lush with huge flowering trees and shrubs, thousands of plants, and as the name implied, a river lined by sidewalks. On each side of the river were restaurants, hotels, and little shops. Stone bridges connected the two sides. Flat-bottomed boats filled with tourists and guides reciting the history of the area floated past. If not for the occasional roar of a truck's engine or the honk of a car's horn, I would've been sure that the rest of the world had disappeared.

I was so enchanted by the place, I wandered the sidewalks and crossed every bridge I came to before starting my job hunt. While I walked, I saw some places with 'Now Hiring' signs in the windows. Not as many as I'd hoped, but it was a start. I decided to try a restaurant called The Old Stone Church. That's exactly what it was—a small, old church made out of stone. Below the name on the black, oval sign it read 'A Fine Dining Establishment.' The finer the place, the better the pay, I figured.

"May I help you?" a man in tux asked when I entered the restaurant.

"Yeah, hi," I said. "I see you're looking for help."

"Do you have any experience?"

He made a disapproving face while analyzing my outfit.

Maybe I should have borrowed something from the rack at Rita's.

"Um, a little." You needed experience to bring people food? It had been a while, but I used to help my mom bring food to the table every night. That must count for something.

"Do you have any references?" the man asked.

"References?"

He sighed in a way that told me he was done talking to me, he just hadn't ended the conversation yet. "Someone who can verify that you would be a top quality employee."

Carol. But the likelihood of her even admitting I was her sister was low. Kaf?

"No," I told him.

"Miss," he said, flipping importantly through papers, "we only hire experienced wait staff who have impeccable references."

"Oh. Gotcha." I held up a peace sign. "Thanks anyway."

All right, fine dining clearly wasn't the best place for me to start. The next place I came to sold Tex-Mex.

"How old are you?" the guy behind the bar asked.

Numerically or chronologically?

"Eighteen," I said.

He frowned. "We're looking for a bartender. Legally you're old enough but we prefer someone with a lot of experience."

I could pop a top on a beer can with the best of them. That's probably not what he meant though.

"Do you need a waitress?" I asked. "I can bring people food."

"A server, you mean?"

Server? Not waitress? Okay, another change of the times. "Yes, sir. Do you need any servers?"

"Sorry. Our wait staff is full. Check back later next week. We might have an opening for kitchen help by then. We tend to go through a lot of dish washers."

Just the wrong place, I told myself. I needed to find a

non-fancy place that was looking for someone other than a bartender. The seafood place needed an assistant manager. I had no experience with that so kept walking. The Italian place needed someone to do bookwork. I'd never even heard of "QuickBooks." The French place was looking for a pastry chef. My only experience with French pastries was the day I ate six chocolate éclairs, and drank three lattés, at a café in this little French village after concluding a wish for a particularly ornery charge.

I passed by a plain, wooden, hand-painted sign for an ice cream parlor and stopped. That could be the perfect place for me. I wouldn't need to know how to mix any drinks—except maybe for a malt and a bartender's certificate probably wasn't needed for that—and I wouldn't have to deliver anything so no waitressing skills…no. No *serving* skills necessary.

The woman at the window—which did have a 'Help Wanted' sign taped to it—wore a nametag that identified her as Emily. Below her name it said "owner." Emily had crazy-long hair done in about a hundred little braids and cinched back in a ponytail. She also had a small, silver nose ring with a fine silver chain that attached to her left earring. Cool. I had to get one of those. Of course that would mean getting my nose pierced. That had to hurt.

"Hi, Emily," I said and pointed at the sign. "You need help?"

"Do you have any ID?" Emily wanted to know.

This was progress. She didn't ask about experience. I didn't need to know the chemical makeup of vanilla versus French vanilla versus New York vanilla. All I needed was an ID. I had that.

I took the driver's license Kaf had given me from my bag and handed it to her.

"Says you're from Colorado," Emily said.

"I just moved here," I said. "Haven't had time to take care of that yet."

"Hmm," she said and handed it back to me. "You got a social security card?"

"I've got a number." I couldn't remember what it was though.

"How about a passport?"

"I thought Texas was part of the US." Seriously, had I crossed a border without realizing it?

"Very funny. You're a funny girl," she said, shaking a finger at me. "Look, the law says I have to have two forms of identification to verify that you're legal to work in this country. That means your driver's license and social security card or passport or birth certificate."

Seriously? I had found possibly the one place on the Riverwalk that would hire me and I couldn't get the job because I only had a driver's license?

"That's all I've got," I said.

I must've looked desperate because she took a little pity on me.

"Sorry. You're young and you've got a great look." She motioned to my outfit. "Perfect for this place. But I gotta follow the rules. If you get hold of another document, come back and see me."

"I understand. Thanks anyway."

"Would you like an ice cream?" she asked as I turned away. "On the house."

I turned back. "On the house is exactly what I can afford."

I figured she'd give me a small cone. Emily was bitchin' though and said I looked like I could stand to gain a couple pounds. So she piled it on until I cried uncle. I sat under an umbrella at a table along the river and ate my triple-scoop bowl of raspberry cheesecake, Rocky Road, and Pecan Brownie with caramel, hot fudge, and whipped cream.

It was late afternoon, almost four, and while I didn't have a job, yet, I felt like I was a step further along on my path than I had been that morning. Gypsy V was legally parked and I wasn't going to starve. Good stuff.

As I sat there, wishing I had one more scoop of ice cream, I noticed a teenage girl across the river. She caught my eye because she was wearing pajama pants. It was a little cooler below street level by the river, but still far too hot for long flannel pants. What kept my attention was the fact that she was going up to every person that she passed and asking…something. Even from the distance, her expression looked pained, like she was desperate. Maybe she was lost or had lost someone. No, she was too calm for that. The crowd was huge, shoulder-to-shoulder in some spots. If I'd lost someone here I'd be frantic.

Most people just walked past her, ignoring her pleas for…whatever. Finally an older couple stopped and listened to her. The girl talked and talked. She even clasped her hands in front of her chest at one point. The woman patted the man's arm—husband and wife I assumed—and nodded at him. He reached into his pocket, pulled out his wallet, and handed the girl some money. She grabbed his hand in hers and lowered her forehead to it. The woman said something, to which the girl shook her head, gave her a big hug, and then the couple moved on.

I'd been watching the scene so closely, I hadn't realized that my entire body had started to shake. Maybe it was from all that ice cream, but more likely it was that the longer I watched, the more the girl across the river reminded me of Marsha.

Their faces were different but their hair was nearly identical. For as long as I'd known her, Marsha had a habit of braiding her hair when she got bored. She'd put a braid in, immediately take it out, and put it back in again. Repeat, repeat, repeat. When we lived in the commune the habit changed a little. She'd put in a dozen or so skinny braids but she wouldn't take them out right away. If she left them in too long, her hair would look really messed up, almost like dreadlocks. That's how this Marsha-girl's hair looked, almost like dreadlocks.

It wasn't just her hair though. Her way of moving, bouncing around like the ball in a pinball machine, reminded me of Marsha toward the end. Someone would send her in one direction, someone else would step in and send her in another. She never admitted it, but I knew Marsha was scared and lost in her own life. That's how this girl looked—a little scared, a little in pain, and a little lost in her own world.

When I came out of my memory-induced stupor, the Marsha-girl was turning away from a walk-up restaurant window with what looked like French fries and a big drink. She chose a seat and shoved fries into her mouth like she hadn't eaten in days.

Those few hours I'd spent begging for gas money at the truck stop had been humiliating. How must this girl feel? Was that what my life would become?

No, I had a home and I'd found a place to eat. The Marsha-girl must not know about Rita's Kitchen. I needed to help her.

I walked a dozen or so yards to a trash can and threw away my sundae bowl. By the time I turned back, the Marsha-girl had already left.

Chapter Nine

After a week, I still hadn't found a job. I also hadn't given up. I knew Kaf could get the certificate and card for me, but I didn't want to deal with the smug *see you need me* look that would surely be on his face if I asked. There had to be someplace out there that wouldn't care if I had experience or worry that I didn't have the right documents. I tried every restaurant along the Riverwalk and those within walking distance of the parking lot. None of them would hire me without the proper documents. At the last hotel I tried, a questionable establishment to say the least, the woman behind the registration desk pulled me aside. Actually she pulled me all the way outside onto the sidewalk.

"Listen," she said, "if you ain't got a social security card or a passport you've basically got two options."

Finally, someone willing to help me. "What are they?"

"One," she held up a finger with a dagger-like nail, "you find a job that pays cash."

"What kinds of jobs pay cash?" I couldn't even find coins on the street. Desperate didn't begin to describe my situation.

"You know, odd jobs here and there."

I needed steady money. Not here and there jobs.

"What's the other option?" I asked.

"Buy a passport."

"How do I do that?"

She looked over her shoulder into the hotel and back at me. "I know a guy."

I may have lost touch with some aspects of the world during my years as Wish Mistress, but even I could tell by her tone this was not the standard way people acquired passports.

"It'll cost ya," she said.

"How much?"

"A few grand."

"Grand? As in a few thousand dollars?"

She nodded. "Probably ten."

"Sister, if I had that kind of bread to spend on a passport I wouldn't need a job."

"Well, I do know of one other way you can earn some money fast." She raised her eyebrows and stared me in the eye.

The slime ball at the truck stop waggling his privates at me had given me a similar look. So those were my choices? Illegal documents or prostitute myself. Well, there was also begging like the Marsha-girl. But that would also fall into the minimal cash option. And pan-handling was illegal in San Antonio, so there was that detail.

I could call Mandy or Crissy. Except I didn't know how to get in touch with them. When they made their wishes their info had appeared in my *genie phone*—as many of my charges had referred to it—but Kaf had taken my phone. I could track them down but then what? It's not like either of them had the money to help me. Maybe I could find a few of those odd jobs the skuzzy hotel lady mentioned. It would take a while, but eventually I'd make enough to go back to them.

Or I could summon Kaf.

No. I was an independent woman. I could figure this out on my own.

My stomach rumbled. I hadn't eaten since breakfast early that morning. That's why ridiculous options were sounding okay to me. Time to go back to Rita's Kitchen. I'd been there for at least two meals a day all week and, like every other person who ate there, I was enormously grateful for the food. It didn't hurt that Rita was a great cook.

At first I figured we'd all keep to ourselves, like that first day of junior high school when few of us knew each other. We'd mind our business, eat our meal, and go on with whatever we had to do. That was true for some, but just like with Marsha, Gail and Janice that first day, I was getting to know some of the other guests.

One family—a mom, dad, and three kids—had captured my attention the first time I saw them. The oldest kid was a boy and the younger two were girls. They dressed well and looked to be an average, middle-class family. If they were sent back in time forty-five years, they could be my family. What had happened to them? Why were they eating at a soup kitchen?

The third time I saw them I smiled and waved. They invited me to have dinner with them.

"You're new here," the mom said.

I nodded. "Just moved to the area and I'm still trying to find a job."

"Good luck with that," the dad said. He told me that he had been a warehouse manager. The mom had opened a little nail salon, her dream, six months before he lost his job.

"We sunk a ton of money into my salon," she said. "It was starting to take off, but we had to borrow from our savings now and then to pay some of the bills. When he lost his job, I had to close up shop and take a job at another salon. Our savings has to go toward our mortgage so we don't lose our house, too. Not to paying bills at a struggling business."

"I've got a few leads," the dad said. "A job might come through soon. It'll be years before she can think about opening her salon again though."

They were a good family. I hoped everything worked out for them.

When I walked into Rita's this time it was only three o'clock, two hours before dinner service. Rita was a blur behind the counter. I swear, the woman never stopped moving. With her back to me she called out, "Dinner isn't until five."

"I know," I said. "Thought I'd just hang out." It was another hot day and the air conditioning felt wonderful.

Rita stopped and gave me a smile. "Oh, Desiree, it's you."

"Hi, Desiree." Leo, a boy about my age, was sitting near Henry, watching him work on his mural and examining Henry's box of brushes and tools. Leo was big but not buff and wore his hair in a buzz cut. Every time I'd come to Rita's, Leo had been there.

"Hi, Leo," I said. "How's your day?"

"Same as yesterday." That was the same response he gave me every time I asked.

The first day I had met him he sat down next to me like we were old friends.

"Hi. I'm Leo," he had said. "I'm eighteen. How old are you? I got to sleep at the bunkhouse last night 'cause they had a bed available." He didn't wait for me to respond, just kept giving me his introduction. "When I was sixteen. I got in a fight. This dude hit me in the head with a metal pipe and now my brain don't work so good no more and I can't get a job."

"What was the fight about?" I asked him.

"A girl," Leo had said with a sort of aw-shucks blush.

"What about the rest?" a man across the table asked Leo. To me he said, "He tells this story to every new person he meets. He likes to leave out this last bit."

"I was mad at the dude," Leo said. "We both liked that girl and he stole her just when she was going to go on a date with me."

"And," the man pushed.

Leo looked down shamefully at his hands. "And I cut him with my knife. Not bad though. It was only a little cut on his arm. He hurt my brain way worse." He pulled out a five-inch knife with a nasty-looking serrated edge on it to show me. The men sitting on either side of Leo immediately stood and backed away.

"Leo!" Rita had charged from across the room. "Why do you have that?"

"For protection," Leo had said as though that should be obvious.

"No," Rita said. "Not only are weapons are not allowed in here, you are not allowed to have a knife. You know that. Your probation officer reminds you about that all the time." She held out her hand. "Give it to me."

Leo followed her to the kitchen and stopped beneath the sign over the door that read 'Employees and Volunteers Only.' He shuffled his toes as close as possible without crossing the line.

"How am I supposed to protect myself?" There had actually been tears in his eyes.

"You don't need to protect yourself in here," Rita had said. "Either way, you're not allowed to carry a knife anymore. You could have hurt that boy badly so the judge told you, no more knives. Remember?"

Because he had broken a rule, no weapons, Rita told him he had to leave the Kitchen for the rest of the day. He could come back in the morning for breakfast. I remained slightly on guard every time I saw Leo after that. He was a good guy, things just didn't connect in his brain like they should.

"So," Rita asked, "How's the job hunt?

"Dead," I told her. "No experience, no job. No documents, no job."

"No documents?"

"All I have is a driver's license and apparently that's not good enough." There was a wash bucket sitting at the end of one table. I squeezed out the rag floating inside and wiped down the table.

"You don't have a social security card?" Rita asked.

I left home without it in 1969. Not something I figured I'd need during a road trip.

"I have no idea where it is."

"Isn't it probably at home where you left it?"

In all the chats we'd had over the week, and we'd had many, this was the first time she had mentioned anything about my home or family. I had no idea what had happened to all the things I'd left behind. I doubted Carol had them. It was remotely possible that she'd kept a few items, but my social security card wouldn't be one of them.

"No," I said, "my stuff is long gone."

Rita paused and gave me that look that she'd given me many times. It said 'what happened to you?'

"Well then," Rita said while setting empty pans in the hot food serving area, "you'll need to get a new one."

"How do I do that?"

"Don't suppose you have a copy of your birth certificate do you?"

I shook my head.

"You'll need to order one of those first," Rita said. "There's a form to fill out with the state you were born in and they'll send you a replacement. Once you have that, you fill out another form with the social security department to get a replacement card."

Right. Get replacement documents for either Gloria Calhoun, a person declared dead in 1970, or Desiree No Last Name, a person who had never legally existed. I had no choice. I was going to have to summon Kaf. Despite being hugely opposed to asking him for help, a little thrill rushed through me at the thought of seeing him.

"Ow," Rita said and held her left hand in her right. "Damn."

"What? Are you okay?"

Rita looked frazzled. Normally she seemed bullet proof. Today she was racing around, trying to do everything at the same time to get set up for the next meal. She looked tired, too. Her eyes were droopy and had big dark circles beneath them.

"I'm fine. Just pinched my finger."

"Don't you have anyone helping you today?" I asked. Normally there were a dozen people buzzing around the place.

She went back into the back room and returned holding an ice cube to her finger.

"My help consists of volunteers and two paid employees. A big church group was supposed to come help serve tonight. There were enough of them that I told Faith, one of my employees, she could have the night off. My other employee is on sabbatical for a month building a school in Guatemala." She let out a hard exhale. "Anyway, the church group had to cancel at the last minute because of transportation problems. I called Faith. She'll be here in a little bit."

"I can help," I said. "I'm just sitting here doing nothing." I raised my voice a little. "I bet Leo can help too. Can't you, Leo?"

He sprang up out of his seat. "What help should I do?"

Rita stopped what she was doing and stared at me for a good long while. Finally she said, "I have one cardinal rule around here: Don't get involved with the guests. I know things about people only because they tell me. I never ask personal questions. It's easier that way."

"But?" I could hear it coming. If the tingles coursing through my body meant anything, a new fork was about to appear on my path.

Rita shook her head and went back into the kitchen. She returned with a pan of food this time and slid it into a warming well on the food table.

"I don't know what it is about you, Miss Desiree," she said. "No, that's not true. I know exactly what it is. You look like Soledad. And because you look like her, I feel like I need to help you. You've been out there every day, all day looking for a job even though everyone tells you no." She paused and zoned-out for a few seconds. A slow, sad smile turned her mouth before she returned to the now. "I'm impressed with your perseverance."

I was dying to know who Soledad was but said nothing. I was afraid that if I did I'd break the spell and she'd retract whatever it was she was about to say.

"I can pay you two hundred dollars a week in cash," she finally said. "I'm legally allowed to pay someone six hundred dollars, well, five-hundred-ninety-nine, before I have to report it as income for tax purposes." She paused again. "That'll give you three weeks of work. Your replacement documents should be here by then and Celia will almost be back from Guatemala."

Six hundred dollars? That was a fortune. To me at least. It would be almost enough to get me back to Mandy and Crissy.

"That would help a lot," I said softly, still afraid of breaking whatever spell was happening.

"What do you think?" Rita seemed hesitant, like maybe she shouldn't be making the offer. "You try it for three weeks. After that you can move on if it's not working for you." She shrugged noncommittally. "Or, if you do a good job, maybe I'll hire you."

"Yes!" I blurted before she could change her mind. "Thank you, Rita."

"Don't thank me yet," she said, turning away. "You're going to have to work hard. We barely get cleaned up from breakfast before we have to start lunch. Then it repeats for dinner. And all over again the next day. You'll go home exhausted every night." Her face softened. "But knowing that you put food in the bellies of hungry people will be the most fulfilling thing you've ever done."

Well, there were a few wishes I'd granted over the years that I'd classify as equally fulfilling. I understood what she meant though.

"Come on then," Rita said waving me into the back room. "We've got a ton of things to do and only forty-five minutes to do them. My customers may be grateful for a free meal, but they expect it on time." She stopped and called out, "Leo? Could you wipe down the tables for me?"

Again, Leo sprang to his feet and stood like a soldier. He even saluted. "Yes, ma'am. Yes, I can."

The first thing Rita did was hand me a 'Rita's Kitchen' T-shirt and apron.

"Don't get me wrong," she said, "I, um, *dig* your style, but those sleeves are a safety risk in the kitchen."

I had on a mini-dress, tie-dyed in these bitchin' psychedelic colors with long, loose bell sleeves. It reminded me of an outfit Janis Joplin wore at Woodstock. I loved the dress, but I could see how it wasn't appropriate kitchen wear.

"Run upstairs to the clothes rack," Rita said. "There should be a pair of pants or a skirt up there that will get you through the shift."

I found a denim skirt up there that fit me perfectly. Too perfectly. I was pretty sure Kaf had manifested it. After I changed, Rita showed me where to wash my hands and gave me a quick lesson on how to use the dishwasher.

A thin woman with big Texas hair walked into the kitchen as I was pulling on a pair of rubber gloves.

"I'm here, y'all can relax now." The woman spoke in one of the strongest southern accents I had ever heard. I'd seen her a couple times during the week but didn't know who she was.

"Faith, this is Desiree," Rita said. "I just hired her. Temporarily. Desiree, this is Faith."

Faith held out a slim hand to me. "Can't tell you how happy I am that you're here, Desiree. There's no such thing as too much help around this place."

"All right," Rita said, "enough chit-chat. Time's flying."

Once I was gloved, Rita put me to work helping with the last of the dinner prep. Tonight's meal was diced chicken and vegetables in white gravy with either mashed potatoes or big, Texas-sized biscuits. The chicken-and-veggie mixture was bubbling in big pots and smelled so, so, so good. There were also shredded-beef burritos and salad.

"We make a lot of burritos here," Rita said. "They're easy, filling and the customers love them."

My stomach growled loud enough for Rita to hear. She glanced at the clock.

"You've got time. Get yourself something to eat. I don't want you passing out while you serve," she said. "Then you can finish cutting up the lettuce for salad."

Easy choice. I went for the chicken-and-veggies over mashed potatoes. It was something my mom would've made. With the first creamy, savory bite, I felt emotion rise up from some deeply hidden place inside me. I'd missed my parents a lot over the years, but never as fiercely as I did at that moment. Maybe it was because I was back in Texas. Maybe it was that since Kaf stripped me of my powers, I'd never felt so vulnerable. Like a little girl in need of protection.

I ate quickly, finished the lettuce, and peeked out the kitchen door. The line went out the front door and, if this meal was like all the other meals I'd been here for, around the corner and down the block. The area by the hand washing sinks near the front door was a congested cluster of guests getting ready for dinner.

As I wandered the Riverwalk and the streets of San Antonio over the week, I'd seen lots of people that must've had grant-worthy wishes. An old man missing a leg struggling to get across the street in his wheelchair. What would he wish for? A new leg? A motorized chair? A Good Samaritan to push him? I couldn't magic a leg or a chair for him, but I was strong enough to push him a few blocks. The look on his face was astonished gratitude.

I'd also come across a little lost girl standing in the middle of El Mercado, the Market Square, where I'd also looked for a job. If I'd had my powers, I would've transported her to her mother's side. Instead I stood next to her and promised to stay right in that spot with her until her mom came back. Not even five minutes later a totally freaked-out woman with two other little kids rushed up to us. She thanked me repeatedly as she hugged her daughter.

My chest had swelled with happiness when the little girl turned to wave at me as they walked away. Knowing I was about to give the Rita's Kitchen's guests their last—or possibly their first—meal of the day filled me with that same happiness. Not quite as life-changing as the wishes I'd granted but still important to everyone in line.

"All done," I told Rita as I filled the lettuce pan on the salad bar.

She told me to man the burrito station on the hot food line.

"How about I woman it instead?"

"Sassy girl," she said with a grin.

Many of the guests recognized me from the past few days. Some wondered what I was doing on the other side of the counter. Some acknowledged me with a silent nod or a wave. Some said nothing, just pointed at what they wanted then quietly sat, ate their meal, and left.

After an hour and a half the line was down to a trickle.

"I can handle serving now," Rita said, moving a pan of burritos to an empty warming well by the mashed potatoes. "Why don't you help Faith clean up in the back? Start by sending the dirty dishes through the dishwasher."

The last hour flew by and soon Rita was locking the

doors for the day. A few of the guests helped out by cleaning up the dining room. It took Rita, Faith, and me another hour to clean up the kitchen and my first day on the job was done.

"I don't have any cash," Rita said. She pointed to a large sign, surely painted by Henry, over the serving line. It said simply 'No money on premises.' Right next to it was another sign that stated 'Rita's Rules: No fighting. No cursing. No weapons...' "I take care of the business end of things from home to inhibit theft."

I'd noticed the bars on the windows and industrial locks on the doors. She must've been robbed before. I couldn't think of any other reason for all that protection on a soup kitchen.

"I'll bring you today's pay tomorrow so you've got a little in your pocket. Otherwise you'll get paid on Fridays like Faith and Celia." She gave me a hesitant pat on the shoulder. "Good work tonight, by the way. Where are you headed now?"

"Home, I guess." It would've been a blast to go out and celebrate my first day on the job. But I didn't know anyone and didn't feel like celebrating with strangers. Besides, I didn't have any money to celebrate with.

"Let me give you a ride."

"I can walk."

"I know you can. But it's getting dark and it's not safe for a little thing like you to walk alone. Besides,"—she shot a quick glance my way—"you're an employee now and as your employer I have an interest in your safety and well-being. I'll be down a body again if something happens to you."

"Gee, thanks for the concern." But I liked that she was joking with me.

Many of Rita's guests didn't even have a stripped-bare bus to live in so I counted myself fortunate. The closer we got to Gypsy V, though, the more agitated I felt about it.

"You live in a parking lot?" Rita asked when I told her

where to turn.

"No, I live in that school bus." I indicated Gypsy V. "My bus lives in a parking lot. For now."

Her eyes went wide and for the first time all day, Rita was left speechless. After a minute she said, "You really do have a story, don't you?"

I shrugged. "Doesn't everyone?"

"Yours is different. I can feel it." She paused before saying, "Faith and our regular morning volunteers are taking the breakfast shift tomorrow so I don't have to be there until a little before noon. I'll pick you up at eleven-thirty for the lunch and dinner shift."

And with that small gesture, along with the bigger gesture of a job, I felt like I belonged somewhere again.

Once inside Gypsy V, I instantly noticed that Bonnie's bent-over near-broken stem now stood tall, the flower proudly showing off its beauty. Maybe Kaf had done it for some strange Kaf reason. I preferred to think Bonnie was getting stronger again. Like I was.

Speaking of Kaf, I held the Zen stone in my palm and placed my thumb over the circle.

Chapter Ten

Kaf appeared right away. No shirt, small orange and green cloud hovering at his feet. I hadn't seen him in ten days. It felt like it had only been minutes ago and like it had been years. Then he spoke in that antagonistic way of his and it was like I hadn't been away from him anywhere near long enough.

"Interesting decorating choice," he said walking up the aisle and indicating the lack of…everything.

"As if you didn't already know," I said. "You probably watched as he tore my home apart. Did you purposely put me on his path? Did you send him to do this?"

"What purpose would that serve?"

"To keep me dependent on you." Even as I said it I was cringing. I'd never been dependent on Kaf. The truth was, I was a little bit now. Despite knowing this, my mouth had taken over and had more to say. "Were you hoping I'd be so distraught I'd summon you right away and beg to be saved?

As though the lack of furnishings would be enough to beat me down."

Suddenly, memories of my charges doing this same kind of thing came to me. Almost all of them, especially toward the end, would end up frustrated with the path their wish was traveling. Things would be going badly or not quickly enough for their satisfaction. So they'd summon me and take that frustration out on me by calling me names or insinuating I'd been purposely torturing them.

"How do you know that you did not cross *his* path?" Kaf asked while running a finger across my all-but-empty shelves. He frowned and brushed the dust left behind from his finger.

"What?"

"Do you know Ritchie's story? Do you know what has become of him after encountering *you*? You were not in possession of the Zen stone until after your sister rejected you." His voice remained steady and infuriatingly calm. "There was no way for you to summon me until after he had stolen your belongings. Therefore no reason for me to have manipulated events."

"You're my Guide," I stammered. "I know you've been watching me the entire time. Are you saying that if had I been in trouble and called out for you, whether I had the stone or not, you wouldn't have helped me?"

"Is there something you needed, Desiree?" Kaf asked as he placed his hands on his hips, in classic genie pose, and flexed a pec. "Hard as it may be for you to believe, I have matters other than you and your wish to attend to."

His cold, business-like manner was like an icicle in my heart. This was standard protocol for a Guide though. No charge was more important than another.

"I need some documents," I said. "I can't get a job without a social security card and I can't get a social security card without a birth certificate."

"Why are you coming to me for this?"

"Because you are the only one who can provide them for me," I said.

"Really?" His swagger intensified. As if this proved his belief that I'd been looking for an excuse to summon him. "How do other people acquire these documents?"

"Well, you're given a birth certificate when you're born," I said. "To get a replacement you fill out a form—"

"Then you should do that," Kaf said. "You desire to be an independent woman, capable of taking care of yourself. Perhaps you should fill out the form—"

"And which replacement do you suggest I ask for?" I arched a challenging eyebrow at him. "The person who was registered forty-five years ago as being deceased? Or the one who was never registered as having been born?"

He had no response. For the first time that I could recall, Kaf had been rendered speechless.

"You assured me," I said, "that you would provide me with everything I needed for my wish to come to a satisfying conclusion. I need documents. Please provide them."

Why did he have to make everything so difficult? This thing we did, the arguing and belittling and taunting of each other, was exhausting. Logically, he was the exact opposite of everything that was attractive to me. He was egotistical, obstinate, and chauvinistic. There was absolutely nothing about him that should have been appealing to me.

But logic had little impact on emotions. I loved him and as hard as I fought it, there was nothing I could do to change that. Why couldn't he feel the same way about me?

He placed his hands together in Namaste and within a few heartbeats, two pieces of paper appeared between them. He handed them to me with a slight inclination of his head.

"I apologize if I offended you in any way," he said with as much formality as if he was speaking to the Emperor of Japan.

"Peace, brother," I flashed him a V. "Thanks for the help."

He stood there, looking uncomfortable. “Is there anything else you require?”

“Nope. That’s all I needed you for.” I held up the Zen stone then tossed it onto my kitchen cupboard. My heart clenched. If he didn’t have any feelings for me, I had to pull away. “I’ll get in touch if something comes up.”

He paused, as if thinking about saying more, bowed his head again, and vanished.

Just as I looked down at the documents in my hand, I realized he hadn’t asked and I hadn’t told him which name to use. I opened my birth certificate and saw immediately that he’d used my same birth date, August eleventh, but instead of 1951 he’d used 1996. Good. I wouldn’t have to explain why my birth certificate said I was sixty-three when I looked eighteen.

I skipped all of the other information and went right to my name. Desiree Inaba. I never chose a last name when I dropped Gloria and become Desiree. For the last forty-five years I’d been simply Desiree, the Wish Mistress. How had he chosen that surname for me?

Chapter Eleven

Rita had said she'd be at my bus by eleven-thirty to give me a ride to work. She arrived at eleven.

"I'm concerned about you living here," she said as soon as I stepped outside.

"I love my bus," I told her.

"I'm sure you do," she said in that way moms have. That way of agreeing with your words while at the same time letting you know you're being an idiot. "This isn't exactly a safe or healthy environment."

"I thought you said you don't get involved with your guests."

Her mouth twitched like she was fighting off a sneeze. Or a smile. "You're not a guest anymore."

"Not that I don't appreciate your concern, but why does where I live matter to you?"

"It'll sound cliché," she said.

"It's not cliché if it's the truth," I answered.

She let the smile break free. "You remind me of my daughter."

"You have a daughter? Where is she?"

Rita turned serious. "Her name was Soledad."

Ah. The mysterious Soledad.

"*Was* Soledad?" I asked cautiously.

"We went through a rough period where we fought a lot," Rita said, leaning against the white van with the navy 'Rita's Kitchen' logo on the side. "Our last fight was huge. We, her father and I, didn't approve of the crowd she hung out with." She shook her head dismissively. "Normal parent-daughter drama. Except that Soledad would become irrational if we told her she couldn't do something. Every time we said no to something important to her, Soledad would run away. She always came back. Except for the last time."

I couldn't ask what happened. I mean literally, I was choked up. Soledad's story sounded too much like my own. Taking off on a road trip because my parents, in my opinion, didn't get it and weren't trying to understand what was important to me. Seeing the pain on Rita's face made what I had put my parents through sting even more.

Rita kicked away an empty beer can rolling her direction.

"I tell everyone this story," Rita said sounding tough again. "This isn't a gift just for you. My daughter is the reason I do what I do. She was only sixteen when she died. She'd been on the streets for four months and was a shadow of herself when I identified her body. I almost didn't recognize my own child. They said she had been doing drugs and most likely working as a prostitute. Someone, her pimp I assume, left her body in a vacant lot. She weighed eighty pounds."

Flash to Marsha, strung out on heroin and LSD and who knew what else, left by the stream to die alone.

"I'm so sorry, Rita."

"Don't be sorry," she snapped and squashed the can when it rolled her way again. "Be smart. I can only imagine what that bus must be like inside."

She shook her head, disgusted, probably imagining a stained, bare mattress on the floor or torn and tattered bus seats as my bed. Gypsy V wasn't what it used to be, but it was better than what she must be imagining.

"Come inside," I said, unlocking the door. "I'd like to show it to you."

I stepped aside to let Rita pass. She climbed the stairs and stopped by the little kitchen near the front.

"Wow," she said. But not with the appreciation I'd hoped for. None of the sparkle and awe Cam had demonstrated after being inside the Victorian gypsy wonderland. Rita frowned a little. "So this is what you call a home?"

For the first time ever, my bus didn't fill me with the warm, cozy feeling it always had.

"It used to be amazing. On my way here, to San Antonio, someone stole it." The memory of waking up to Gypsy V being gone surged back in a painful wave. "He didn't get far, but he stole all my money and food and stripped the bus of everything he could take." I laughed and indicated my bell-bottom jeans with the bandanas sewn in to the sides below the knee to make them even wider elephant-bells. "Everything except my clothes."

I walked slowly down the aisle and pointed out where the heavy velvet and lace curtains that separated the eating area from the living area used to hang. Where the other pair had hung to designate the sleeping and bathroom area.

"There used to be these great tin tiles on the ceiling and small crystal chandeliers." I pointed over the tub and went to the closest window. "Gorgeous silk scarves used to hang here as curtains."

Rita said nothing, but her face was a mask of sadness.

"Even now," I said, "it's not that bad. I'm going to fix it

back up." I placed a hand on my little refrigerator and waved the other at the counter. "I still have a kitchen. I just can't afford food." I laughed and Rita opened her mouth to speak but I stopped her. "The bed. You should've seen it. Covered with a crushed-velvet spread and the softest sheets ever made."

"Sounds like it was quite a place," Rita said gently.

"It still is," I said, offended, as though she'd just called my baby ugly.

"How long did it take you to make it what it was?" Again, the emphasis.

"Oh, you know,"—forty-five years—"I added to it a little over time. I traveled around and came across bits and pieces that fit perfectly with all the other bits and pieces."

Tears threatened as I looked around and suddenly saw that my beautiful bus was nothing but a box of bones. The velvet and lace and tin and crystal had given her character and made her beautiful. First Kaf and then Ritchie. They stripped out what had made us magical and left two skeletons behind.

"Sweetheart," Rita started.

"This is my home," I said too loudly. "My nest. My pad."

"Your pad?"

Damn. I had to stop using hippie words.

Rita's eyebrows furrowed. She wanted to ask. I could see it on her face. When we were talking about my clothes that first day before I went out to look for a job, she had that same *what are you* look that all of my charges had gotten. The great thing about being a Wish Mistress was that I could tell everyone the truth about myself. Some took longer than others, but they always believed. Now if I revealed my true self, people would think I was cracked or tripping.

Rita sat in the driver's seat, which left me the floor.

"Soledad was pretty," Rita said. "Long dark hair. Big, round black-brown eyes. She was on her high school's track team, got good grades..."

She paused, looking through me to the past and smiled at something she saw there.

"She wanted to go to school at Texas A&M to study horticulture. Being an urbanite, her term, always surrounded by concrete and steel, she loved anything lush and green. She especially loved our weekend trips to Hill Country where we could be close to nature." Rita grew quiet for a few minutes and wiped her eyes. Her voice was soft and choked with emotion when she spoke again. "I don't usually share that much about her with people."

"Why me then?"

She held out her hands, indicating my bus. "You let me into your world. It's obvious that was a big thing for you. I felt like I should repay the gesture."

In a little more than a week, Rita had gone from a stranger to a mother-figure for me. While part of me was leaping for joy, another part of me was standing back. Probably because I couldn't reveal my true self to her the way she had to me. Not unless I was willing to risk her thinking I was crazy and breaking the connection we'd just formed.

"You can't stay in this bus," Rita said, sounding more than ever like a mother.

"It's my home," I said with far less conviction than a few minutes earlier.

"It's not a home." Her voice was sharp, insistent. "It's no better than the crack houses you… That Soledad used to live in." Her cheeks flared bright red and she closed her eyes to calm herself. "I believe you when you tell me what your bus used to be. I can see the ghosts still here, so maybe you will be able to rebuild it. But right now, honey, it's a shell. This is no place for a girl to live." She held up my parking permit. "Besides, this is expired. You need to either get another one or move on."

"I can't afford another permit," I said, my throat

tightening. "Where am I supposed to go?"

She rubbed her hands over her face and blew out a slow breath.

"I know a place." She looked at her watch. "We've got to get to the Kitchen now. I'll show you later."

☮☮☮

When we walked in Rita's Kitchen's front door, we found one of the dining room tables full, but not with guests. There was a group of older ladies sitting there, drinking sweet tea, and playing poker.

I gave Rita a questioning look and she shrugged. Faith came out of the back and over to us.

"What's going on?" Rita asked and tilted her head toward the table of ladies.

"These are the church ladies," Faith said. "They felt so bad about leaving you without help yesterday that they came today."

"That's great," Rita said. "We already had plenty of regular volunteers scheduled for today. We'll do a service dinner tonight."

"That's what I was thinking," Faith said.

"What's that?" I asked. "A service dinner?"

"That means the guests will remain seated this evening," Rita said. "We take their orders and bring their food to them."

"Like a restaurant," I said, nodding my head in approval.

"Exactly." Rita straightened her shoulders and held her head high. "Our guests love it when we do that."

"*I* love it when we do that," Faith said, placing a hand over her heart. "There are few things in life more personal than someone bringing your food to you. Too many of our guests feel unimportant because of their situations. We do what we can to help them feel a little better about themselves."

I understood then why Rita kept her distance from people. Listening to Faith, all I wanted was to help everyone. I could feel something waking up in me. A flicker of that same incensed passion I had when Marsha, Gail, Janice, and I would talk about women's rights. These people deserved better than to feel unimportant.

Rita looked at Faith and arched an eyebrow. "Flowers?"

"Oh," Faith put her other hand to her heart, "yes."

"Run over to the florist," Rita told me, "three blocks right and two left. Ask him for his droopies."

"Excuse me?" I asked.

"That's what he calls the wilting flowers he can't use in arrangements," Rita said. "He gives them to me at less than cost. A steal for me and he makes a little of his money back."

Along the way, I swear I saw the Marsha-girl. She was just rounding the corner at the end of the block. By the time I'd run up to look for her, she was gone. I needed to get back down to the Riverwalk and look for her. If she was still begging, she needed to know about Rita's.

The florist gave me so many flowers I couldn't carry them all and he had to give me a ride back to the Kitchen. I thought of the commune and the wildflowers we'd weave into our hair as I filled two-dozen little vases with water and flowers and set them around the dining room. It was such a simple thing. But having just spent a week depending on this place for my survival, I understood how big the simple things could be.

"Gather around, please," Rita said a few minutes before we started serving dinner. "There are a few rules that I need you to understand."

The church ladies and I formed a half-circle around Rita.

"We don't offer seconds," Rita began. "If we can't give seconds to everyone it's not fair to give it to anyone. Next, you need to maintain personal space. Shake hands or pat shoulders, but do not offer hugs."

I raised my hand. "Why? Not that I'm a hugger. Just

curious."

"Fair question," Rita said. "The majority of our guests are people like you and me who have simply come on hard times. A few of them, however, have psychological or emotional problems, which can make them aggressive or even violent. Leo is one such guest. I tell you this so you understand, not to single him out. Sometimes he, or others with a similar condition, will misinterpret a hug as a sexual advance."

There were shocked gasps from a few of the church ladies.

"Too much physical contact can upset him," Rita continued. "It's either over stimulating or he feels confined and it upsets him. If he gets upset, his off button doesn't always work. It's unlikely but it is possible that he could hurt someone."

There was some murmuring from the group.

"I understand if this makes some of you uncomfortable," Rita said. "There are plenty of things you can help with in the kitchen if you'd prefer."

A couple of the ladies raised their hands so Rita sent them in back with Faith to help the regular volunteers there.

"Another really important rule," Rita said. "Do not, no matter how badly you may empathize with someone's situation, offer them money. Again, if we can't give to everyone we don't give to anyone. We're here to provide food." She pointed to the reading corner. "The big bulletin board there has information about available jobs in the area, housing assistance, and even educational opportunities. I can put them in touch with other organizations as well if what they need isn't posted there."

Then she went over some minor details. Where the clean dishes were. Where to stack the dirty ones. Where to find more napkins and flatware. She and I would dish up the food, the ladies would deliver the plates.

The service started out like any normal dinner. The fish

tacos disappeared almost immediately. There hadn't been many of them though so Rita had made extra Tex-Mex meatloaf.

"I'm a vegetarian," a twenty-something guy near the serving tables said.

"We have salad," the church lady taking his order suggested.

"What about some protein?" he asked. "What's a bowl of lettuce going to do for me?"

Rita overheard him, too.

"You know the rules, Kyle," she called out loud enough that everyone heard, but not so loud that it sounded like she was scolding him. "This isn't a restaurant. If you can't find something you like today maybe you'll have better luck tomorrow."

He grumbled, but said he'd take meatloaf and a salad.

"He does that every time he comes in," Rita told me quietly as we filled plates with meatloaf and baked potatoes. "He's fine with whatever we're serving, just angry about having to come here. Someone told me he was on track to be a VP at a local bank but was let go days after signing a lease on a high rise apartment. Had to forfeit a huge down payment on the place."

"For someone who doesn't get involved," I said, "you sure know a lot about your guests."

"I care," she said avoiding eye-contact with me, "and I listen. I just never ask directly. They get attached to me if I show too much interest. I can't let that happen. I'm only one person, there's only so much I can do."

I nudged her shoulder with mine. "And what keeps you from getting attached to them?"

I was teasing, but apparently hit a nerve.

She gave me a sideways glance and quietly admitted. "Why do you think I keep doing this? It's not because there's any money in it."

Everything was going fine until about halfway through

dinner. That's when a couple of the church ladies started taking pictures. "To show the rest of the folks at the church," one of them said.

After the third camera flash, Hazel, a tiny, gray-haired woman who came in a few times a week freaked out.

"Save your souls!" Hazel screamed and dropped into a fetal position on the floor. "Everyone, protect yourself. They're trying to take your soul!"

Half the dining room ignored her. The rest of them either left the building, moved to the perimeter of the room, or dropped to the floor with her. Leo rushed to her side.

"Hazel," Leo said, "what is wrong? Are you hurt?" He glared at the church ladies. "Did someone hurt you?"

"Protect your soul," Hazel cried out again.

"What did you do?" Leo demanded of the church ladies.

The two ladies stood there with their mouths hanging open. One shook her head, the other stared at Hazel.

In the blink of an eye, Leo had grabbed a fork from the table. He held it in front of him like he was prepared to stab anyone who came close and stood protectively between the church ladies and Hazel.

"Stop taking pictures," Rita called as she rushed over. "Leo! Put the fork down."

Leo's eyes blazed as he swayed side-to-side in agitation. "But they—"

"Put the fork down now," Rita said, leaving no room for argument. "And you need to go outside."

"But I—"

"Now, Leo. Leave the building." Rita turned her attention to Hazel and crouched down next to her. "It's okay, darlin'. They're all done. Your soul is safe."

"Three flashes," Hazel said, her wails calming slowly. "Three prayers. Three flashes, three prayers."

Rita stayed by Hazel's side as the tiny woman rocked and chanted three unintelligible prayers. Those who had dropped to the floor with her muttered as well but different words than Hazel's. When she was done, Rita helped Hazel stand up and settle back at the table to finish her dinner.

"Everything's fine," Rita called out to the dining room. "Everyone back to what you were doing." She turned to the horrified church lady still holding the camera. "It's okay. Really. Hazel just has a fear of cameras."

"She's done this before?" I asked.

Rita nodded. "I pulled out a camera one day to take a picture of Henry's mural. I've been doing that for months. Every time he comes in to work on it, I take a picture when he's done for the day. I'm putting them in a little portfolio for him." She shook her head. "One day Hazel was here when I took a picture. I don't know who told her that cameras steal souls, but she obviously believes it. Problem is, there are cameras everywhere these days. I'm trying to find a therapist who will see her free of charge." She laughed and quickly slapped her hand over her mouth. Then she whispered, "She thinks therapists make you smaller every time you talk to them."

"Ah," I said. "Because they're shrinks."

Rita nodded. "Guess she figures she's small enough as it is." She motioned toward the front windows where Leo had his hands and nose pressed against the glass. "I'm going to go talk to him."

"He was only trying to protect her," I said.

"I realize that," Rita said, "but we have rules and he broke one. Again."

Rita stood outside with Leo for a long time and Faith took charge of the service. The rest of dinner went smoothly. No other rules were broken, except for 'No Profanity.' That guest had Tourette's though so the outbursts weren't really his fault. With all of the volunteers helping, we were cleaned up and out the door half an hour after the last guest left.

"Thank you so much," Rita told everyone as we left. "I always need help and you all were great. Come back anytime."

A few said they'd definitely be back, clearly gratified by the experience. Others looked shell-shocked by the dose of reality they'd gotten.

"Come on," Rita said to me as she locked the building door. She led me to her van. "I'll show you where you can park your bus."

She pulled up next to my bus and told me to follow her. So I fired up Gypsy V and trailed the white van through the city streets.

We drove a few miles away from the downtown area to a nice, neat neighborhood with simple, older, single-story homes. Rita pulled into one of the driveways and all the way into the garage. Confused, I waited in the street to find out what I was supposed to do.

Rita came out to the bus and I opened the door.

"There's a decent sized yard in back," she said. "Plenty of room for your bus."

"Is this your house?" I asked.

"Yep."

Seriously? "You want me to park my bus in your backyard?"

"It's an offer to keep you from getting towed." She kicked at the pavement a few times and let out a few heavy sighs. Finally, she looked me in the eye. "You can park back here and use the bathroom in the garage. I'll take a few dollars out of your paycheck for utilities. It's a way for you to keep living in your bus and still be safe. No strings. You can leave at any time."

"You're sure?" I asked.

She pulled her wallet out of her purse, poked around a bit, and handed me a piece of paper.

The paper turned out to be a picture of a young girl. I had to admit, our resemblance was uncanny. If I was Hispanic, I could be Rita's daughter.

"I'm not crazy," she said quietly. "And I'm not trying to turn you into her or be your mom or anything like that." She blinked a few times and then nodded as though assuring herself this was a good thing. “If someone had shown my Soledad a little kindness, maybe she’d still be alive. I’m just doing for your mother what I wish someone would have done for me.”

Chapter Twelve

I couldn't turn her down. Not just because I had few other options. I'd heard thousands of wishes straight from people's souls over the years so I knew a genuine wish when I heard it. I couldn't remember anything more honest. Rita really wanted to help me. By letting her do this for me, I'd be filling an empty spot in her soul, too.

Rita's fenced-in backyard was long and narrow and mostly dirt. I backed the bus in—no easy feat, but Gypsy V seemed to do most of the work herself, literally—and parked next to the garage beneath a big pecan tree. By the time I stepped out, Rita was out there, laying down a big piece of Astroturf and setting up a lawn chair and small table.

"Now you have a yard," she said with a satisfied grin. "I want you to feel like you're at home."

I jerked my thumb at Gypsy V. "I'm always at home."

Rita nodded. "You know what I mean."

"I do. Thank you for this."

"Like I said, just doing for you what I wish had been done for my daughter."

Next she brought me a set of sheets for my bare bed, a fan, and an extension cord she'd plugged into a socket on the outside of the garage. She went back inside and came out fifteen minutes later with a tray of cut-up melon and strawberries, crackers and cheese, and a pitcher of sweet tea.

"The meatloaf disappeared," she said. "We didn't get any dinner. It's getting late so I just grabbed some quick stuff."

She stood there like a sprinter waiting for the starter's pistol to go off, the signal that I needed something else. I was the one who should have felt nervous. I was invading her home after all.

"You don't have to do all of this for me." I gestured to the food in her hands. "I'll be fine with what I've got."

"I know, but I want to," she said as she set the tray on the little table. She got another chair from the patio off the back of her house and joined me.

The sky showed nothing but stars and the temperature had dropped to make a warm and humid but not unbearable night. It was nice.

"So how did you get into the soup kitchen business?" I asked and popped a little cube of cheese in my mouth.

"I started things rolling about a year after Soledad died," she began. The pain of the memory etched deep lines across her forehead and around her eyes.

"If you don't want to talk about it, that's okay," I told her. "I didn't mean to bring up bad memories."

She shook her head. "It's good for me to talk about it. And it's actually sort of,"–she paused to find the right word—"cosmic the way it came together."

Cosmic? Sister was speaking my language.

"What happened?" I took the cushion off the chair, sat down on my little patch of Astro-lawn, and pulled my legs into full lotus to hear the story. The muscles in my legs cried out in relief with the stretch. I wasn't used to standing all day.

"About six months after Soledad ran away that last time," Rita said, "it became obvious she wasn't coming home. Eight months after she left, they called to have us, my husband and me, come down to the morgue to identify her body. Our marriage fell apart after that and we decided to get divorced."

"That's rough," I said. "I'm sorry. Do you ever see him?"

She nodded her thanks while shrugging off my condolences. "Rarely. He lives in a little village in Mexico with his family now. It's all good. We parted as friends."

She got lost in a thought for a minute. I said nothing, just let her think.

"The day the divorce was final," she said, "I stopped for a bottle of wine. Partly to celebrate the ordeal being over and partly to drown my sorrows. I must've looked like a pretty sad case because the clerk at the liquor store asked if I was okay. I gave him the quick version of my story. He felt bad for me and said he wished things could be different." She paused and smiled. "Nice man. I'll never forget him. Large Asian guy with a black ponytail. Anyway, I said I wished so, too, and he handed me a lottery ticket. 'To your new future,' he said with this formal little bow."

Shivers ran through my body. Had she…was it possible that Rita had received a wish? No, probably not. If she would've said the clerk had been a female it might be true. But Kaf only had female Guides, not one male. Unless Kaf had taken on a wish of his own? I couldn't imagine him doing that though. It would have been beneath him. I couldn't believe he hadn't passed me and my wish on to someone else.

"It was a winning ticket," Rita said with an amused smile.

"Far out. How much?" I asked, figuring she'd say a

couple hundred, maybe a thousand.

"One point five million."

"No way!"

She nodded. "The store owner told the local paper and television station and they came and interviewed me. It was all very exciting."

The houses in her neighborhood, Rita's included, were simple homes, nothing fancy about them. She clearly hadn't spent the money on her house.

"So what did you do with the money?" I asked.

"I invested enough to make sure I'd have money to live on when I get old," she said. "With the rest I opened the Kitchen."

"Groovy," I said, for which Rita shot me a look. I was trying hard to kill the hippie-speak, but words still slipped. "Not many people would do something like that."

"I did it in Soledad's honor," she said and sat a little taller. "I even thought about calling it Soledad's Kitchen at first, but everyone would want to know who Soledad was. At the time, I thought it would be too painful. Now I realize that talking about it helps."

She was right. Since the start of Mandy's wish and throughout almost every minute of Crissy's, Marsha had been on my mind. I thought of all the fun we had together, how much I worried about her, the pain of her death, my guilt over believing I'd let her die because I hadn't done more for her. Or maybe I'd done too much. I didn't know. I'd never have an answer to that question. Sitting in Mandy's Haven a few weeks ago, telling her and Crissy about Marsha helped a lot. If I would've said something to someone sooner, maybe I wouldn't have gotten so bitter and been so hard on my charges.

Most of the pain and guilt I'd been carrying around for decades were gone, but there was still something left that made me feel uneasy. Whatever it was, it had poked at me when I was at Carol's house. She'd been talking about what had happened to Marsha's parents after she died…

"In two weeks," Rita said, "the Kitchen will celebrate its fifth anniversary. A reporter from a local TV station will be coming to do a story. She's the same reporter that came when I won the lottery. Five years ago she was fresh out of college and they gave her silly little local interest pieces to cover. I don't think they ever even ran the 'Local Woman Strikes it Rich after Clerk's Generosity' piece. One day, a few weeks after I won, she called to ask what I planned to do with the money. She came to the grand opening and shows up every year on the anniversary."

"That's pretty gro—great," I said, almost slipping again.

"She anchors on the weekend shows now so has some pull over which stories air," Rita said. "She says this year they're going to do ninety-second live something-or-others on the noon, five, and six o'clock news and a whole five minutes on the ten o'clock show. That's a lot of promo for my little Kitchen. I'm hoping for some good donations this year. I've got plans for expanding our services."

We sat outside for another hour, sometimes talking, other times just relaxing in the warm summer evening air. Finally Rita said, "It's late, time for bed. We have to be back to work by five. We're just doing simple scrambled eggs with ham and cheese tomorrow. Pancakes, too."

"Sounds delicious. Sleep well, Rita."

She opened her mouth to respond, but nothing came out. Instead, she raised her hand in a little wave and went inside.

The fence surrounding the yard, the pecan tree covering Gypsy V like a canopy, and the knowledge that Rita was only a few feet away comforted me. I lay down on my mattress with the fresh-smelling sheets and started to drift off immediately. I slept better than that night than I had in I don't even know how long.

☮☮☮

After the uneventful breakfast service was done the next day, Rita handed me some sheets of paper and gave me an assignment.

"These are all the restaurants and businesses along the Riverwalk that give us donations," she said. "Go to each one and find out what they plan to send over this week. I make out the menus for the week after I know what we have to work with."

"Can't I just call?"

"You could." Her tone told me that was wrong, wrong, wrong. "A personal connection makes a big difference. People are willing to give more to actual people than they are to voices."

"I'll go connect then," I said, looking over the list. It had the name and address for each business, the person to talk to, and what they'd given last time. "This looks like a lot. Is it enough to feed everyone all week?"

"No. Not even close. The donations give me a good start. We have to shop for the rest once we figure out what we've got to work with." She handed me a map of the Riverwalk, all of her contributors highlighted. "Take your time. I've got lots of help this afternoon. Get to know the managers."

Before starting on the list, I stopped at the ice cream shop first.

"Hey. You're back," Emily said. "Do you have your card? Can I hire you yet?"

After Kaf gave me the card and certificate—with the name Desiree Inaba on each—I remembered that Rita had said it would take three weeks for replacement copies to arrive.

"I had to order replacements," I said, answering but not answering her question. "I wanted to thank you for being so nice to me. I was pretty bummed out that day."

Emily nodded. "Just paying it forward. The job is still yours when your card comes."

I explained what I was doing with Rita's Kitchen and

she was impressed.

"I noticed the T-shirt," she said, pointing at the logo over my heart. "Good for you. Wish I had something to donate. I try to run with minimal inventory though."

"That's okay, I wasn't looking for anything from you. Just wanted to stop and say hey."

"It's good what y'all are doing." Emily leaned on the counter and twisted a few of her many, many braids around a finger. "Stop by again sometime."

I gave her a little wave and moved on to the first restaurant on the list. It was The Old Stone Church, the same fine dining place where I'd tried to get a job. In fact, the dude in a tux who told me I didn't have enough experience was there again. The contact name on my list matched the name on his badge. Lucky Rita had given me the T-shirt or he'd probably kick me out this time.

His eyes narrowed and his head titled. He remembered me but couldn't seem to figure out why.

"I was here a few days ago looking for a job," I supplied.

"Ah, yes." He wrinkled his nose and wiggled his fingers near his waist. "The fringed vest."

Brother was rippin' on the fringe?

"I've got a job now," I said and pointed at the logo on my T-shirt. "Do you know what Rita's is?"

He looked at me like I was a moron and pointed at the papers in my hand. "We are on your list, correct?"

"Yes."

"We made a contribution last time, correct?"

"Yes."

"That would indicate I know what Rita's is." He returned to the papers on the podium in front of him, effectively dismissing me.

My list showed that this place hadn't given much last time though. Not in comparison to the neighboring restaurants, which suggested it was him and not me. I sure hoped he didn't treat Rita this way, like she was a nuisance and he didn't have time for her. Because knowing Rita, she'd take the abuse if it meant more food for her guests. I stared at the list, trying to hold back the words that wanted to burst, burst, burst out of my mouth. I didn't call him a snob. I didn't tell him he was a tool, ruled by The Man. I didn't tell him he was what was wrong with society. Instead, I thought again of Glenn and his respectful negotiation tactics.

"This is obviously a restaurant with very high standards."

Tux-man studied me for a moment, probably trying to figure out a way to disagree with me. "Indeed."

"I'm new to the area," I said, "but I'm sure you have a respected reputation around town."

He stood taller and raised his chin. "Something we pride ourselves on."

I nodded. "You set the bar."

He actually blushed the tiniest bit.

"Imagine the influence you could have," I said. "Obviously you cater to a certain clientele. Not everyone has the money to enjoy a meal here, but a generous donation from you could have a snowball effect." The tilt of his head said he was listening. The purse of his lips said he knew what I was doing. "Not only would you encourage other restaurants to reach for that bar, you'd feed those who can't come here."

I held my breath. I'd either just scored big or was about to lose this game.

He narrowed his eyes at me and cleared his throat. "It so happens that the night manager fat fingered an order of extra-thick pork chops. We never freeze our meat and it is doubtful that we could sell all of the inventory even if it was a half-price Special of the Day all week. We planned to write the excess off as waste. You may let Rita know that she may have them."

"Thank you," I said and did my best to not show my disgust at the thought of throwing away perfectly good food.

"She'll be very happy."

"You're welcome." He tried to maintain a stern expression, but the corners of his mouth turned up a little bit. "Now shoo. I have work to do."

I flashed him a peace sign on the way out. "Have a beautiful day."

I felt that I'd grown as a person. I got my point across without letting my indignation take control. I'd possibly made a friend, or at least less of an opponent. And I got what were surely killer pork chops for our guests.

I behaved myself at the rest of the places on the list as well. None of them were rude to me and they gave decent donations. Not quite as generous as last week, but I was new and they didn't know me yet. Next time would be better.

After I'd gone to all the businesses on one side of the Riverwalk, I crossed a bridge to start on the other side when I saw that girl again. The Marsha-girl with the sort-of dreadlocks. A young mom had just handed her a bill. She was begging again. I needed to help her. I had to let her know about Rita's.

"Hi," she said when I got close. Her forehead wrinkled and her eyes, heavily lined in black, were heart-wrenchingly sad. "Do you have a little money you could spare?" She clenched her hands together at her chest. "I'm so hungry. Just a dollar?"

Something seemed different about her today.

"What's your name?" I asked.

"Dara," she said. "Please, can you spare even a dollar?"

Rita's warning about giving financial aid echoed in my head.

"I don't have any money, but I know where you can get a meal for free." I pointed at the logo on my shirt. "Rita makes great food."

Her expression shifted, like she wasn't sure what she should do with this information. No one had told her about soup kitchens before? I understood what Rita meant about wishing someone would have done something for her daughter.

"Lunch goes until two so if you head over now there should still be plenty available. And," I gently added, "if you need help, you know, with a place to live or whatever, Rita can give you names and numbers." I pointed on my map to where we were and where the Kitchen was. "It's just a few blocks. Go get a good meal."

Dara took my hands in hers and her eyes filled with tears. "Thank you *so* much. This is really nice of you."

"You're welcome. I'm glad I could help."

She walked past me toward the nearest staircase and I continued to the next restaurant on my list, feeling like I'd done something really good.

I took a dozen or so steps and stopped. Her clothes. That's what was different about her today. The first time I'd seen her she was wearing flannel pajama pants. Today she had on jeans shorts and a new-looking Alamo T-shirt.

That didn't mean anything. Maybe she wasn't homeless. Maybe she was like some of the people who came to Rita's who had homes and jobs but sometimes couldn't afford both food and rent. That would explain why her makeup looked freshly applied and not like it had been on her face for days and days. The Alamo was a short walk from the Riverwalk. Maybe she'd been begging over there and someone took pity on her and bought her a shirt.

Still, there was something about Dara. I ran back to the stairway and up to street level to find her. She wasn't anywhere around. Either she was on her way to Rita's or had found another crowd of people to beg for money. Or…

A memory from life in the commune came to me. There were only about twenty of us who permanently lived there. At any given time there were another ten or so drifters who would stay a day or two or sometimes a week and be on their way again.

Then there were those we didn't especially like but

tolerated. The weekend hippies. They spoke the hip talk and wore the rad clothes, but unlike the rest of us, they had steady jobs. They floated in every weekend to get away from society and be one with nature, their cars stuffed full of food and supplies for us. Once they'd gotten enough peace, love, and bug bites, they went back to their comfortable homes with central heating and running water.

I had the distinct impression Miss Dara was like those weekend hippies, playing the role of beggar for some reason. She was on my radar now and I'd be watching for her.

Chapter Thirteen

I spotted Dara a few more times over the next week but was riding in Rita's van both times so couldn't talk to her. She was in high tourist-traffic areas both times—once near El Mercado, where people shopped and ate, and once on a busy, downtown street. Her hair was always the same, those loose, messy semi-dreads, but she had on different outfits each time. As if her reminding me of Marsha wasn't enough to keep my attention, the fact that I now wondered if she was legit or scamming people turned my interest into an obsession.

"Do you need me to do the rounds with the restaurants again?" I asked Rita on our way back from Costco.

"We usually only go once a week," she said. "There's no harm I guess. Just go to those who couldn't give last time and ask specifically for fresh fruits and veggies. We're running very low on produce. Otherwise we'll go raid a farm or two I know of."

"We'll do what?"

"There are a couple of farms in the area that I go to. Occasionally the farmers will pick out the less than perfect items and set them aside for me. Other times they let me wander the field after they harvest and take anything left behind."

"You pick up food off the ground?"

"Desiree," she said with a sigh that made me feel ten kinds of dumb, "vegetables come from the ground. There's nothing wrong with this food. It either fell off the truck or the harvester missed it. It's not like I'm picking up half-rotted, worm-ridden produce for my guests."

Point taken.

"This is what you were born to do, isn't it?" I asked, wondering where my new path was leading me. To something that would allow me to make a difference to people like Rita did, I hoped.

"It does feel a little like a calling, I guess," Rita said. "It's like a scavenger hunt at times and I loved doing those as a kid."

A few hours later, I entered the Riverwalk. Everyone at the restaurants remembered me but I didn't spend as much time chatting with them as I should have. I was distracted and on alert for Dara.

"You in a hurry today, Desiree?" the assistant manager at an American-style restaurant asked. She and I had bonded the last time I'd stopped in. I'd had my old love beads wrapped around my wrist as a bracelet. The beads brought back memories for her and we talked for a long time about the music at Woodstock. Her parents had taken her. She'd only been six at the time, but she described events just as I remembered them. Maybe we'd even crossed paths in that farmer's field.

"We're a little short-staffed today. I need to get back and help Rita," I lied. The place was actually packed with Boy Scouts. One of them was working on an Eagle project building shelves in the back room and planters on the roof where Rita wanted to grow herbs. The boy brought half his troop with to help with the project and they also helped serve during meal times.

"Too bad. I like talkin' with you," the hostess said. "Even though you're a kid, you get it."

I felt bad. I'd seen Dara everywhere. It wasn't like I wouldn't run into her eventually. So I stayed and we chatted a little more about Woodstock and then about the protests over the war in Vietnam. She was impressed with how much I knew about the events back then. I'd never forget. If only I could tell her that I'd been right in the middle of them.

Rita had been right about that connection thing. That extra time not only bonded us further, it turned into a crate of tomatoes too soft for the restaurant to use in salads or on sandwiches but would be perfect for Rita to use in soup or spaghetti sauce.

I popped in to a steak house and got a promise for twenty-five pounds of just-starting-to-sprout potatoes and just-starting-to-soften onions. I couldn't believe the food some of these places deemed unusable. I never realized how much food got wasted. In the commune, we ate every morsel and if there were scraps, they went in a compost bin to be turned into fertilizer for our gardens. Like Rita told me that first day I met her, if you're hesitating you're not hungry enough.

With one place left on my list, I spotted Dara on the other side of the river. Today she had on Capri-length jeans and a white T-shirt. She was talking to a couple of guys—in their mid-thirties I'd guess—with that same pained, I'm-so-hungry look she had every time I saw her.

The way they were looking at her sent a cold chill up my back despite the hundred-degree day. If they were somewhere more private, Dara would be in big trouble.

I entered the door of my last stop, a bakery, and the manager gave me a thumbs down as soon as he saw me.

"Sorry, Desiree. Still nothing to give today," he said. "Next week for sure."

"No sweat, George. It happens," I said while marking on my list. "See ya later."

Too late I realized he was saying more to me but I'd already spun and walked away. My focus was already on Dara. I had to talk to her before this obsession I had with her took over my life.

I found her right away, went into stealth mode, and followed. She seemed to have a system: Females, whether walking alone or in groups, she let pass by. She homed in on old people like a bee to pollen. Guys, mid-twenties and over, were other hot targets. Especially if they were in a group and had been drinking.

I gathered intel for about an hour. Her system earned her money every third or fourth time, and in that hour she had stopped a couple dozen people. Assuming she got only a dollar from each person, she was making six to eight dollars an hour. Not a living but enough to buy a meal.

"Hi, Dara," I said as I joined her on her stroll down the sidewalk. "Remember me?"

Her eyes narrowed as she thought and then they went wide.

"The free food place," Dara said. "I couldn't find it." She frowned and her eyes took on that hungry, pained expression. "Would you have a dollar to spare so I can buy lunch?"

"You didn't get enough from all those other people?"

Her face froze. She appeared confused. Or was it that she'd been caught in a con?

I hooked my arm with hers and dragged her over to an open table at a restaurant. A waitress…I mean server was there in moments.

"What can I get you girls?" she asked.

"We'll have a large order of fries and two sweet teas," I said.

"Oh, no. Unsweet tea for me," Dara said. When the woman left to fill our order Dara turned to me. "Thank you *so much*."

"For what?" I asked.

"The food."

I laughed. "Oh, you're buying."

Her face froze again. "What? I…I don't have any money."

"Of course you do," I said. "Look, I've been watching you for nearly an hour. Not sure how long you've been trolling the Walk, but I'm willing to bet you could buy just about anything I ordered."

Dara folded her hands in her lap and lowered her head.

"You're busted, Dara. Is your name really Dara?"

She nodded.

"You're not homeless," I said.

She leaned forward, head tilted to the side. "What makes you think that?"

It was more a question from an actress wondering why her role was failing than a person being accused of lying.

I sat back in my chair and listed everything I'd noticed. "Your hair looks messy, but it's perfectly messy. You style it that way. Your makeup is also perfect, not a smudge. Except for where you wanted one." She smiled, taking that as a compliment. "You're wearing a T-shirt that is blindingly white. Your manicure isn't chipped." I looked down at her flip-flopped feet. "Neither is your pedicure."

She paused before saying, "I never claimed to be homeless."

"What's going on, Dara?"

And the flood gates opened.

"I've only been doing this for a few weeks. The first time was because I forgot my purse and didn't want to run all the way home for lunch money. I asked a man in an expensive suit if he could spare a few dollars for a burger. He coughed up a twenty just like that." She snapped her fingers.

"So you're not legitimately hungry?"

She looked at the watch tangled among a dozen string bracelets on her arm. "It is lunchtime."

"You know what I mean."

"It's sort of become a game," Dara said. "Sometimes I only ask women, but they don't usually give me anything unless they're older or don't have too big a bag that they'll have to dig through to find their wallet. Sometimes I only ask grandparent-looking people. Guys who've been drinking are the most generous."

"I noticed," I said. The last group she targeted today were guys. "You know they thought you were a prostitute at first, right?"

Dara paled. "They…um…no they didn't."

The waitress brought our fries and drinks and asked for the money right away. "Not that I don't trust you girls, but you'd be shocked at how many people eat and dash at these outside tables."

I kicked Dara under the table and was shocked by the wad of crumpled bills she pulled out of her pocket. She might be making a living at this.

"How old are you?" I asked.

"Eighteen."

"Where do you live?"

She waved vaguely down the Riverwalk. "Over that way. Are you a cop?"

"A cop?"

"Yeah, like an undercover whatever?" she asked and shoved three fries in her mouth.

"No, I'm not a cop."

"Someone from the county? You out here rounding up kids?"

"No."

"You're not a cop and you're not from the county. Then why do you care what I'm doing?"

Good question.

Dara was very pretty. She had these round, rosy cheeks and this big, bright smile. She reminded me a little of Mandy, but her resemblance to Marsha was hitting me again. She sat casually slumped in her chair with her legs crossed. Her foot swung constantly and she kept plucking at the bracelets running up her right arm. A habit, like Marsha braiding and unbraiding her hair.

"Why do I care?" I repeated. "At first it was because you remind me a lot of an old friend. Also because I thought you were hungry and I wanted to help you." I studied her, trying to get a vibe on her. "Now, I'm not sure. I believe paths cross for a reason. For whatever reason, we were meant to enter each other's lives."

Or was this planned? She was almost too much like Marsha. Did Kaf have something to do with this? Was Dara a part of my wish journey like Rita seemed to be? I felt my obsession with this girl rise a notch.

Dara's rosy cheeks had blushed even rosier. She was hiding a lot from me, but I'd figure it out. If I'd learned one thing during my Wish Mistress gig it was patience. Things generally surfaced if you waited long enough.

"So you're out here begging strangers for money because why? You're bored?"

She munched on some fries as she considered the question. "I guess. But I seriously had a need the first time."

"You're eighteen and you have a home…somewhere." I locked eyes with her and she broke away almost immediately. "You could easily get a job. I know the lady at the ice cream shop not far from here. I bet she'd hire you. You've got the right look."

If Dara was truly in need, this would have been a life changer for her. Or something she'd consider strongly for at least a second. Instead, she shrugged in that dismissive way that only a girl who was definitely not homeless and definitely not poor could.

I picked up the bag of fries and my paper cup of tea and

stood.

"Hey," Dara said. "I paid for those fries."

"Come with me then," I said, dangling a fry behind me like a worm on a hook as I walked away. "I want you to see something."

Chapter Fourteen

We stood on the sidewalk across the street from Rita's. It was nearly two o'clock so lunch service was almost done, but the dining room was still full. They all probably wanted to stay out of the heat today. The thermometer read over one hundred.

"Never heard of this restaurant," Dara said. "Is it any good?"

"This is the soup kitchen I told you about. You know, when I thought you had no money for food?"

Dara watched everyone inside and said, "Huh. So all these people…" Her question faded away and I didn't fill in the blanks. "They're all homeless?"

"Some of them are," I said. "They are all hungry. Or would be if not for Rita's."

"Why did you bring me here?"

"You admitted that begging is a game for you," I said. "I just wanted you to see that being hungry isn't a game. Not to the people who eat here."

She crossed her arms tightly and didn't respond.

As for me, my blood was racing through my veins. My heart was beating with life it hadn't felt since sitting by the campfire on our way to Woodstock, talking about women's rights and what we were going to do about it and other injustices. We had the passion but lacked a plan to really make a difference. This had to be the reason Rita and I landed on the same path. I could help make a difference not only for those in need, but help educate those who didn't understand the plight. Starting with Dara.

The Beatles "Revolution" started playing in my head. Damn, this felt good.

"Do you get that what you're doing isn't a game?" I asked.

She gave me a don't-know, don't-care shrug. I took her by the arm and led her across the street. She hesitated, like I was taking her someplace horrible, even though a few minutes earlier she thought Rita's was a trendy, retro diner.

The family who reminded me of mine was back in the corner, probably playing Scrabble. They did that a lot. Another table held a group of teenagers. They didn't come in often, but when they did, they always came in together. They joked around with each other and talked about where they could crash that night. Henry was working on his mural. Leo hovered close by him, always fascinated by how he could turn the little pots of paint into life-like pictures.

"Life's path just takes a bad turn for people sometimes. Dig?"

"Dig?"

Damn. "Do you understand that?"

"Oh. Sure."

"That's what this place is," I pushed. "An alternate path until they find their way back to the one they want to be on."

"I'm not stupid," Dara said, taking a step away from me. "I know bad stuff happens and that everyone's life is different."

I was pushing too hard, too fast.

"You're right. You're not stupid. I apologize." She told me she'd been begging because she was bored. That meant she needed something to do. "You clearly have a talent."

She did the little half-shrug again, but her face brightened.

"Oh, come on," I said. "You bring in a pretty decent hourly wage with your begging game, don't you?" Another shrug. "What if you could use that talent to help the people here?"

She looked at the tables full of teens. They'd just burst out laughing at a joke maybe or a funny story.

"Are *they* homeless?" Dara asked.

"They stay sort of incognito and don't talk much. What I've been able to piece together is that one of them got kicked out of his house and three of them are runaways who met up on the streets a few months ago. I don't know about the other three."

"Where do they sleep?" Dara asked, studying the group closely.

"Wherever they can. Last I'd heard they'd found an abandoned building about a mile from here."

Dara said nothing for a minute. Then, "What did you mean I could help?"

I pulled the list of restaurants and businesses out of my back pocket and smoothed it out on the table in front of her.

"These are the places on the Riverwalk that donate food or supplies or whatever they can to us. I've got another list of businesses near El Mercado. One of my jobs is to go to them every week to see what they have to give."

Dara was curious, but distantly. She was sniffing at the worm. I needed to get her on the hook.

"What about instead of begging for money that I don't think you need," I said, "you come with me. You talk to the people at the restaurants. See what you can persuade them to donate." She turned her attention to her bracelets. I was losing her. "I'm issuing you a challenge. I did pretty well last time I went around. See if you can get more than I did."

She turned to look sideways at me.

"There are a few really fine bartenders you can flirt with."

Her head snapped up and she bit back a grin.

"And what if I do?" she asked.

"Get more than me?" I was pretty sure that saying she'd get the satisfaction of helping those in need wouldn't work with Dara. "Why don't you give it a try and then you tell me."

Rita came out of the back and announced that lunch service was finished. Half of the guests got up to leave even though they could have stayed. Leo, who had been watching us from the second we walked in, came over until he was standing two feet away, his focus firmly on Dara.

"I think he likes you," I teased but she didn't respond. Her eyes were wide and she took a step closer to me. Leo was sort of intimidating, big as he was, so I whispered, "He's harmless. Probably fascinated by your hair."

"Who is she?" Leo asked in his too loud voice. "She's pretty. Will she be my girlfriend?"

Dara's eyes went even wider with panic.

"I thought you wanted me to be your girlfriend," I told him. "Are you tossing me aside for someone else?"

"Sorry, Desiree."

He wasn't apologizing, more stating a these-things-happen fact. Dara gave him a nervous smile and little finger wave.

"Have you been here all day, Leo?" I asked.

"Yeah."

"Maybe you should go out for a while. Get some fresh air." I guided him to the open door and gave him a little nudge out onto the sidewalk. "Come back later for dinner."

"Will she still be here?" he asked. "What's her name?"

Dara looked at me like she was waiting for me to save her.

"He's not going to hurt you." I leaned in and she bent to hear me. "Tell him your name. It'll make him happy and he'll go."

She cleared her throat. "So, your name is Leo?"

His mouth dropped open, like her speaking to him was the most amazing thing that had happened to him in a long time. Sadly, that might be the truth. He nodded.

"Nice to meet you. I'm Dara."

It was the verbal equivalent of a little pat on the head. Fortunately, for Leo, that was plenty.

"Dara," he said as though trying to find the best fit for her name in his mouth. "Dara." He turned and walked away repeating, "Dara" in a different way every few feet.

"Told you," I said.

"Who's this?" Rita asked, holding out trash bags in one hand and a bucket with soapy water in the other. I took the bags and she started wiping down tables.

"This is Dara," I said. "She might be able to work with us."

"Uh," Rita said, "we'll need to have a little talk about that first. I'm not looking to hire anyone else."

I shook my head. "That's not—"

"Well I'm not looking for a job," Dara snapped and left the building.

I ran after her. She couldn't get away. Not when I was so close to showing her a better option. She'd probably go right back out and beg again. She didn't get it. It was like Russian roulette. She'd pulled the trigger with that group of guys earlier and walked away. Eventually she'd stop the wrong person and the bullet would come out.

"Marsha, wait. I'll explain things to Rita." She kept walking.

"Look," Dara stopped and turned toward me, "I don't need you, whoever you are, to save me. I'm fine by myself, thanks. And who's Marsha?"

I hadn't realized I'd slipped. As Dara walked away from me, I thought of the many times Marsha had done the same thing. Gone off with someone in the commune, usually a guy, who she thought could give her what she needed. Sometimes that was simply a shoulder to cry on. Sometimes it was someone to party with. That last time it was whoever had given her the heroin.

"Just think about what we talked about." I thought of Mandy and Crissy and the many, many other people I'd granted wishes for over the years. "Trust me, it feels good to help other people." I didn't know what else to say so repeated, "Think about it."

She spun without answering and walked away.

"What's going on?" Rita asked when I went back inside. "Who is that girl?"

"Her name is Dara," I said. "I've seen her all around town begging."

"You know the deal here," Rita said. "We give food to the hungry. If she's homeless—"

"She's not homeless," I said. "That's what she said at least. I don't think she needs the money either."

While we cleaned up the dining room and started on dinner prep, I told Rita what I'd learned about Dara and how I thought she could help us. Then I told her about Marsha, minus the 1969 details. By the time I was done pleading my case, she'd softened. Well, softened for Rita.

"You really think she's going to come back?" she asked.

"I have no idea," I said. "But if she does I don't want to turn her away."

"You should've cleared this with me first," Rita said. "How old is she? If she's a minor we'd need a parent's permission for her to volunteer."

"She said she's eighteen."

Rita grumbled. Something about minors and the hassle she went through getting all the permission slips so the Boy

Scouts could work on those shelves and planters.

"She may or may not need food," I said, "but she does need help. That's what we do, right? Help those who need it?"

This is what I'd always wanted. To be a voice for those who couldn't or didn't know how to speak for themselves. Dara was a lost soul, I could see it in her eyes. She probably did have a home. And a family. But something was missing for her or she wouldn't be playing this game.

Just like something was still missing for me or this wish would be done now. But what that thing was, I couldn't say.

"Fine," Rita said like I'd been bouncing around, pestering her for an answer and she couldn't take it anymore. "If she comes back and can prove she's eighteen, we'll give her a chance to show what she can do."

I went to Rita, gave her a hug from the side, and laid my head on her shoulder. "Thank you. She'll be my project."

"Like you're not enough of a project yourself," Rita said in her gruff-love way and pushed me off. "Go away. You're rounding off all my hard edges." She gave me the same amused but exasperated look that I'd only ever gotten from my mom. "Don't take in any more strays, you hear me?"

I gave a noncommittal shrug.

"I'm serious, Desiree. We don't need to be opening ourselves up to trouble that way."

We prepared that night's dinner, but Faith ran the service with a group of volunteers from an elementary school PTA. That meant Rita and I had the night off. Well, I had the night off. Rita rarely stopped working. Since she didn't have to work the dinner shift, she set to work on the mountain of paperwork on her desk at home. Why the woman didn't fall over from exhaustion I couldn't say.

I knocked on her back door and she called out, "You don't have to knock. Just come in."

"Don't want to risk seeing you in your undies," I said, walking into the kitchen. "Do you have any cleaning supplies?"

Rita pointed toward a narrow closet next to her refrigerator. "What're you cleaning?"

"My bus. There isn't much left in it, but I thought I'd clean what's there."

I spent hours scrubbing Gypsy V. It was the first time I'd ever had to clean it myself. Before I could wave my hand and take care of the mess magically. As much as I missed being able to do things like that, there was something back-to-nature satisfying about doing it the normal way. It took longer than I thought it would and I was tired by the time I was done even though the bus wasn't that big.

"Desiree," Rita called from her backdoor. "Come have some dinner."

I went inside to find broiled chicken breast and baked apples.

"You're going to have to start charging me for food along with utilities if you keep feeding me," I said.

She swatted at me like I was pestering her again. "I always make too much. I'll end up throwing it away if someone doesn't help me eat it."

Right. Rita was the queen of lcftovers. The only other person I'd ever seen morph leftovers into a whole new meal that way was Mandy.

I washed the dishes afterwards and cleaned up her kitchen in payment. Then I took a cool shower to wash away some of the heat of the day. When I got back to my bus, I stepped inside and slammed my shins into something big. I clicked on the lights and found my chair, my favorite cozy reading chair, the one Ritchie had stolen, back in its spot.

The something big I'd slammed into, however, was sitting in the chair.

"What are you doing here?" I asked Kaf as I tightened the towel wrapped around me.

"Returning your chair," he said as if that should be obvious.

I squinted at him, trying to figure out his angle. "Why?"

As he stood, a small cloud of orange and green smoke appeared at his feet and the bus filled with his sweet-and-spicy, bitter-and-sour aroma. I reminded myself that he was my Guide. Just like when he was my boss, there were protocols we had to follow. Maybe he missed me and this was the excuse he'd come up with to see me.

"The last time I saw you," he said, "you accused me of purposely placing Ritchie on your path. I wanted you to know that I did not. Your encounter with Ritchie occurred all on its own."

"Okay," I said simply. He'd been here a whole three minutes and neither of us had said anything nasty. That had to be a record for us. "Why my chair? I mean of everything he took, why my chair?"

"It was one of the first things you acquired when you became a Guide," he said. "Of everything you had in here, I thought that it would hold the most sentimental value for you."

Sentimental value? Since when had Kaf given half a thought to sentimental value? Of course, he had kept that strip of my shirt.

"Why only my chair?" I asked. "He took a lot of stuff."

His cheeks reddened slightly. "Consider it a memento."

"I think you missed me and needed an excuse to stop by," I said with a flirty grin.

He took a step closer and let his eyes roam over the towel that was barely covering me. "Do I need an excuse?"

My mouth had gone dry or I would have said no, never. Instead I just stood there, wide-eyed and longing to kiss him.

He smiled, pleased with the effect he'd had on me and turned as if preparing to leave.

"Can I ask you something?" I blurted before he could.

"Of course," he said, turning partway toward me.

"The last name you gave me. Inaba. Why that one?"

He paused before saying, "It was the first one that came

to me."

"Inaba is the first name that came to you? It's sort of unusual, don't you think?"

He said nothing for so long I didn't think he was going to respond. Then he said, "My family has always been fond of it."

And he disappeared, leaving only his scent behind.

Chapter Fifteen

Rita knocked on Gypsy V's door early—four-freaking-thirty early—the next morning. It's not like I had a nightlife. Maybe I'd switch over to lunch/dinner instead of breakfast/lunch so I could sleep in. I really wasn't a morning person. Since I didn't have a car, getting to work would be a hassle though. The Kitchen was too far to walk from Rita's house and there was nowhere to park a bus.

"Why do we have to be there so early?" I grumbled as Rita drove and listened to boring, too-early-for-a-DJ radio.

"Because breakfast happens in the morning. It's only been a week. You'll get used to it."

Three other volunteers were waiting for us when we got there. Getting breakfast ready wasn't so bad with all that help. I even had time to slam down three or four cups of coffee. I'd only gotten about two hours of sleep because I'd been laying there all night, agonizing over my new last name. Had Kaf given me his last name? If he had, did it mean anything? Or had it really been the first name that had popped into his head?

These questions, and many more, distracted me to the point that Rita kicked me out of the kitchen.

"I don't know what's going on with you today," she said, "but you're a danger to yourself and others. Go fill napkin holders or something."

That didn't go much better. I pinched my finger while snapping one of the holders shut and ended up with an ugly blood blister. With about twenty minutes left to breakfast service, Dara entered the dining room and walked right up to me.

"So," she asked, "what do you want me to do?"

She wouldn't look me in the eye and didn't seem to know what to do with her hands, but she was there. What had changed her mind? Maybe she'd been out begging again and something bad happened. Or maybe she had gotten bored with begging, too, and wanted something different to do.

"Glad you came back," I said. "We still have some French toast sandwiches left. Have you eaten?"

"A latte and a cinnamon scone."

She said this so casually it had to be a common thing for her. I pictured her tossing a twenty on the counter and absently letting the coins she received as change slide into the tip jar. I wasn't sure the others in line could have come up with twenty dollars between them. Some of them couldn't come up with equivalent of the tip change.

Dara must've realized how that had sounded to the people around us. Her cheeks flamed pink and she said quietly, "I've eaten."

"Why don't you just hang out," I said and gestured to the reading corner. "Breakfast is almost over. You can pitch in and help with cleanup if you want to."

Once she had shown her ID to Rita as proof that she was eighteen, Dara did help with cleanup. She swept the floor, but her side-to-side motion only stirred up the dirt and made it obvious she'd never held a broom before, let alone used one.

"Tell me about yourself," Rita said as the three of us sat and drank iced tea during the half-hour break before starting lunch.

"Desiree already told you," Dara said. Her attitude was *I can be here or I can go have another scone*.

Rita slapped her hand down on the table, not hard, but enough to get Dara's attention.

"I've worked really hard," Rita said, "to make this place a success and that has meant following rules and laws. Even though you are here on a voluntary basis, I need to know certain things about you. For example, do you have a record? Do you have probation restrictions that I need to be aware of?"

"No," Dara said with a sigh.

"Do you use drugs? Desiree told me you beg for money on the streets. Do you turn tricks, too? Because I won't risk bringing that kind of trouble into my place."

"God," Dara said with an expression of disgust and horror. "No. Nothing like that."

"Told you that's what people would think," I said. Dara replied with a death glare.

"I'm willing to let you help," Rita said, "but I expect to be treated with respect and for you to tell me what I need to know." She waited for Dara to respond. When she didn't she slapped the table again. "Well? Say *something*."

"I'm not on drugs," Dara said, "and I'm not a whore. No, I'm not homeless. I live,"—she waved vaguely at the front door—"not too far from here. No, I'm not poor. The begging thing, it's just a thing. It's just something to do."

"You need to stop," I said for probably the tenth time.

"You act like I'm an addict," Dara said, crossing her arms and legs. "You don't know me. It's not like that."

She was right. I didn't know her. I couldn't get a read on her at all and it was driving me nutty.

"I'm sorry," I said.

She gave me a little nod in acceptance.

"So?" I asked. "Are you prepared to step away from the dark side and use your talents for good instead of evil?"

"Whatever, Obi-Wan," Dara said.

In the forty-five years since I had nearly died alongside that road, I'd never felt like anything but an eighteen-year-old. The eye roll she'd just given me made me feel about a hundred-and-eighteen.

"Look," Dara said, "I told you I'll help. If you want me, tell me what you want me to do. If you don't, I'm out of here."

Rita tapped her fingers on the table as she glanced between us. Finally she said, "Take her to our restaurants over by El Mercado. Our fifth anniversary is next week Wednesday. A reporter from channel 12 will be here with her camera to cover it. So will someone from the paper. The attention should raise awareness and help bring in funding so I can, hopefully, hire more fulltime people." She rubbed her hands over her face and looked more tired than if she'd been running all three services for days. A flick of her hand dismissed us. "That's your mission. Go. Get as much food as you can to make this thing as nice as possible."

We hadn't even gotten to the street corner when Dara said, "I'm not a bad person."

"Never said you were."

"I'm not lazy or spoiled or whatever it is you're thinking about me."

"I'm not thinking anything about you. I don't know what to think. You won't tell me anything."

She continued as though I hadn't spoken. "I can't help what I'm given. We can't choose the lives we're born into."

I couldn't argue with her on that point. What was her life though? And why was she so unhappy with it?

"Money doesn't always mean a perfect world," she said and got very quiet.

So, Dara's family had money.

Marsha's family had money. Her father had been someone important at one of the biggest companies in town. Her mother, one of San Antonio's high society ladies. Marsha had been alone most of the time, as Dara seemed to be, and despite plenty of money, like Dara seemed to have, Marsha's world was far from perfect. As soon as we'd left town on that first day of August, Marsha let loose—flirting with every guy she came across and trying every joint and acid tab offered to her. It got so bad Stan couldn't take it anymore.

"I'm done," Stan had said to her when we had stopped for gas somewhere in Oklahoma on our way to San Francisco. "I'm not playing this game anymore. Do what you want. You can come with me or you can stay with them, but I'm gonna split."

She wouldn't go. I never knew if it was because she didn't want to go home again or because she didn't want to be with him anymore. I assumed it was going home that she couldn't handle. She never wanted to be at her house and spent as much time as possible with either me or Stan. He had made her over-the-moon happy. I never understood how she could just stand there smoking a joint, watching him walk away like it was no big deal. My best friend completely fell apart after that and nothing I tried helped. I could see the light at the end of the tunnel for her and it wasn't salvation, it was a train. I wasn't about to let Dara go down the way Marsha had.

"Hello," Dara said and waved her hand in front of my face.

"Sorry," I said. "Thinking about something else." Something to do with Marsha and her life at home…

"Well check back in," Dara said. "What are we doing here?"

I handed Dara the list of businesses and the map. "All our stops are highlighted. Go in order on the map and we won't miss anyone."

Our first stop was an Italian bistro a block from El Mercado. The make-your-stomach-growl aroma of garlic hit us from ten feet away.

"They gave me day-old bread last time," I said.

"What's wrong with day-old bread?" Dara asked.

"Nothing," I said, "but if they want to give it, we'll take it."

I introduced Dara to Arturo, the manager, and they immediately started chatting. In Italian. I knew the girl had secrets, but I hadn't expected that. By the time we left, Arturo had agreed to give us not only bread, but two pounds of cheese and twenty-five pounds of pasta for the fifth anniversary.

"What, no meatballs?" Dara asked him, in English, with a flirty tilt of her head.

Arturo laughed and shook a finger at her. "You gonna be a pip to deal with, Miss Dara." He laughed and walked away. I half expected him to turn back and say, "For you, of course I will give the meatballs, too."

"That was fun," Dara said when we were back on the sidewalk. "We do need meatballs though, right? I mean, what's a spaghetti dinner without meatballs?"

"You speak Italian."

"Yep," she said, jotting notes on the list. "Learned it in school. You ever been there?"

"To school? Sure."

Forty-five years and I never learned another language? What was I thinking?

"Very funny," Dara said, and made a face at me. "I meant Italy. You should go sometime. It's totally fun."

"You've been to Italy?" I asked, trying to fit in another piece of the Dara puzzle.

She nodded like this was normal but gave no other details.

By the time we'd finished the list, Dara had secured

enough donations for not only the anniversary dinner, but two other days' worth of meals as well.

"Dessert," she said, studying the map. "We didn't get anything for dessert."

I was beat by this point. It was another steamy-hot day and my two hours of sleep the night beforc, thanks to Kaf-related thoughts, had worn out long ago.

"Dessert isn't that important," I told Dara. "We've got plenty of food coming."

She shook her head and mumbled, "Got to have dessert. Isn't a party without it."

Before I could object again, Dara ran ahead to a bakery on the corner. She came back out five minutes later, jotting more notes on her list.

"Did you get something?" I asked, sitting on a bench in the shade.

"Sheet cakes. Enough to serve five hundred."

I nearly fell off the bench. "Are you kidding me? This place isn't even on Rita's list."

"It is now," Dara said with a proud lift of her chin. "New manager."

I checked over the list on the way back to Rita's. Dara had gotten donations, generous donations, from almost everyone.

"Did I do as well as you did?" she asked.

"You did pretty well." She had totally blown away my best day. "So? What did you get out of this?"

"A warm fuzzy feeling," she said with a sassy grin.

"Do you want to do it again?"

She nodded, no sass attached.

"Impressive," Rita said with reserved enthusiasm but an approving nod when she saw the list. "Okay, you can help, but strictly on a volunteer basis. I will give you free meals though."

"Doesn't everyone get free meals?" Dara asked.

Rita winked and walked away.

The next day when Dara came in the Boy Scouts were there working on the shelves.

"Who are all the little park rangers?" she asked.

"They're not park rangers," I said. "They're Boy Scouts. They've been working on some projects for us."

"And they're not all little," Dara said, staring into the back room. "That one's hot."

"Which one?" I asked. But there was one who stood out to me as hot. His name was Wyatt. He was sixteen or seventeen and had dark, chin-length hair that hung in a curly mop across his forehead.

"Gotta love a man in uniform. I should go say hi," she said. "Do a good deed, or whatever it is that Boy Scouts do, and be neighborly." She made a beeline toward Wyatt and looked back at me with a flirty over-the-shoulder smile.

She stood in the back room, disrupting the progress on the shelves, long enough that Rita finally stepped in. She gave Dara a T-shirt with the Kitchen's logo.

"Go get more donations," Rita said.

"Can't I help them?" Dara asked with a little pout.

"Do you have any idea how to build a shelf?" Rita asked.

"No, but it can't be that hard. Wyatt could—"

"Go," Rita said and spun her toward the door.

Not only did she get tons more food donations but also cleaning supplies, napkins, paper towels, and even paint. Enough that Henry could finish the Hank mural and start on another wall.

"Imagine the good she could do if she really cared," Rita told me on the way home that night.

"She cares," I said, balancing Henry's box of paints and brushes on my lap. He'd agreed, via a hesitant and silent nod, to let me borrow his set so I could start fixing Gypsy V. I promised to bring the box back each day.

Rita shook her head. "It's a game. Dara's got nothing to do. I'll be surprised if she's still around next week."

Once home, I found a work light in Rita's garage and got to work on Gypsy V's restoration. I stood there with my eyes closed for a few minutes meditating on where my path had been and where I'd like it to take me. As soon the paint-filled brush touched the side of the bus, I entered a zone more intense than that joint Ritchie had given me. My hand and the brush became one and worked independently from my mind. I had no idea how much time had passed, but when I stepped back to check out my work, I found a new peace sign where the big, black blob had been. My words of love and harmony restored to their pre-graffiti state. How had that happened? I'd intended to give the bus a new look for our new adventure.

"Looks great."

I jumped and spun, my heart pounding, to find Rita sitting in a lawn chair fifteen feet away with a beer in her hand.

"It's like magic," she said and took a small swig from the bottle, her eyes never leaving mine. "The paints match exactly."

I stepped back farther and adjusted the light to shine on more of the bus. She was right. It appeared that I wasn't just repairing Gypsy V, I was returning her to what she had been. Exactly what she had been. That shouldn't have been possible. The paints I'd just used were nothing like those that I'd used decades earlier. And when I looked down at the pots of paint I'd borrowed from Henry, they were all full, like I hadn't used them at all.

There was only one explanation.

The Zen stone clattered on the counter inside confirming my suspicion.

Chapter Sixteen

Why the same paint job?" I asked Kaf.

"I do not know what you are talking about," Kaf said, lounging in my chair. Making it smell like him.

"I wanted the bus to have a new look," I said. "Something that better represents my new journey."

"And you believe I had something to do with the outcome? That would be interfering." He leaned his head against the back of my chair and closed his eyes. "I understand why you are fond of this piece of furniture. Very comfortable."

I stood, studying him, trying to decide if I should believe him or if he was trying to rile me again. "Why didn't it change?"

"It did change," Kaf said, eyes still closed. "The graffiti is gone."

"But it went back to what it was." I said this more to myself than to him, pondering more than expecting an answer. What did it mean that Gypsy V wanted the same image? Or that the cosmos wanted her to have the same image? Or that, subconsciously, I wanted her to have the same image?

Kaf rose, slowly, from my chair. "If that was all you required, I will be leaving now."

"Inaba was your last name," I said before I could stop myself or he could go.

He said nothing at first and then, "Indeed it was."

"And you gave it to me."

What response did I want to that?

Again he said nothing and time seemed to stop as I waited. His eyes locked with mine. He reached out and brushed something from my cheek with his thumb and let his palm remain cupped to my face for a heart-stopping moment. Skin-on-skin.

"Indeed I did."

He placed his hands palms together, lowered his head to me, and vanished.

☮☮☮

Whenever I had a quiet moment, my head filled with thoughts of the whole name thing. He hadn't given me a satisfactory answer. But then, I hadn't actually asked a question.

Fortunately the eve of anniversary day was chaos and excitement so I didn't really have time to obsess, too much, about it. Rita, Faith, and I worked non-stop we made a couple hundred breakfast burritos, sliced meats and cheeses for lunch subs, prepared gallons of spaghetti sauce, placed hundreds of meatballs on trays for baking, and pre-boiled dozens of pounds of pasta. While we did that, Dara took care of the dining room. She'd commandeered nice tablecloths for the day from a local linen service and transformed the dining room.

“She’s making it look too nice,” Rita grumbled.

“Is that possible?” I asked, amused at how she refused to ever be completely satisfied. There was always room for improvement with Rita.

“Yes, it is. We need the donations. If it looks like we have enough already, people won’t give as much.”

It was nearly ten o’clock when Rita declared everything ready and said we could leave.

“You need a ride,” I told Dara as I sniffed my shirt and hands. It would take days before I no longer smelled like onions and garlic.

“I’m good,” Dara said.

“I wasn’t asking. It’s late. You can’t walk home alone in the dark.”

“The Riverwalk is still packed with people,” she insisted. “I’ll be fine.”

She must’ve been tired or was getting comfortable with us because that was the first hint of a clue as to where she lived. Why was that such a big deal?

“Then we’ll drive you to the Riverwalk,” I said as she crossed her arms in silent protest. “We’ll follow you if you don’t let us take you.”

“Fine,” she said and I thought she was agreeing to a ride. “Follow me.”

So we did. She walked five or six blocks to the closest Riverwalk stairway, turned, gave a little finger wave, and disappeared down the stairs. Part of me wanted to run after her, but the Riverwalk would be packed this time of night. She had probably already been absorbed by the crowd.

Once home, I planned to crawl into bed and crash. About two seconds after I’d closed my eyes, Rita pounded on Gypsy V’s door.

“What?” I called from the bed.

“Come out here and sit with me,” she said.

“I’m tired, Rita. We’ve got a big day tomorrow. Go to bed.”

"Can't sleep. Too wound up." When Rita got nervous, she got chatty. I heard the groan-sigh that only came from someone finally sitting down after a long, hard day followed by the *shhh-click* of the lid being popped off of a bottle.

"I'll just keep yelling to you if you don't," she said. "Then the neighbors will get mad and call the cops."

Wouldn't want that. I stumbled across the bus, stubbed my toe on the chair, and nearly fell down the stairs. Rita was in a lawn chair with her feet soaking in a tub of water and a beer in her hand. She had placed a stone, about the size of a bowling ball, on the little table. A six- or eight-inch flame was dancing out of a hole in the center of the stone like a genie from a bottle.

"What is that thing?" I asked of the stone.

"Too damn hot here in the summer for a real fire pit. This gives me the ambience."

"You got any more beer?" I asked

"You're only eighteen."

Physically. I was dying to tell her my truth. She'd never believe it though. No one around here, except my sister, would believe it. Since I couldn't do magic anymore, there was no way to prove I wasn't making up a crazy story.

"I'm with a responsible adult," I said, daring her to contradict that one. "I think I can handle one beer."

She relented and jerked a thumb over her shoulder at the house.

"When's your birthday?" she asked when I sat in the chair next to her, an already-sweating bottle in my hand.

I hadn't thought about my birthday in years. Forty-five of them to be exact. The last one I celebrated was during the road trip to Woodstock. It was a low-key celebration, we were at a campsite in the middle of the woods after all. Marsha never told me where or how she got it, but somehow she had come up with a cake. Guess that's what best friends do. They make the ordinary something special.

God, I missed her.

"August eleventh," I told Rita.

"That's only ten days away," she said.

"Really?"

"Tomorrow is the first," she said. "I opened Rita's Kitchen on August first five years ago tomorrow." She looked at her watch. "Which is only minutes away."

My birthday was in ten days. The first year in forty-five years that I'd become older. I sucked down two or three big swigs of my beer as that sank in.

"Why are we still up when we have to be back to work in about five hours?" I asked. She looked ready to drop, but I could tell her brain was in hyper mode.

"There's going to be a camera crew, a newspaper reporter and photographer. People will come in off the street when they see the news van parked in front of the building. Faith said something about having contacted a radio station, too."

Rita stared without blinking into the tiny fire for so long I finally said, "You're going to burn your corneas."

"Then there's Dara." She switched topics without warning. "I can't figure that girl out. I don't know what her angle is, but you were spot on with her. Whether she realizes it or not, she cares about people."

"She's a kid," I said. "She's looking for her path."

And even though I didn't have magical abilities anymore, maybe there was still a way I could help her find it.

"Regarding paths," Rita said, "have you found yours?" Her phone chirped before I could answer. She pulled it out of her pocket, looked at the screen, and smiled. She clinked her bottle against mine. "It's midnight."

August first. It was my anniversary of sorts, too. A more bittersweet one than Rita's. This was the day all those years ago that Glenn, Marsha, and I took off on our road trip. My eyes filled with tears as I realized it was also the last time I'd seen my family. And my friends, Janice and Gail. I couldn't believe I never said goodbye to any of them. I tried blinking the tears away, but they spilled uncontrollably down my face regardless.

"Why the tears?" Rita asked.

"August first is a significant day for me, too." I wiped my hands over my face.

"Significant," Rita repeated. "Not special though?"

"It was the day I left home," I admitted. "The same day my brother joined the military."

"Why don't you go back?" She looked at me over her beer bottle. "I'm sure they'd love to see you."

"I tried to see my sister. She sent me away. My parents are gone."

"I'm sorry," Rita said. "What about your brother?"

The tears started again, harder than before. I couldn't say the words, so I just shook my head.

"Where did he die?" Rita asked, placing a comforting hand on my knee.

"Viet—," I started to say but bit off the word and waved my hand vaguely. "Somewhere in southeast Asia." I put the bottle to my mouth to stop more stupidity from escaping.

She caught it. I could tell by the questioning lift of her eyebrows. She didn't ask me more though. Instead she said, "You and Dara are an awful lot alike."

I set down my bottle and wiped my face. "How do you figure?"

"Neither of you will reveal the full truth. You've got stuff locked away so tight, no one can crack through to the inside."

I laughed. "You wouldn't believe me if I did tell you."

She said nothing until I looked at her. "Try me."

Maybe it was the fact that I was about ninety-nine percent sure Rita had gotten a wish. Maybe it was a combination of the beer and the fact that I was drop-dead exhausted from our work day. Whichever it was, I suddenly heard myself say, "What if I told you I was born more than sixty years ago?"

My mouth went dry. What the hell was I doing?

Rita's expression didn't change. Her only movement was involuntary, a small twitch at the corner of her left eye.

"I'd say that you're remarkably well preserved. That or you wished on a falling star and it came true."

She wanted to hear more. It was there in her voice. I wanted to tell her everything, but my breath caught in my lungs, trapping the words inside me. Good! I couldn't risk the truth. I couldn't let her think I was a whack job. If I was wrong about the wish, everything would be ruined. She was letting me live in her backyard. Letting me come and go from her house as I chose. She still hadn't taken any money from my paycheck for utilities. She welcomed me as if I really was her daughter. The chance at being a member of someone's family again, to be a daughter again? That was a dream too big to risk.

"Are you anywhere near ready to go to sleep?" I asked and a yawn broke free. More because I hadn't been breathing for the last minute or so than because I was tired. In fact, I was wide awake now. My brain buzzing with questions I had to know the answers to.

She waited a long beat, probably hoping I'd volunteer more about myself. When I didn't she said, "I'm worried something's going to go wrong tomorrow."

"What could go wrong? The food is ready. We made three times as much as we normally do. No way we'll run out. The dining room looks bitchin'. Dara did a great job."

"Yes, we checked all of our boxes," Rita said. "There is one factor we can't control. The guests."

I shook my head. "They'll be fine. We've been talking this up for days."

"Hazel," Rita said flatly.

Hazel, God love her, was indeed a few leaves short of a joint. Everything had been fine with her since that day with the church ladies and the cameras though.

"Maybe she'll stay away tomorrow," I told Rita through

a yawn.

"What if she comes, reacts to the cameras again, and Leo tries to defend her again?"

"Then we take the opportunity to talk on camera about mental health."

"Unflappable," Rita said with a shake of her head. "You really get people."

Since my first day as a Wish Mistress more than four decades ago, I'd granted wishes to people of every conceivable mental state. Most were healthy and normal, but a few were full on crazy. It wasn't their fault. No one can help how their brain is wired. Like the man who wanted a giant, invisible, dome to be placed over his town that would keep the evil forces out but still let the sun in. It was a legitimate wish, he truly wanted it. I, of course, didn't encapsulate his town. I encouraged him to write a book about it instead.

"Everything will work out the way it's supposed to tomorrow," I told Rita and yawned hugely again. "But if we don't get some sleep, we're not going to be alert enough to fend off the crazies and you'll look like a fool on camera. Not to mention the big circles you'll have under your eyes. Bigger circles. You look awful."

She kicked my leg gently. "Fine. Go to bed." She stood to go inside her house but stopped and turned back to me. "I can tell you're not ready, but when you are, I'd like to hear the rest of your story."

Chapter Seventeen

Not being able to tell Rita the rest of my story was killing me. I really, *really* wanted to, but before I could tell her the truth about me, I had to know the truth about her first. I sat in my chair and watched lights go on and off from her kitchen to her bedroom at the back of her house. When all the lights had gone out and stayed out, I assumed she had gone to bed and it was safe for me to summon Kaf.

I placed the Zen stone in the palm of my hand and before I could even touch the circle, I could sense him.

"I didn't summon you." I hadn't turned to face him, but I knew he was there. If I threw myself into his arms, he wouldn't feel more real.

"You were about to," he said and the sound of his voice made my breath catch.

I turned and my heart ached at the sight of him. It was almost worse having him there in front of me. Missing him left the possibility that my hopes and dreams of us being together could really happen. As he stood before me though, his eyes anywhere but on me and his jaw clenching and releasing, he seemed farther away than ever. But maybe his distance meant he was flustered being around me, too.

"I need to ask you something."

"Ask."

"Did Rita make a wish?"

He waited a long time before answering, his way of maintaining control over a situation. "Everyone wishes for something at some point."

"You know what I mean. Did she make a wish that was granted? And were you the 'large Asian guy' who handed her that lottery ticket?"

"Why is this so important to you?" he asked as though exasperated by me and my bothersome questions.

What happened? The last time we were together he was almost flirty, for Kaf, telling me about giving me his name. Now he seemed to want to be anywhere except in my presence.

"Why," I asked, echoing his chill, "is it so hard for you to answer a simple question?"

He paused again and closed his eyes as if trying to remember. Kaf never forgot. He remembered every wish he'd ever deemed grantable.

"Yes," he said simply.

"Yes she received a wish? Yes it was you who gave her the ticket?"

"You know how this works, Desiree. A wish is made. My job is to determine if it is one that should be granted. My girls decide the details after that. Or have you forgotten already?"

His *girls*. I bristled. He used the word specifically to aggravate me.

"Did she realize she'd receive a wish?" I asked. "Or did she just think she'd gotten lucky?"

"Her wish was to be able to feed the hungry and help

runaways. I would have to look back for the specifics."

In his big book, he meant. His enormous leather-bound compendium of every wish he'd granted. It was a foot wide, two feet long, and more than a foot thick. A few weeks ago, when he summoned me to his cave, he had the book open, three or four inches back, to my page. That's technically when my wish started. So four inches equated to about fifty years' worth of wishes. That meant Kaf had been ruling over the Guides for a century and a half.

"Why are these details so important?" he asked.

For a moment I thought he was reading my mind and meant the details I'd just been calculating in my head. Then I realized he meant the details about Rita.

"You arrived before I summoned you which tells me you were listening to the conversation I just had with her. Can't you connect the dots?"

"You revealed your true age," he said.

"No. I asked her what she would think if I told her I was born more than sixty years ago."

"You are looking for a confidant. Are you not comfortable on your own like you wanted?"

Why did we always have to play this game? The verbal equivalent of keep away. I liked to argue my point as much as anyone did, maybe more. But I was tired of arguing with Kaf.

"She trusts me enough to bring me into her home and business. I want to repay the favor by entrusting her with something big as well."

"But you do not trust her enough already?" he asked, crossing his arms over his chest, making it appear even more massive. "Your trust is conditional? Extended only if you have a guarantee that she will believe you when you reveal what you are?"

Damn it. He was right. Except for one minor thing.

"What I was," I corrected. Surprising that he slipped on such a detail. After the dramatic way he relieved me of my responsibilities, I'd think he'd be happy I wasn't around anymore. Or maybe that was exactly it. Maybe he missed me. "Remember? I'm no longer yours. In your service, I mean."

"What you were," he conceded softly. He locked eyes with me and I could tell he wanted to say more. Why, even now, couldn't he just say what he felt?

Why couldn't I?

Outside the bus came a noise that sounded like something being knocked over and then a muffled cry. I opened the door. The area was dark, the only light the soft glow coming from inside Gypsy V. One of the lawn chairs was on its side but I didn't see anything else unusual.

"Hello?" I called out. "Is someone there?"

No response. I scanned the area once again but still saw no one. Maybe an animal had been nosing around out there.

"Have I adequately answered all of your questions?" Kaf asked once I'd closed the door. "Are you done with me?"

The cold coming from him had turned frigid. I couldn't figure out what game he was playing, but I didn't want to play it anymore. It hurt too much. At times I was sure that he loved me, too. At other times it felt like he could barely tolerate being in the same space with me. I'd been under his control for nearly fifty years. Despite my feelings, it was time for me to fully take charge of my life.

"Yes, I'm done with you."

Chapter Eighteen

I went to bed after Kaf left, but he'd gotten me too worked up to sleep. I tossed, then turned, wondering what I should do with myself. I could keep working with Rita. If she wanted to keep me on at the kitchen. Or I could get a job somewhere else. Emily at the ice cream shop still wanted to hire me. Or I could take a different path altogether and finally go to college. If I kept working, pretty soon I'd have enough money to go back to Mandy and Crissy. That had been my plan for the last two weeks.

Could I really leave Rita and the friends I'd made here though?

"They're genuine," I said to myself. "They don't feel indebted because they received a wish."

You think Mandy and Crissy feel indebted, a little voice in my head asked. *You think they're not genuine friends?*

Guilt, so strong I nearly spewed, slammed into me. Of course they were genuine.

"I could beg Kaf for my powers back."

Do you really want to be a Wish Mistress again?

"Just exploring options. It's nice to magically clean clothes or make a hot dinner."

Yeah, it is a drag having to make all your own decisions. You're right. It's easier to let the wishes decide where you're going and what you're doing with your life.

"You calling me lazy?"

Maybe you're running away because you're getting too close to people here.

"Oh, what do you know?" I snapped and rolled onto my side.

☮☮☮

When we got to the Kitchen at five the next morning, Dara and all the other volunteers were waiting for us. Everyone in regulation 'Rita's Kitchen' shirts except Dara. She had on a T-shirt with a big cartoon hand making a peace sign, ripped jeans that were more rips than jeans, and a Rasta-striped beanie covering her semi-dreads.

"Nice shirt," I said.

"Yeah. Couldn't find my Rita's shirt. This one was in my closet this morning. Don't remember buying it." She shrugged. "It's cool though."

Very funny, I thought at Kaf. Or whomever. For all I knew the entire harem gathered around to watch The Desiree Show in the little cloud he enchanted to be like his version of a television. Any one of them could and would do something like that just to let me know I was being watched.

Was that comforting? Not sure. I never had gotten very close to any of them. I was the rebel, the outsider who wouldn't live in the castle with them.

"Is everything okay?" I asked Dara. "You look like you've been up all night."

"I'm good," Dara said. "It's just…nothing. Everything's

fine. Are we ready to do this?"

She almost revealed something. Almost opened a hairline crack to let me peek through into her world. If I pushed, the crack would most likely seal back up rather than open wider.

"Is Wyatt going to be here today?" she asked with a little bounce.

"Nope, sorry. Rita said no Boy Scouts. There's enough going on here today." I gave her a shoulder bump. "You'll have to find something else to occupy hours and *hours* of your time."

Today's assignments put me on the serving line and Rita floating around to supervise and talk to people and reporters. Since Dara wasn't dressed properly, and Rita couldn't find the box of T-shirts since the Boy Scouts rearranged the back room, she was to stay in the dining room.

"Answer questions," Rita told her. "If the commotion upsets anyone, talk to them and try to calm them down. Keep an eye especially on Leo and Hazel, if she comes in. Let me know about any problems right away."

"Rita," I said, "everything will be fine. Relax."

She was so tightly strung this morning she couldn't even back straight out of her driveway. She ended up partway on the front lawn and nearly hit her own mailbox.

Breakfast service was half over when the news anchor and camera crew arrived. Rita rushed over to hug the woman leading the crew through the dining room. She had camera makeup and big hair and was dressed in jeans and a nice blouse. She looked like she belonged on TV but seemed right at home in the Kitchen at the same time. Rita waved me over.

"Desiree, this is Cristina," Rita said. "Desiree is new here and already a huge help to us."

Cristina gave a wave across the dining room to Faith and then held out her hand to me. "Has she been panicking?" She tilted her head at Rita.

"Completely," I said.

"I'll talk with you somewhere quiet later on," Cristina told Rita and shooed her into the back. She checked her watch and to me said, "In the meantime, I need to do some live interviews. I surely want to talk with you. Who else—?"

That's when Cristina noticed Dara.

"Are you a guest here?" Cristina asked. "Would you be willing to talk with me on camera for a little while?"

In half a blink, Dara transformed from the confident donation gathering girl of the past few days, into the beggar girl I'd first seen. She seemed to shrink before my eyes. Her shoulders rounded and fell forward. Her eyebrows softened and scrunched together a little. Her forehead wrinkled. Her lips pursed into a slight pout. Her expression had become the one I'd seen her wear while trying to get money from unsuspecting tourists on the Riverwalk. I took a few steps closer and was about to suggest Cristina interview one of the families or out-of-work professionals there having breakfast.

But Cristina put her hand to her ear, nodded while listening to what was being told to her in her earpiece, and told her cameraman, "They're ready for us." The interview, live on the morning news, was underway.

"Good morning, San Antonio," Cristina said. "Many of you may recognize my location today, Rita's Kitchen. Five years ago today the owner, Rita Morales, opened this soup kitchen not far from the Riverwalk. To celebrate the anniversary, we'll be broadcasting from Rita's throughout the day, telling you about the hungry and homeless in our community and how you can help. Let's start by meeting a young woman who captured my attention the moment I walked in."

Cristina held out her arm and motioned Dara over.

In a business-like but empathetic voice Cristina asked, "How long have you been coming to Rita's Kitchen?"

"Not very long actually," Dara said, the pained, hungry-girl look plastered on her face for all of the San Antonio metro area to see. "I just found out about Rita's Kitchen.

That's Desiree." She pointed to me and the camera panned my way long enough for me to give a little wave. "Desiree stopped me on the Riverwalk one day and told me if I was hungry I could come here and get a free meal."

So far, no lies.

"On the Riverwalk?" Cristina echoed, prompting.

"I was there hoping to get something to eat." She paused, nodded her head side-to-side as though making a decision, and admitted, "I was begging. I'm not proud of that but the people there, the tourists especially, can be so generous." Then she gave that bright, infectious smile of hers. "I don't have to do that anymore though."

"Do you have a home?" Cristina asked. "Or is your situation like so many of the others here and your home is the streets of San Antonio?"

"I have a home," Dara said. "It's all right. Not the one I would choose if I had the choice."

Not the one she would choose? Dara had a home with plenty of clothes and money for scones and lattes. What was wrong there that made her so unhappy?

Cristina's cameraman held up his hand with his fingers splayed wide. Five more seconds? Cristina made a circle motion with her finger. Keep rolling?

"What's your name, sweetheart?" Cristina asked.

"Dara."

"How old are you, Dara?"

She looked down. "Eighteen."

"And how long have you been living like this?"

Dara got quiet and her eyes filled with tears. What I wouldn't give to have magical access into her life. Not understanding her was killing me.

"This has been my life for as far back as I can remember," Dara said.

I had to know where she lived. I had to know the truth about her life. If she needed help, if something was going on in her home that made her want to stay away, I had to help her.

Like Marsha wanted to stay away, the little voice in my head said.

"Oh, Dara." Cristina placed a hand on her arm. "You're so young to be living this kind of life."

"Rita and Desiree are helping me," Dara said, brightening a little. "If it wasn't for them, I'd probably still be down on the Riverwalk begging for my lunch."

She turned and looked right at me. Her eyes were sad but she still gave me a smile.

"Wow," Cristina said, looking straight into the camera. "If Dara's story doesn't touch your heart, I don't know what will. Stay tuned to channel twelve throughout the day for more stories like Dara's and to learn more about Rita's and other organizations in the area and how you can help."

As soon as the camera was off, Cristina's phone rang. The dining room had all but frozen in time during the interview, but was now buzzing to life again. Leo and some of the other guests pulled Dara into a corner to grill her with questions. I got pulled back to the food line to fill plates.

"The camera loved Dara," Cristina told me as she tucked her phone into her back pocket. "That was the studio. Apparently the phones over there are lighting up over that interview."

"Really?" I asked.

"Absolutely," she said. "Nothing draws people in like a live interview. They know this is happening here and now and that inspires them to help. Donations are already coming in on the hotline the station set up."

I glanced across the dining room to Dara as I placed a breakfast burrito and scoop of home fries on a plate and handed it to a woman with two babies—one strapped to her front, the other on her back.

"How's your day going, Jackie?" I asked her.

She gave her standard thumbs-up and tired smile but said nothing.

"The guys," Cristina said with an eyebrow waggle, "want to know if Dara has a boyfriend."

In Dara's mind she did. Poor Wyatt. He had no idea what he was in for.

The cameras had to move to a corner by the windows at the front of the dining room. They'd started at a table near the front door but a crowd had gathered there to watch the interviews and it became impossible for guests to get in. During the break between breakfast and lunch, Cristina recorded an interview there with Rita to be aired during the five-minute special report slot on the evening news that night.

During that same time, a camera crew from another news station showed up wondering if "that girl Cristina interviewed" was still around.

"It's your hair," I told Dara as I removed one of the breakfast pans and inserted a pan of ham and cheese subs to start the transition to lunch.

Dara reached up to touch a dread. "What about my hair?"

"I don't know how you make it look like that every day," I said, "but it's easy to believe that you slept under an overpass last night. Cristina says you're attracting a lot of attention for Rita."

"I am?" She smiled, like this was great news.

"Yep. I don't like that you turned on the beggar girl thing, but you're helping bring awareness to a big problem. Just don't forget that it isn't a game."

"I know that," Dara snapped. "You make it sound like I planned it or something."

Was she embarrassed? The way she wouldn't look at me said she might be.

"I heard what you said about your home not being what you'd choose. You know if you want to—"

Some kids came up to her before I could finish my plea for her to talk to me. Dara had become a pseudo-celebrity for the day. Parents stopped by with their kids. Most of them were the activist types, wanting to bring more awareness of social injustices to their kids. Everyone, kids included, should know about the realities of life.

Some people handed Dara money ("We just want to help you, you poor thing.") which she shoved in her pocket.

I promptly took the money to put in the donation box Rita had locked in the walk-in cooler. It made her beyond nervous to have that kind of cash in the building.

"You're not in need," I told Dara. "Remember?"

"I wasn't going to keep it," she insisted.

For the first time that day I wasn't sure I believed her.

Unfortunately where there is good, there is almost always bad as well. Some of the bad came from people out front on the sidewalk waving signs that said 'Drain on Society' and my old favorite 'Get a Job.' There were also people who came in with their children to use the situation as a threat or a shaming tactic.

"See what can happen to you if you don't do your homework," one mom told her son while pointing to Henry. "This is what we tell you. You don't get good grades, you end up living on the street."

I couldn't stand by and listen to that. Partly because I couldn't stand for anyone to talk about Henry that way. But also because I wanted to help educate the public about the truth of people who were hungry or living on the streets.

"Sorry to interrupt," I said forcing myself to remain polite. "I wanted to let you know that man's story."

"His story?" the mom said like she couldn't care less about his story.

"Yes, ma'am. He used to be a marketing executive. He not only isn't a dropout, he has two college degrees." I looked at her son and she hugged him in closer to her. "Bad things can happen to anyone. It's not always that the person did something wrong. Places like Rita's Kitchen are for anyone who needs help whether that's for a day or a year or more."

The woman looked up at her husband and they looked at me, but not with gratitude. I was ruining their lesson. They needed to understand the truth though. More importantly, their kid needed to understand so he didn't grow up believing a lie.

"This isn't a lifestyle choice our guests have made," I continued despite the glares. "They would love to have secure jobs and a warm home where they could make their own meals just like you've got."

The woman spun away, grabbing her son's hand, and walked away.

"Peace-out," I called after them as they left. I could only provide the knowledge. What the recipient did with it was out of my hands.

And then, while Cristina was filming another live interview for the early-evening news with Rita about Henry, things went from bad to worse.

A cream-colored limo pulled to a stop in front of the Kitchen. Everyone turned to look and I could only imagine who was coming to donate now.

A man in his mid-to-late twenties, wearing a chauffeur's hat and dark suit, got out of the driver's seat and walked around to open the back door for a woman. She was tall, nearly six-feet in her heels. She had on a beige suit and white blouse. Her hair was done up in an intricate twist. She looked ready to take on the world.

"Dara MacDonald," the woman said in a tone that could only mean Dara was in big trouble.

Dara rose slowly from the couch in the reading corner, almost as though she'd been expecting this.

Who was this woman? And why was she so angry with Dara?

"Ma'am," I said in a hushed voice, "they're filming a live news segment over there."

"I'm perfectly aware of that," the woman said. Her

voice, which held what sounded like a soft, Scottish accent, got louder rather than softer.

Cristina stopped talking to Rita and said something to her cameraman. He turned the camera away from Rita and Henry and followed Leo as he did his shuffle-walk over to the woman.

Leo stood close, stared the woman in the face, and called out, “Dara? Do you know this lady?”

“Of course she knows me. I’m her mother.” Before any of us could react, she pointed at Cristina and said, “You and the rest of the news stations that have interviewed my daughter today need to know that she’s been feeding you one lie after another.”

Chapter Nineteen

Cristina crossed the dining room in about two seconds. She had that hungry look reporters get when something big was about to happen in front of them. And they were still live as far as I knew. She held out her hand, "Cristina Worth, channel—"

"I know who you are," the woman said. "I'm sorry to interrupt your broadcast but I feel it's important that everyone knows the truth. You are interested in the truth, aren't you?"

"Of course I am," Cristina said.

"Good," Ms. MacDonald said. "Then you need to understand that my daughter, Dara, is not hungry. She is not homeless. In fact she comes from a very fine home."

Rita had gone pale. She looked at Cristina and shook her head in a plea to turn off the camera. Fortunately, Cristina was the only reporter left in the Kitchen, but surely damage had been done.

Cristina put her hand to her earpiece and then turned to the camera. "The station has informed me that I need to sign off at this time. Tune in to our ten o'clock newscast for an update on this story. For now this is Cristina Worth, channel twelve news."

The camera light went out a heartbeat later and Ms. MacDonald asked Cristina, "Is this how you always handle breaking news?"

"Ma'am, I'm not saying you're not telling the truth," Cristina said. "Before I destroy the reputation of someone I've known for over five years, I'd like to learn all the facts first."

"Fair enough," Ms. MacDonald said, pushing her shoulders back.

The group of teens had been hovering near Dara all day. When a camera was on her, they scattered, but welcomed her to their table when there was no chance of any of them ending up on the news. Now they descended on her in the reading corner, trying to find out what was going on. Leo shoved his way through the huddle, though, and pushed everyone back, refusing to let anyone get too close.

Rita, still pale but back in control, motioned for all of us—Cristina, Ms. MacDonald, and me—to follow her to the corner.

"I need everyone to go back to their dinners," she told the crowd. "If you've already eaten, I'd like you to leave the Kitchen now. It's been a long day and we need to talk to Dara. We'll see you all tomorrow."

Leo refused to leave. "This lady is mad at Dara."

"We don't know what's wrong," I told him gently, trying to soothe him. "We're going to talk to her and find out what's going on."

"Dara needs a bodyguard," Leo said. "I will stay." He stood next to her, arms crossed like he was there for the long haul.

I motioned to Dara to talk to him.

"It's okay, Leo," Dara said.

"She is your mom?" Leo asked.

"She is."

"She is mad at you?"

"Seems like it, doesn't it?" Dara glanced at her mom, who was standing next to me, and back to Leo. "Everything will be fine. I promise." The more she tried to comfort Leo, the more agitated he got until he was swaying side-to-side.

I motioned for Dara to follow me toward the front door. She did and as I expected, Leo followed her.

"My mom used to hit me when she was mad," Leo volunteered.

"I'm sorry about that, Leo," Dara said. "That's awful."

"I don't want you to get hit."

"She won't get hit, Leo," I held the door open for him. "I won't let that happen. Go on now. We need to find out why Dara's mom is so mad."

Leo still wasn't convinced but took another step toward the door and then wrapped Dara in a hug.

"No, Leo," I said while Dara pushed him off. "What are the rules about touching?"

"Not supposed to," Leo said and hung his head.

"Right. Go on," I said. "We'll see you for breakfast."

By the time we'd finally convinced Leo to leave, Rita had brought a tray full of coffee mugs to the reading corner. Cristina was off to the side, talking on her phone.

"You're Dara's mother," Rita stated more than asked. She handed her a steaming mug and took the seat next to the woman on one couch. Dara and I sat across from them on the other couch. "I'm Rita Morales."

The woman nodded her thanks for the coffee and said, her accent a little stronger now, "Finola MacDonald. Yes, I'm Dara's mother." She took a sip of coffee, raised an eyebrow, and said as though surprised, "This is very good."

Rita made killer coffee.

Ms. MacDonald leveled a glare on Dara that would have

crumpled any other human being. Dara sat taller though and pushed back her shoulders, ready to deflect whatever might be coming her way.

"I saw you on television today," Ms. MacDonald said with icy formality. "Imagine my surprise."

"I figured you would," Dara said and turned to Rita and me. "She has the news on all day. *All* day."

She figured she would? I had no idea what was about to be revealed, but had the awful feeling that whatever it was, Dara had set it up.

"I was sitting at Dulles International," Ms. MacDonald said," waiting for my connecting flight home when the texts and phone calls started. Friends and employees calling to let me know my daughter was on the news."

"I need to get back to the station," Cristina said. She sat in one of the lounge chairs near the couches, cup of coffee in hand. "Ms. MacDonald, will you give me a quick rundown on what you're talking about, please? I'm still planning to run the five-minute story on Rita's Kitchen tonight, but I'll need to address your…outburst first."

If she meant to embarrass Dara's mom, it didn't work.

"Is it standard practice for your guests to lie on camera?" Ms. MacDonald asked, more to Dara than Rita.

"I didn't lie," Dara said. "Everything I said was the truth."

Rita stiffened and sat taller. "Okay, what's going on?"

"What has my daughter told you about her life?" Ms. MacDonald asked.

"I haven't—" Dara started, but her mother held up a professionally manicured hand—short nails, nude polish—and silenced her instantly.

"Please," Ms. MacDonald said, "I'd like to hear from Ms. Morales first."

Everyone, even our guests, called Rita by her first name. The fact that Ms. MacDonald didn't was supposed to be a sign of respect. By the way Rita shifted in her seat, it intimidated her instead.

"I really do need to get back to the station," Cristina apologized. "Can you tell me something that will explain this? And hopefully diffuse it a little? Calls for donations dropped almost instantly."

Ms. MacDonald turned to face Dara. "No lies? Tell them how old you are."

Rita spun so quickly toward Dara, I worried she'd give herself whiplash.

Dara sighed and deflated. "Fifteen."

"Fifteen?" Rita nearly bolted across the coffee table. "You told me you were eighteen."

"That's what I heard on the news as well," her mother said.

"She showed me an ID that confirmed it," Rita said.

"You have a fake ID?" Ms. MacDonald asked Dara.

Rita turned to Cristina. "I didn't know. I promise."

Cristina patted at the air for Rita to calm down. "Rita, I know you follow the law to the letter. Dara…misled us, but nothing other than an accusation was made on the air. I'll do my best to diffuse the situation, but if that doesn't help, we'll do a follow up interview. Okay?"

Rita slumped against the back of the couch and nodded at Cristina. By the time Cristina had gathered her things and walked out the door, there were only fifteen minutes left to the regular dinner service. Rita told Faith to close early then clean up and head on home.

"Do you have any idea," Rita asked, slamming her hand on the coffee table so hard all of the mugs jumped, "the trouble I could get into if something had happened to you while you were here or out, by yourself, collecting donations? And then you lied on camera?"

"Only about my age," Dara defended herself and shot a smug look at her mother.

"You led everyone to believe that you were a guest here," Rita said. "That's more than enough. I could be totally discredited. Everything I've been working for—"

Rita stopped, closed her eyes, and calmed herself.

Dara opened her mouth, but no words came out.

"And you," Rita spun on Ms. MacDonald now. "How could you do this? You should have come, quietly, to me rather than storming, ranting and raving, through my front door."

"For all I knew," Ms. MacDonald said, "you were aware of Dara's status and chose to ignore it. I expected you had fully investigated her."

"I did," Rita said through clenched teeth. "*Your daughter* lied to me."

The more they argued over who was more wrong, the worse I felt. I was responsible for Dara being here. If I wouldn't have interfered, if I wouldn't have insisted she come with me…

"Everyone needs to chill out," I said. "Bad stuff happened. Everyone should've done something different. None of that changes the now. Let's all take a deep breath and figure out how to fix this." I was the only one who did. So I tried a different route. "I know this doesn't excuse the lie, but Dara has been a big help to us. She's been going around to local businesses and asking for donations. Rita says she's never received more in a single week."

"That doesn't surprise me," Ms. MacDonald said. "My daughter is very good at persuading people to give her what she wants."

Dara sighed. "Mother."

"I don't think," Rita said, calmer now but with a mom-look that echoed Ms. MacDonald's, "you fully appreciate the trouble you may have caused by lying about your age. I'm not allowed to let minors volunteer here without parental permission. If anyone else knows that you're only fifteen and they report this, the penalties could shut me down."

"Sorry, Rita," Dara said. "Really, I am. I would've brought a note if I'd known. Oh, that's right,"—she looked at her mother—"Mom's been away on business. Again."

There were zero good vibrations coming off those two.

"Other than lying about her age," Ms. MacDonald said, ignoring the jab, "and begging on the streets, have there been any other issues?" While the comment made Dara wince, Ms. MacDonald seemed genuinely concerned if not a bit embarrassed.

"No, Finola," Rita said. "Desiree's right. Today marks five years that we've been open and Dara was a big help in the preparation for the event." Rita gave Dara a smile. Thin and quite chilly, but still a smile.

"Congratulations on your success," Ms. MacDonald said and hesitantly added, "Rita. I realize you may not want her help any longer, but if you do, I'm happy to give her permission to keep working with you."

I had a good instinct when it came to people. Granting all those wishes over the years and learning the reasons behind the wishes made me confident in my ability to form spot-on first impressions. Both Dara *and* her mother, however, had me stumped.

One second Ms. MacDonald seemed like a cold-hearted businesswoman. The next like a worried mother. Maybe there was a reason for that. For all I knew Dara could have a police record. Maybe she was a shoplifter. Maybe she held monster parties and let her friends trash the house when her parents were away on business.

I didn't believe any of that though. I believed, like I had from the start, that Dara was simply bored and lonely. She found a way to get some attention and it worked perfectly.

"In exchange for letting Dara help you," Ms. MacDonald said, "I'd like to give a donation to your business." She took a checkbook from her purse, wrote a check for ten thousand dollars, and slid it across the table.

Rita stared at the check, her eyes bugging out for a moment.

"I assumed she was a legal adult." Rita narrowed her

eyes first at me and then at Dara. "That's the only reason I let her volunteer with us."

"Dara has a guardian who is supposed to be aware of her comings and goings when I am gone," Ms. MacDonald said and made a disapproving face. "It seems there is a communication problem there that I will have to address. Dara should simply have asked her, Elena would have cleared it with me and then given her the necessary permission to volunteer her services here." She pushed the check a little closer to Rita. "The structure here and your good influence would be a good thing for Dara."

"Ms. MacDonald," Rita said, pushing the check back at her, "this is not a daycare."

"And I don't need a babysitter," Dara said.

We all gave her a look that questioned that and she sank into the couch cushions with a pout.

"Consider it support for the positive effect you are having on our community," Ms. MacDonald said of the check. "And an apology for the lie my daughter told." She picked up the check and held it out to Rita.

Rita stood, without taking the check, and pointed at Dara. "You, come with me."

They went into the back room where I'm sure Dara was getting a good dose of what-for and how-come. While we waited, Ms. MacDonald finished her coffee and sat with her hands in her lap, legs crossed at the ankles.

"Would you like some more coffee?" I offered.

She tipped her head back and rotated it side-to-side. "That would be lovely."

She thanked me—sincerely, not just politely—when I set the re-filled cup in front of her. She took a sip, let out a coffee-sigh, and sat quietly. I got the impression she appreciated the silence.

"I saw you on the television as well. You're Desiree, correct?" she asked and I nodded. "Dara's father and I travel a great deal for our work. He's in Taiwan right now. I just got back from London."

"That's hard on a kid," I offered. "Not having her parents around."

Then again, my dad had been home every night and that didn't mean my life was better than Dara's. My dad was a hard, unhappy man. Things were often tense simply because of him.

"Dara attends a private school," Ms. MacDonald said. "For most of the year she's around people her own age." She stared blankly at her coffee cup.

"So she's alone all summer?"

"No, this is unusual," Ms. MacDonald said. "Usually she spends her summers with friends. She was supposed to this year, too." She waved a hand as if wiping away the details of that topic off a chalkboard. "Plans fell through. Long story."

She spent the summer with someone else's family?

"Ms. MacDonald," I said, "this is really none of my business, but I think Dara is not only bored, but I think she misses you and her dad. When you said you saw her on the news, she said she figured you would. That sounds to me like she was trying to get your attention."

"Well it worked, didn't it?" She took another sip of coffee. "We always take a family vacation at Christmastime. I suppose we could make more of an effort to go somewhere in the summer as well."

Rita and Dara came out of the kitchen and while Dara looked like she'd gotten a lecture, she didn't look like her world had collapsed.

"Dara and I have an understanding," Rita told Ms. MacDonald "With your permission, she will publically apologize for lying and explain what she's learned since coming here."

"Of course," Ms. MacDonald said, softer now than she had been.

"In exchange," Rita said, "she can continue to help until school starts in a few weeks. Desiree will need to go with her to collect donations however. First, to make sure she sets the record straight with the businesses that donate to me. Second, because I won't let a minor in my service run around town alone. Even though it seems she's good at that."

Ms. MacDonald nodded, like the deal had been closed. "I apologize for the problems I have surely created for you."

Dara looked surprised by that.

"I did not handle this any better than my daughter did."

At this, Dara rolled her eyes and shook her head.

"To be honest," Rita said, "I questioned whether she was really eighteen. The fact that she refused to tell us where she lives was a sign. I should have trusted my instinct."

"I will do whatever I can to help with the fallout," Ms. MacDonald said.

"I want you to know," Rita said, "Dara is a good kid. I wasn't so sure of her at first, but she's grown on me. I like having her around. The guests do, too."

"I'm glad to hear that," Ms. MacDonald said. "I will draft a permission letter tonight and messenger it to you tomorrow. It's been a long day and I'm sure we would all like to go home now. Come along, Dara. We obviously have some things to talk about. We'll stop for dinner and have a chat."

While a bit formal, it sounded like a nice offer to me. Maybe Ms. MacDonald wanted to talk about a family vacation. I thought of my own mom. What I wouldn't give for one more vacation or even one more dinner with her. Hell, I'd even welcome a humiliating confrontation like Dara had just suffered.

"No thanks," Dara said, sharp as the edge of a knife.

"Dara," Ms. MacDonald exhaled heavily. "I just got home last night and am a bit jet lagged. I'd like to go home."

"Go then," Dara snapped.

"Okay, ladies," I said, playing peacekeeper again. "Ms. MacDonald, how about Dara comes with me for a little while. We'll talk and I'll have her home in an hour."

She opened her mouth and then held up hands in surrender. “Fine. I’m too tired to argue.” To Dara she said, “One hour. We need to talk.”

Chapter Twenty

I was dead on my feet. We'd all been going at full speed since four that morning, and I'd only gotten two hours of sleep last night. All I wanted was to go home and drop into bed. I might not even bother to get undressed. So naturally, Dara was in performance mode and it was drama to top all dramas.

"I can't go home," she said, for the second time because I hadn't reacted the first time.

"What do you mean you can't go home?" I asked and laid my head on the table in the dining room. "Of course you can."

"You saw her," Dara said of her mother. "She's like a prison warden. She monitors everything I do."

"Wasn't she away on business?" I asked, my eyes too tired to blink so they stared at Henry's mural.

"Yeah."

"Isn't she gone a lot?"

"Yeah, but—"

"How can she be like a warden if she's gone all the time?" I sat up and pushed my drying-out eyes shut. "And your dad travels too? Talk about minimum security." Dara crossed her arms and pouted. "Are you home by yourself all the time?"

She shook her head. "Dad doesn't travel as much as she does."

I waited for more, but Dara wouldn't say more.

"Look," I said, "I understand why you're so mad. If I was home alone with nothing to do all summer, I'd be pretty hacked-off, too."

She turned away but tilted an ear toward me. God, how many times had Marsha stood in that same pose? The *you're not on my side but keep talking, I like what you're saying* pose. Sometimes she aimed it at me, other times at her boyfriend, Stan.

"Okay, ladies," Rita came out of the back room, turning off the main lights as she did, leaving only the security lights in the corners on. "I would've preferred a different ending, but overall this day could not have gone better. Like Cristina said, the cameras only caught the accusation, no one knows for sure that Dara lied. Maybe Cristina will work her magic and things will turn out better than I fear. Either way I'll deal with the chaos the MacDonald's have created tomorrow. I want to end the day on a positive note. Ice cream all around. My treat."

As sore as my feet were, as numb from exhaustion as my body was, ice cream sounded really good. We moved the van closer to the Riverwalk and walked to Emily's shop.

"You made it just in time," the girl, not Emily, at the window said. "I was just about to close up."

"Are you new here?" I asked.

"Yep, Emily just hired me a couple days ago."

A fork disappeared from my path as I realized she got the job Emily said she'd hold for me. No bad karma there though. As far as Emily knew, I had a job at Rita's. Would Rita still want to give me a permanent job after all the drama today? I'm the one that pushed, pushed, pushed for Dara to help out. I should have left everything alone. I just couldn't stop myself from interfering in people's lives.

"We'd like three cones," Rita said.

"Easy peasy," the girl said. "And nothing but the scoop to clean."

We found some seats next to the river beneath a canopy of twinkling lights and sat to enjoy our treat. Couples walked by hand-in-hand. One big guy made me think of Kaf. What would it be like to go on a date with him? Kaf, I mean. To talk about something other than wishes. To stroll hand-in-hand like that and do something together that wasn't wish related. The only personal things I knew about him were that he was Japanese and that he'd been stuck at whatever his age was for a very long time. I didn't know how he got his powers. I didn't know how long his indenture was. I didn't know if he had a boss. I'd never heard him refer to a higher up. I didn't know if he'd left a family behind like I had.

"Desiree?"

I blinked to see Rita and Dara staring at me.

"Hmm?" I asked.

"Your ice cream is melting," Rita said and nodded at the cone in my hand.

I looked down to see that the nighttime heat was making the ice cream run in a little stream down the cone and over my fingers.

"You totally checked out," Dara said. She looked over her shoulder to see if something was going on behind her that caught my attention. The guy that reminded me of Kaf was still there, holding his girlfriend's hand while she leaned to adjust her shoe. Dara turned back with a smirk.

My face flushed hot, so I hid behind the cone, licking the drips. I had to stop thinking about him. I'd just told myself last night—was it really only last night?—that I was going to take control of my life. The best thing was to move on without him. The vibe he was giving me said that's what he wanted. Then again, he gave me his name. God, he was making me crazy!

We were all wiped-out, too tired to do more than sit and eat. Rita—who had been near exhaustion before today—looked like she had black eyes, the circles had gotten so deep. Her skin had turned a lovely coordinating shade of gray. Even constantly chatty Dara was quiet. Although I think it had more to do with her mom than the work day.

Once the last bite of the last cone was eaten, we all agreed it was time to go. Rita groaned as she stood.

"I'm not getting out of bed until noon tomorrow," she said.

"You told Faith you'd be there at eleven-thirty to help with lunch," I reminded.

Rita swore softly. "Fine. I'm got getting up until eleven. Let's go home." She looked at Dara. "I know your mother told me I'm not responsible for you, but I'm not letting you walk home anymore. Where do you live, I'm driving you."

"Told you, I'm not going home." Dara said. "I'll go with you."

"No," Rita said leaving no room for argument. "You cannot stay with me."

The stubborn streak I'd seen in Dara over the past week was just a warm up for the silent protest she was giving now. She refused to get out of the chair. In fact, she grabbed on to the seat in a move worthy of any protesting hippie.

"Call your mother," I finally said. Rita needed to get home and I was too tired to argue with Dara. If she was as much like Marsha as she seemed to be, this could go on all night. "Let her know you'll be at my place for a little while."

Except for Kaf's unannounced appearances, only two other people had ever been in my bus. Rita and Lexi, Mandy's imaginary friend come to life. And I wasn't sure that Lexi counted because I wasn't entirely sure Lexi was a person.

"You're not staying all night," I said. "You can hang out for a little while longer if your mom says it's okay."

Dara texted instead of calling. Ms. MacDonald called back immediately and wanted to talk to me. She wanted to know where I lived. Did anyone else live there? What did I mean I lived in a bus? All your standard, concerned-mom questions. She also wanted Rita's address. She'd send her driver to pick Dara up at eleven.

Rita went inside the second we got home and must've gone directly to bed. It was only nine-thirty but all the lights in her house were out within minutes. Lucky her. I was going to be up for a while.

I unlocked Gypsy V and held the door open for Dara. I'd already warned her about what Ritchie had done to it.

"This must've looked so cool," she said, walking down the aisle.

Like I had with Rita, I described what used to be where—the curtains, the chandeliers, the tin ceiling tiles.

"This is my kitchen," I said of the four-foot square section toward the front. "Rita feeds me every night so I don't really use it right now."

Dara walked down the aisle toward the bedroom, passing by my tiny bathroom as she did.

"A claw foot tub?"

"I'm not using the bathroom either." No water hook ups in Rita's backyard like at a campground. "She lets me use the little bathroom in her garage."

"A bathroom in her garage?" Dara asked, making a face.

"Came with the house," I said. "It's not fancy, but it's clean."

"So can I stay with you?" Dara asked, bouncing on my bed.

"Get off my bed," I said from the front of the bus. "Already told you, you're not staying."

She came back up the aisle and draped herself over my

recliner. "I could live here."

"Come outside," I said. "You're getting too comfortable. Besides, we need to talk."

As her head dropped back, her shoulders slumped forward. Talking to me, clearly, was a major drag.

I started up the little fire bowl then got two glasses and a pitcher of water from inside the house. When I got back outside Dara had her shoes off and her feet propped up on the other chair.

I handed her a glass and swatted her feet off my chair, "Talk."

"About what?" Her voice was eager, like maybe we were going to have some deep, heart-to-heart, girlfriend bonding discussion. She was avoiding. She knew what I wanted to know.

"About you," I said. "Your mom and dad. Where you live."

I'd never realized how important knowing about people was to me. When a wish would come in, I'd immediately know anything about my charge and her or his life that was important to the wish. Usually that meant pretty much everything since the wishes meant putting the charge's life on a new path. Understanding the past made creating a new future easier.

"What are you so afraid I'll find out?" I asked.

"Nothing."

This was becoming like a game of who could go the longest without blinking. I had no intention of losing. "Tell me something then."

She gave a hollow, nervous-sounding laugh. "What are you, some kind of shrink?"

"No." That was possible now though. I could go to school near Mandy and Crissy and get that degree I'd always wanted. "Talking helps though. One little thing. Where do you go to school? Your mom said it's some private place?"

"What right does she have to tell people about me?"

"She's your mom," I said with a shrug. "If she talks about you it must mean you're important to her."

"Doubt it."

"Come on," I prompted. "Where do you go to school?"

She sighed hard. I know, I'm exhausting.

"Livingstone Prep."

Victory! But it wasn't enough. I wanted more.

"Never heard of it," I said. "Where is it?"

She crossed her left leg over her right and kicked her foot. "Between Glasgow and Edinburgh."

"As in Scotland?" That confirmed Ms. MacDonald's accent.

"Yep."

Not what I expected. By 'private' I figured she wore a uniform and the limo dropped her off in the morning and picked her up at night. Never would've guessed it meant boarding school.

"I sense," I said, trying to keep it light, "that you're not happy about that."

"I go there because my mom went there," Dara said. "And her parents. And on and on." She stared at the fire bowl. "I didn't have a choice. I never have a choice."

Until the women's movement in the 60s and 70s, women had few choices for their lives—mother, teacher, secretary, nurse, store clerk. The lady doctors and lawyers and psychiatrists were few and far between. Same grossly-unfair deal for minorities. That had been my whole fight. All I wanted was for women and minorities to have choices.

"I understand," I said.

"Yeah, right."

If I wanted Dara to share with me, I was going to have to share with her.

"I live in a bus because I ran away from home when I was seventeen."

"What, like a year ago?" She was actually intrigued by this. The look on her face and the way she was eyeing up

Gypsy V said that running away was an okay option if she had someplace as cool as my bus to live in. Not the result I was shooting for.

"If I could go back I would," I said and the entire seven months from the time I left until the time I almost died flashed before me in one psychedelic blur. "It was a mistake."

"So why don't you?"

"My parents are dead." This stopped her cold. "My brother is dead. My sister is still alive, but she's so mad at me for running off she doesn't want anything to do with me anymore."

After a minute of awkward silence, Dara gave a sheepish smile. "So I shouldn't run away?"

"I don't recommend it," I said. "New topic. Where do you live?"

She didn't respond. But this time the non-response said something. The fact that she was keeping so stubbornly quiet told me I was getting closer. But to what?

"On the Riverwalk," she finally volunteered.

"There's nothing but hotels, restaurants, and shops on the Riverwalk."

"Right," Dara said, refilling her water glass. "I live in a hotel."

"I didn't know people lived in hotels."

"They do when their mom owns the building. She bought this one like five years ago. We moved here so she could 'keep an eye on her new employees and bring the place up to standards'. She and my dad liked it here enough that they decided to stay."

Ms. MacDonald owned hotels? Something about that meant something.

"Well," I said, "guess that's not all that different from an apartment."

"Except without neighbors. The only people I see regularly are the employees and business travelers who stay there a lot." She stared, unblinking, at the flame from the fire rock. "I'm in Scotland most of the year. I don't know anyone here."

"All right, so that's why you're bored. Isn't there something you like to do?"

She shrugged. "I like computers. Developing software and apps and stuff."

I didn't know much about that. I used to have a cell phone. Kaf took it away. Company perk and since I wasn't with the company anymore, I couldn't keep the phone. When I had a computer, that Kaf also took away, I received emails. That was about as tech-savvy as I got.

"Isn't there a summer camp or something for that?"

Dara kicked at my chair. "Maybe. Don't know, didn't look."

"You can't complain about being bored if you're not willing to help yourself." Whoa. That sounded exactly like my mom's voice coming out of my mouth.

Dara looked at me like I was the lamest person ever. In my defense, being an eighteen-year-old with sixty-three years' worth of life lessons totally messed with my cool factor.

"Okay, next topic."

"No more topics."

"Tell me more about your mom and dad."

"No."

"Why not?"

"What's the big deal anyway?" Dara asked while lining her bracelets up perfectly on her arm. "Why do you want to know all this stuff?"

"Because when people don't want to talk about their families, it usually means they're unhappy with them for some reason." A massive shiver ran through me, like a ghost from the past had just shoved me.

"What's the matter?" Dara asked.

"Nothing," I said, confused. Something was trying to

break free.

"You said talking helps. So talk."

"You're lonely," I said.

"I mean it, Desiree. Time for you to talk—"

"No, I am." I tapped my head. "It's right there. Something to do with you being lonely." I got up and walked a circle around the chairs, the crispy grass of Rita's lawn poking my bare feet. "I was thinking that sometimes when someone doesn't want to talk about their family it's because something is wrong."

Flash of Marsha, leaning against a tree, waiting for the acid tab she'd just place under her tongue to take effect.

"My family is fine," Dara said defensively. "They're gone a lot but it's not like my parents abuse me."

"Abuse?" I wandered toward Gypsy V.

"They *don't* abuse me," she repeated.

"No, not you."

Another flash of Marsha and I remembered everything. My knees gave out. I dropped to the ground next to my bus and threw up.

"Oh my god, Marsha." Tears streamed uncontrollably down my face.

Dara was at my side, helping me to my feet.

"Come on," she said. "Come sit down. Are you okay?"

I nodded my head, then shook it.

"What did you remember?" Dara asked.

The one thing I'd kept locked away. The one thing that I absolutely should have helped with and didn't.

"Marsha was my best friend." My voice broke as a few fresh sobs escaped me. "She was one of the people I ran away with."

"Where is she," Dara asked.

"She's dead."

Like most people, Dara didn't know how to respond to that. Finally she simply asked, "Dead?"

I nodded.

"You remembered something about her?"

"Marsha's life was similar to yours," I said. "Wealthy parents who were gone a lot. When they were home, she didn't want to be there."

Dara squirmed. "I told you—"

I held up a hand. "I know. What I had pushed to the back of my brain for so long was the reason why she didn't want to be at home." My tears started again, with less force this time but just as much sorrow. "She was high all the time at that point, like she couldn't stop. One day I told her maybe it was time for us to go home where she could get some help. She went ballistic. She started ranting about how I had no idea how much worse it would be there. I told her that things would be different. We'd been gone a long time and her parents would realize how important she was to them. That they'd probably be around a lot more."

Marsha's response was crystal clear in my head now, but I couldn't get the words to come out.

"That would be a good thing, right?" Dara asked.

"That's what I thought," I said, my head in my hands. I needed to just say it. To put the words out into the world once again so they'd be out of my head and I could move past them. "Marsha told me that ever since she was nine years old, anytime she'd be home alone with her dad he'd…touch her."

"God," Dara said, making a face, "that's disgusting."

Disgusting didn't begin to describe it.

"I'd known Marsha since we were twelve years old. She never told me."

"Why would anyone tell anyone about that?" Dara asked. "Even a best friend."

"I should have known!"

"Desiree, how could you possible know *that*?"

Dara was right. Still, "She was my best friend. I could have done something."

"No matter how badly you want to," Dara said, "you

can't fix everything."

My brain spun with trying to prove her wrong. Dara didn't know about the magic. If Marsha would have made a wish Kaf could have… What? What could he have done? Mistakes can be admitted to and forgiven, but once a thing is done it can't be undone. Maybe Marsha could have learned to move past what her father had done to her, but she never would have forgotten.

"Feel better now?" Dara asked.

"A little. It's going to take time for me to forgive myself." She started to object and I stopped her. "You're right, I know there's not much I could have done. I wish I would have known though. I couldn't change what happened, but I might have been able to stop it from happening again."

Dara nodded and let her head drop against the back of the chair to stare at the sky.

I did the same. I missed the stars I used to see when Gypsy V was parked in the middle of the Rocky Mountains. The sky there was huge and dark and I could see so much more of the universe. As much as I loved it there, I was definitely lonely and a little bored. I didn't turn into a beggar, but I did take my loneliness out on my charges. Poor Mandy. She had suffered so much. Crissy, too.

"I get it," I told Dara quietly. "I understand that people do stupid things when they're lonely."

"God! Will you stop already?" Dara said and slapped her hands on the arms of the chair. "You're like three years older than me. Stop sounding like such a mom. You don't need to impart your wisdom, or whatever, on me. I mean seriously, were you ever cool?"

Ouch. I liked to think I had been. "It's just that I've been through a lot."

"I don't care." She emphasized each word. "We just had this nice bonding moment. Time to leave the rest alone now. I'm fine. I don't need a shrink. Quit trying to fix me." She paused to catch her breath. "You are right about one thing.

I'm lonely. So what I could use is a friend. Can you be that?"

Dara was right. I was about the lamest person ever. Here I was trying to help her with this grandiose gesture of analysis and understanding and all she really needed was a friend. Just like Marsha needed me to be. Just like I could really use right now, too. Be a friend to makc a friend. The easiest and best gift ever.

"Yeah," I said. "I can be that."

At the stroke of eleven, the long cream-colored limo pulled into Rita's driveway. The same chauffer, the guy in his twenties, from earlier got out. He took two steps toward us and Dara jumped up and called out, "I'm coming. Be right there."

He gave a little head-bow, went to the back passenger's side door, opened it, and waited for her.

I stood and Dara hugged me.

"Thanks for talking to me," she said. "I'm sorry about your friend."

I nodded. "Talk to your mom. Trust me, things aren't as bad as you think they are."

She made a face but didn't argue.

Despite being to-the-bone exhausted, I couldn't sleep. Now that I'd remembered a little, the rest of Marsha's story had come back to me, too.

"I tried everything," Marsha had said, too numb from the drugs to even be emotional. "I pushed him away. I hid in my closet. I cried. I even threatened to tell Mom once." She shook her head. "You know what he'd say?"

I couldn't respond, too shocked and repulsed to speak.

"He'd say 'You don't have to be scared of me, baby. I would never hurt you.'" She took another long drag from her joint. "Never hurt me. The bastard."

She hadn't remembered telling me. I'd asked her about it once when she wasn't so stoned. She called me names and accused me of making up lies about her.

No matter what Dara said, I should have known. Never

wanting to be home that way, it wasn't normal. Had I been that wrapped up in myself, and ironically in the plight of women, that I couldn't see even a hint of how much my best friend had been hurting?

Marsha, I now realized, had been the subconscious driving force behind my life. That's why I'd insisted on learning every detail of my charges' lives. I couldn't risk missing something that important again. That's why I'd become so obsessed with Dara. That's why I'd likely become obsessed with many more people. I didn't save Marsha, but I'd do whatever was necessary to save others.

Chapter Twenty-One

Ms. MacDonald's accusations had spread. The donations, which had been coming in fast and furious, died to a trickle. Some donations had even been revoked, the giver claiming that if Rita wasn't responsible enough to verify a volunteer's age, what else was she letting slip past.

Cristina told Rita the best thing was for her to do another interview. She came back with her cameraman and talked to both Rita and Dara at the same time.

"Rita did check," Dara said as the camera recorded her apology. "I showed her a fake ID." She handed it to Cristina. "Take it. It's caused too much trouble."

"Why do you have a fake ID, Dara?" Cristina asked.

Dara shrugged. "The standard reason. To get into clubs. The point is, I lied and I'm really sorry." She looked straight into the camera, no beggar-girl routine this time. "Don't let my stupidity stop you from doing the right thing for Rita and her guests."

Donations picked up again, but nothing like what they had been.

The day after the interview I answered the phone and the woman on the other end asked for Desiree.

"I'm Desiree," I said. "Who's this?"

After a pause the woman said, "It's Carol. Don't hang up."

"Okay." I was too surprised to do anything but listen.

"I saw you on the news," she said, her voice tense, nervous-sounding. "That's how I knew where to find you."

Why was she calling? Was she going to tell me now that I had to leave San Antonio, too? That being out of her house and neighborhood wasn't far enough away?

"I'd like…I thought you might want to come for dinner."

"Dinner?"

"I understand if you don't want to. I was really hard on you when you stopped here that day, but you have to understand—"

"When?" My sister had just invited me back into her home. I didn't need to understand why.

Carol let out a huge sigh. "I have to go out of town for a few days. I'll call you again once I'm home. Let's tentatively say a week from Saturday?"

"Groovy."

"Gloria," she said. "I mean Desiree. I'm sorry."

"Me, too. And it's okay if you call me Gloria."

I hung up and wondered if that had been a joke of some kind. I half-expected to see Kaf leaning against the wall laughing. That was crazy though. Kaf never laughed.

"Are you okay?" Rita asked, finding me sitting at a table in the dining room.

"Yeah. I think so." I told her about the call and she pulled me upright into a hug.

"That's the best thing I've heard in days," she said. "Make sure this happens. Second chances don't come around all that often."

Then I did laugh. "Tell me about it."

"Where's Dara?" she asked. "I thought she was coming in today."

"Worried about her?"

"No," she insisted with a tone that said she absolutely was. No matter what she had told Ms. MacDonald, now that Rita knew Dara was only fifteen she did feel responsible for her.

"She texted me. Her mother is leaving town again and wanted to have breakfast with her first."

"Texted you? I didn't know you had a phone."

"I do now." I held it out for her to see. "Dara had it delivered to me last night. She wouldn't let it go. 'Friends text each other.' 'How am I supposed to talk to you?' 'Everyone has a phone.' I told her I couldn't afford a phone. So she got one for me."

Rita tapped buttons, slid images around the screen, showed me the games it would play and all the things it would do. "Nice. It's got just about everything. Lots of apps. You'll need to set up an email account."

"Will it make a phone call?" I asked.

She gave me a strange look as she handed it back to me. "I've never met anyone as old-school as you. Even actual old people embrace technology."

I shrugged and stuck the phone in my back pocket.

Lunch service was nearly over when Dara finally walked in.

"How did breakfast with your mom go?" I asked.

"Fine. I guess," Dara said. "This will be a long trip. I'll be back to school before she comes home." She tried to make it seem like it wasn't a problem, but I could tell it bothered her. "We talked and she said she was sorry she hadn't been home more over the summer." She swallowed hard. "She's going to try to stop by and see me."

Stop by Scotland. She really did have a different life.

"That's nice," I told her. "She's making an effort."

"Hi, Dara." Leo had been waiting all morning for her to show up. He moved in like he was going to give her a hug, but she held out a hand to stop him.

"No touching, Leo."

"I waited for you," he said and clasped his hands together tight enough to make his knuckles turn white. "You weren't here. I don't like it when you're not here."

That's when Dara noticed the Boy Scouts in the back room.

"Hang on, Leo," she said. "I need to go say hi to Wyatt."

Standing next to me, Leo started to sway side-to-side and made little moaning noises.

"What's wrong, Leo?"

"Where is Dara going?"

"She's not leaving again, don't worry. She's just going to say hi to the boys."

"Does she like that boy?" Poor Leo. He was so love struck.

Dara looked wide-eyed at Wyatt, like she did every time he was around, and laughed a little too loudly at whatever he was telling her.

"Yeah," I said, "I think she does."

"Is he her boyfriend?" His swaying got more intense.

"They barely know each other," I said, trying to soothe him.

"I know Dara," Leo said.

"Yes, you do."

"I like Dara."

"She likes you too, Leo," I said.

He changed from aggravated swaying to happy bouncing and I realized I'd probably just made a mistake.

Rita came out of the back, clapping her hands to get everyone's attention.

"All right," she said. "Lunch is over. Everyone needs to leave. The Scouts are going to do a project for me and we need the dining room. Go get some fresh air, but stay out of the sun. We'll see you for dinner."

Rita didn't kick people out very often, but now that the Scouts were done with Wyatt's Eagle project, they agreed to assemble to-go bags. Even though the Scouts came with at least two leaders every time, having that many minors volunteering at once made Rita nervous.

"They could slip and fall in the kitchen," she'd said that morning.

"They could slip and fall in their own kitchen," I'd said.

"What if one of them gets hurt?"

"What if a plane falls out of the sky and lands on the building?"

She didn't appreciate my attempt to settle her down and decided to just empty the dining room to be safe.

"Go on, Leo. We have a lot to do," Rita said as she went into the back.

"Why isn't Henry leaving?" Leo asked.

"He needs to finish his mural," I told him. "A company saw Rita talking with Cristina about him on the news. They want to come and look at his work. If they like it they might hire him."

Henry had been in the zone all week, working to finish his Hank the Dog mural. I even saw him smile a few times.

Leo swayed faster and when he started rubbing his hands up and down on his thighs, it was time for an intervention. Breaking the touching rule, I placed a hand on his back and guided him to the door.

"Why don't you go back to the Riverwalk," I told him. "See if anyone falls in today."

He'd come in one day laughing so hard he had tears running down his cheeks. Some girl had been texting and walking and went right over the edge. Lucky for her the river was only three or four feet deep. All she had to do was stand up.

I felt bad making him leave. I didn't know where he went when he wasn't at the Kitchen. The bunkhouse, sure, but where else? I wondered that about a lot of our guests. Many of them had jobs or families or something to get back to. The rest had nowhere to go. Or, more likely, they had no *one* to go to. Shortly after I'd started working in the Kitchen, Rita told me it would be easier, on me and the guests, if I kept a distance.

"Why?" I asked, unwilling to turn off my humanity. "They're people just like you and me. Aren't they entitled to a little compassion and human contact?"

"Words and meals," Rita had said as we drove to Costco to buy more food and supplies. "We greet them with a sincere hello and a warm pat on the back. We give them a hot, tasty meal."

"I hate how you say 'them' like they're a group of outcasts. How can you be so cold?"

She slammed her hands against the steering wheel. "Damn it, Desiree. Cold? You think I don't care?" She pulled over and shoved the van into park. I thought she was going to kick me out. "We're one small business and there are nearly four thousand homeless people in this city. I can't do everything for them. I can't give them food *and* shelter *and* a job. No matter how badly I'd love to. I can only do one thing. I chose to give food to as many people as I am capable of. Don't you dare tell me I'm cold. If I try to give more than I do, I'll give everything." Her voice cracked. "I'll give until I'm empty and then I'll have nothing left."

She put her hands over her face. I hadn't seen tears, but she'd probably gotten good at stopping them as soon as they threatened. I knew she was passionate about her work, but I'd had no idea how deeply that passion went.

"That's how I am," she said. "I'm an all or nothing person. I don't know how to be any other way."

This went against everything I'd been doing for the last forty-five years. Every person who had crossed my path had a need and it was my job to help them fulfill it. How was I supposed to be around these people every day, every one of them with a real need, and not help them get what they needed most?

"You have agreed to work with me," Rita said, putting the van in gear again and looking over her shoulder to pull away from the curb. "That means you either follow my rules or you go somewhere else. My guests know how much I care about them. I show them with the food I make for them. I show them by giving them a clean dining room where they can be proud to sit and eat." She slapped the back of her hand against my leg. "I show them by choosing only quality people to work with me."

"It's just so hard," I told her, aching with wanting to do more.

"It is," Rita agreed. "But we can go home at night knowing that none of our guests will die from starvation or malnutrition. Not on our watch."

I had wanted to go back to my bus that day and get the Zen stone. I was going to tell Kaf he had to give me my powers back. The thing I'd always wanted was to help masses of people. There had to be a way to tweak the magic. Why did it need to be for only those whose wishes had been granted? Why couldn't I use that power to help those who had an obvious need but hadn't made a wish? I could help everyone in the Kitchen. Everyone in San Antonio.

But now, after my revelation about Marsha and why I'd always dug so deeply into my charges' lives, I knew giving wasn't the right answer. Giving was a temporary solution. I had to help them help themselves.

Rita understood this. The lottery she'd won gave her the money, but she did the work. She didn't offer jobs to many, but she did tell her guests about available jobs when she found out about them. She told them where they could go for housing and medical help. Who was I to question what had been working so well for five years?

"All right, volunteers," Rita called out. "Gather round, take a seat."

I was still standing by the front door. Leo hadn't gone to the Riverwalk like I'd suggested. Instead he was sitting on a bench across the street, elbows on his knees, staring at the Kitchen. He was probably hoping to catch a glimpse of Dara. His crush was turning into an obsession. I needed to talk to Rita about what to do about him.

The Boy Scouts scattered among the tables. Dara sat next to Wyatt. I stood next to Rita.

"Something I've been wanting to do here," Rita said, "is provide sack meals to go. Sometimes our guests don't have time to stay because they need to get back to work. They might have a family member at home who can't make it here to eat because they're sick or unable to leave their home for whatever reason. Now that you're finished with those great shelves, I want to fill them with to-go sacks. We got a nice donation of breakfast items a few days ago so we'll fill breakfast sacks today."

"I'll help them," Dara said which I immediately translated to mean *I need to be within two feet of Wyatt at all times*.

Even though Dara was left "in charge" of the project, Rita sent me out every ten minutes or so to monitor progress. The first couple times I popped out, Dara and Wyatt were moving from table-to-table as though connected by an invisible tether. By the end of the task, Dara and Wyatt were in full-on flirt mode, bumping shoulders and laughing too loudly.

Once all the bags were filled and placed on one of the new shelves in the store room, it was almost time for dinner service. Since we had enough volunteers, we did another sit-down dinner.

"We've done a lot of those lately," Rita said. "They're going to get used to it."

Her tone was gruff—as it almost always was—but the glint in her eye said she was happy to give the guests special treatment.

"Rita's going to float between the back room and dining room," I told Dara. "I'm going to dish up the orders and the Scouts can deliver. Do you think you can help me?"

"Sure."

"All you have to do is put pasta on plates," I said, knowing she was totally zoned out and hadn't heard a word I'd said. "I'll fill soup bowls."

"Yep. Okay," Dara mumbled. "No problem."

"And then we'll perform a ritual sacrifice in the middle of the dining room."

"How is she?" Rita stood next to me and asked like a doctor checking on a critical patient. She and I had been hiding in the back watching the Dara-Wyatt courtship for the last ten minutes.

"If I didn't know better," I said, "I'd say she was high on something."

"She is," Rita said and fluttered her eyelashes at me. "On Wyatt." She had to call Dara's name three times before she heard.

"What?"

"Can you turn it off for two hours?" Rita asked.

"Turn what off?" Dara looked like she'd just been jolted awake from a deep sleep.

"The lovey-dovey eyes," Rita said and let out the laugh she'd been holding in.

Dara turned the color of a bad sunburn.

Leo was the first in line for dinner. He washed his hands and stood across the food line from Dara.

"I went to El Mercado yesterday," he told her. "I got to watch some people do a dance called a mamba. It looked like lots of fun."

Dara laughed. "I think you mean mambo. A mamba is a snake."

"It looked like this," Leo said and showed her a few steps. "'Cept they did it real fast."

"Yep, that's the mambo. You're a good dancer, Leo."

His smile nearly split his face in two and if he bounced any harder he'd shoot himself across the dining room.

"Do you want to dance with me, Dara?"

She was in too good a mood. She just might do it.

"Dara," I said and shook my head. She gave me a quick thumbs up.

"I can't right now, Leo," she said. "I'm busy helping with dinner."

Wyatt took a bowl from me and a plate from her. Their eyes locked. Dara looked shyly away. I couldn't help laughing at them.

"Will you later?" Leo asked, no longer bouncing.

"What?" she asked. "Maybe. We'll see. Why don't you go sit down now? One of the boys will bring you some dinner. Rita made pasta primavera and meatball soup tonight. You don't want to miss out."

I went to her side once Leo walked away.

"You need to be careful," I said quietly. "He's got a major crush on you."

"I know," she said with a grin. "Isn't it cute?"

"No," I said. "Not cute. He's been sitting across the street for three hours waiting to come back in and see you. Leo doesn't process things the way other people do. You can't tell him you're going to dance with him."

She flicked a hand at me. "We're buddies. He's fine."

"Just dial it back," I said. "Okay?"

Instead of going to his normal seat near Henry's mural wall, Leo took the first available chair as close to Dara as he could get. It happened to be Wyatt's table because close to Dara was where Wyatt wanted to be, too. When Leo realized this, he glared at Wyatt. When Wyatt tried to put a dinner plate in front of him, Leo said, "I want someone else to get my dinner."

When Wyatt tried to set the food in front of him anyway, Leo shot out of his chair and pushed Wyatt hard enough that the tray flew out of Wyatt's hands and Wyatt fell to the floor.

The dining room went silent as Leo pulled his fist back, ready to strike just as Dara appeared at Wyatt's side.

"Oh my god, are you okay?" Dara asked Wyatt.

Leo pulled his punch but left it frozen in midair like he might let it fly if Dara moved out of the way.

Rita charged through the kitchen doors, demanding to know what was going on. I stopped her and told her I'd handle it.

"He broke a rule," she said and pointed to the big *Rules for Guests* sign on the wall. I was pretty sure she meant rule number three: *Disruptions and outbursts will not be tolerated.* "He needs to leave the building."

"It wasn't really his fault," I said and she arched an eyebrow at me. "Well, it was, but you know Leo. He's upset because of the Dara-Wyatt thing."

She gave me a look that felt like the one I used to give my charges. The one that said, *just remember, you asked for this*.

"Fine. Handle it." Rita sighed like she was exhausted. The circles under her eyes had gone black again. She pulled on some plastic gloves and took over for me on the serving line.

"Leo," I said and gestured for him to follow me.

He looked down at his feet and shuffled after me out the front door to the sidewalk.

"What's going on?" I asked.

"Dunno."

"I think you do," I said. "Are you mad at Wyatt?"

"I guess."

"Tell me."

"Is he Dara's boyfriend? 'Cause he should not be. I should be her boyfriend. I saw her first."

"She likes him, but I don't think he's her boyfriend."

"She likes him." He moaned as he said this, like it was the worst thing that had ever happened to him.

"Leo, I need you to focus." I had a quick flash of the

commune and the members tripping on acid who always thought the world was coming to an end. “You shouldn’t have pushed Wyatt. That’s not the right way to deal with anger.”

“Sorry.”

“Don’t tell me. Tell Wyatt.”

He crossed his arms tight in a clear not-gonna-happen stance.

I took a centering breath and tried again. “You know I’m supposed to kick you out now, right?”

“What?” His eyes went wide.

“You broke a rule, dude. Rita says if you break a rule you have to stay away for a whole day.”

“Don’t make me go, Desiree,” he begged. “I’m sorry. I will not do it again, I promise.”

He looked like he might cry. Because I was determined to not make people learn lessons the hard way anymore I told him, “I’ll let you stay if you apologize to Wyatt.”

“Oh, thank you, Desiree.” And I immediately doubted my choice because he reached out to hug me.

“Leo! No hugging.” He pulled his hands back and looked at his feet. “We just talked about rules and immediately you almost broke another one. Last warning, brother. Next time you’re out. You get that, right?”

“Yes, I do,” he said and nodded emphatically. “I get that.”

“And you heard what I said about apologizing to Wyatt?”

He dropped his head back, in a great imitation of Dara. “Fine.”

“Good. Go give proper apologies to Wyatt and Rita.”

His forehead furrowed. “I did not push Rita.”

“But you did knock the food she made to the floor.”

“Oh.” He played with his fingers. “Do I still get to have dinner?”

“That’s up to Rita.”

He shuffled over to Wyatt and, through teeth clenched so hard I couldn't figure out how the words got out, said, "I am sorry that I pushed you."

Wyatt held out his hand. "Apology accepted."

Leo shook his hand very quickly and went to the kitchen door, stopping with his toes on the line right beneath the 'Employees and Volunteers Only' sign and waited for Rita to come out. Despite how tough she was a minute ago, Rita reluctantly got him another plate of pasta and bowl of soup.

After dinner was over and everything had been cleaned up, we all stood on the sidewalk to wait for one of the Scouts' parents to get there. Dara and Wyatt sat on the doorstep, shoulders touching as Leo watched from across the street.

"I'm done with my project," Wyatt told her. "It's been fun hanging out with you."

"It has," Dara agreed.

"Are you here every weekend?"

"I'm not an employee," Dara said. "I kind of set my own schedule."

"That's cool," Wyatt said, running a hand through his curls. "If I knew you were going to be here, I could come back to help next Saturday."

"If I knew you were going to be here," she said, "I'd be here."

I chose that moment to squeeze in between them. There was about to be a kiss and that would lead to more kissing and then other things. Despite the free love that flowed through Woodstock and the commune, I always believed that a girl should know a guy for a while before sticking her tongue down his throat. More importantly, Leo was about to blow again. If he did, it was pretty much a guarantee that punches would fly.

"Desiree?" Dara hissed at me.

"Save it," I said. "Besides, his ride is here."

A light blue minivan pulled to a stop in front of us and a

second later the side door slid open.

"Sorry!" The mom inside called out. "Sorry, I'm late."

Six of the khaki-shirted boys followed the two troop leaders to their vehicles parked down the street. The remaining four piled into the van.

"See you," Wyatt said to Dara. "I'll try to come next week. I've got your number."

Dara nodded. "Text me."

Dara sighed as the van door closed again. She sighed harder as the van pulled away. "Isn't he great?"

I rolled my eyes. "What do you know about him?"

That released a flood of information.

"His name is Wyatt Stewart and he's fifteen. He's got a little brother and two older sisters. He likes camping and kayaking and all of this cool outdoor stuff. He says now that he's finished the shelves and the planters, he's gonna be an Eagle Scout."

"Do you even know what that means?"

"Nope," she said. "But he said it like it's something important so, you know, it must be cool." She sighed again. "I can't believe I have to wait a whole week to see him again."

Rita came outside followed by Faith.

"I want you to go on home now," Faith said in her strong accent. "Desiree? Darlin', you need to take Rita home and put her straight to bed, you hear?"

"What's wrong?" I took the car keys from Rita. Her face was translucent gray and she looked ready to fall over.

"This happens every year," Faith said, trying to ease my fear. "She works herself to a frazzle over the anniversary and then ends up sick. She'll be fine. She'll sleep like the dead for a good twelve hours and by this time tomorrow she'll be right as rain. She'll be looking for pancakes when she wakes up."

This happens every year.

Faith and Rita had a history together. For the first time,

watching as Faith held Rita upright, I understood that. They were friends, close friends. Probably best friends. Rita wasn't as alone as I'd thought. She didn't *need* me in her life. Not really.

"I don't know how to make pancakes," I said mostly to myself. How hard could they be? Rita had cookbooks. I could figure out pancakes.

"I'll bring some over," Faith said, not missing a beat. "Heat them up in the oven. She doesn't like them from the micro. Says they get chewy that way. Slather on some butter and strawberry jam, not syrup." She slipped in front of Rita and looked her right in the face. "But she needs to go home and go directly to bed. Doesn't she?"

Rita nodded without even trying to argue. She must have felt as bad as she looked.

"Stay here," I said. "I'll go get the van."

Dara and I took Rita straight home and put her to bed. It took about a minute and she was out cold.

"Do I get to stay here tonight?" Dara asked.

"Do you really think you'd enjoy sleeping on the floor of my bus?" I asked.

"I could sleep in the chair," she said.

"You're not sleeping in my chair." I had a better idea. "I'm taking you home."

"Oh," Dara said and stuck her lip out a bit. "You can drop me by the Riverwalk. I can—"

"I'm taking you all the way home," I said. "Tonight you're going to show me where you live."

I taped a note to the middle of Rita's refrigerator. *I'm bringing Dara home. Call me if you need me. Faith will bring pancakes.*

Dara barely spoke on the way. Her hands stayed folded in her lap until it was time to point out a turn. Otherwise she sat there looking like she was waiting for the world to implode.

Finally, she pointed at a six-story building that took up

an entire block. It was an older hotel, but perfectly maintained. Balconies with overflowing flower arrangements hanging from wrought-iron railings dotted the creamy-yellow exterior. Very charming.

A sign etched into the archway over the covered entrance said *Hotel MacDonald Riverwalk.* I pulled in and came to a stop near the valet podium behind a Lamborghini that was without a doubt the sleekest, shiniest thing I'd ever seen. This was where Dara lived? It fit but I couldn't help but wonder if she was deflecting again.

"Okay," Dara said, breaking her silence. "Thanks for the ride."

"I'm coming in with you," I said before she got out of the car.

"That's okay. I'm good from here."

"See, this is what friends do. I let you into my home. Now I get to see yours."

She got quiet again. This was basically the argument she used to justify getting me that phone. *This is what friends do.* Finally she shook her dreads back and straightened her shoulders. "Fine."

A man in black pants, white shirt, and an orange-and-black tartan vest appeared next to the car. He opened my door and asked, "Will you be staying with us for the evening, Miss?" Then he noticed Dara and any worry I had about her deflecting vanished. "Oh. Miss MacDonald." He seemed a little flustered. Probably because she was getting out of a delivery van instead of a stretch limousine. Or a Lamborghini. "Good evening."

"Hi, Gary," Dara said with her normal, breezy attitude. "He'll take care of the car for us, Desiree."

Gary handed me a token the size of a poker chip with a coat of arms on one side that, I assumed, represented the MacDonald clan. "Call down and give us the number on the token when you're ready for your van, Miss." He inclined his head toward me and offered me his hand to help me out of the van. Classy place. Killer service. I was already digging this hotel.

As we entered the lobby and made our way to the elevator, at least a dozen employees wearing some version of orange-and-black tartan—vests, kilts, skirts—said hello to Dara. She returned the greetings and called everyone by name. For someone who only lived here a few months out of the year, she was well known. And by the smiles on everyone's faces, well liked.

When we got in the elevator, Dara tugged on a leather cord around her neck, hiding beneath her shirt. A key dangled from the end of the cord and she stuck it in the keyhole on the elevator's button panel.

"What's that for?" I asked.

"It's my house key."

I got a funny feeling.

"And your house would be…?"

"The penthouse."

Chapter Twenty-Two

The elevator door opened to a large oval foyer. A four-foot round, clear-acrylic table sat at the center on the gleaming, dark hardwood floor. The most mind-blowing chandelier I'd ever seen, pinecone shaped and made of twisted glass tubes, hung above the table. It was a deep-orange shade at the wide top and faded to lemony-orange at the pointed bottom. I couldn't stop staring at it, which I'm sure was the intent. The tubes cast a rainbow of squiggly citrus-colored shadows on the walls that I at first thought was wallpaper.

This was just the foyer. I was almost afraid to see the rest.

There were three doors on the wall opposite the elevator, one straight across, one directly to my left, the other to my right. In the 60s and 70s there was a television game show called *Let's Make a Deal*. The contestants had to choose one of three doors and their prize was whatever was behind that door. Sometimes it was something far out like a shiny new car. Sometimes the thing was a real drag like a rusted-out bicycle with a bent wheel. Dara's foyer made me feel like I was on that game show.

Dara pointed to the left-hand door. "That way is to the bedrooms. Mine, my parents', and the guest rooms." She jerked a thumb at the right door. "That's the servants' quarters. Let's go this way."

We went through the center door and entered a seriously big room. Sixteen or twenty Gypsy V's would probably fit in there. It spanned the entire width of the space with floor-to-ceiling windows that looked down on the Riverwalk and out at San Antonio.

Straight ahead of us facing the wall-of-windows was a curved, dove-gray leather sofa, probably twenty-feet long. Pillows in shades of the chandelier were scattered along the sofa and perched on the five matching chairs across from it. A two-foot-oval glass-and-chrome table sat in front of each chair. A miniature version of the foyer chandelier hung over each table.

To my left was another sitting area. Six leather chairs in ombré hues from white to cream to dove-gray to steel-gray and finally black sat in a half-circle in front of a fireplace. A massive painting that looked like a geometric jumble of shapes in various shades of orange hung from mantel to ceiling.

To my right was a sleek gourmet kitchen done in gray tiles, stainless steel, and gleaming chrome. I immediately thought of Mandy and could picture her cooking in there. Between the kitchen and the wall of windows sat an acrylic dining table. Twelve smoky-gray acrylic chairs lined it. Chairs covered in fabric that exactly matched the painting sat at the head and foot.

That was the entire room, other than a piece of orange pottery or a small vase of orange flowers placed here-and-there. Mind-blowing in its vast simplicity.

Dara went to a door on the window wall that led out to a balcony. She waved for me to follow. A long, narrow pool that looked like it was dropping over the side onto the Riverwalk below took up the center of the balcony.

"Isn't it cool?" Dara said of the pool. "It's called an infinity pool." She pointed to a control panel on a short pedestal near the wall. "You can turn on a current and swim for miles. There's a glass wall on the outside edge that makes it feel like you're going to swim right off into the sky."

Dark rattan lounge chairs were scattered about in pairs. A large umbrella and small table sat between the pairs.

"I don't even know what to think," I said, coming out of my shock. "You really live here?"

Dara frowned. Except for explaining the pool to me, the only time she'd smiled since we left Rita's house was while greeting the employees downstairs.

"This is why I didn't want to bring you here. Now you're thinking about me differently. I'm not just Dara anymore. Now I'm Dara *MacDonald*."

That was it. When Dara told me her mom owned the hotel I got a little tingly feeling. When I saw the name on the building it happened again, but I still hadn't put it all together. Even I, secluded in my bus in the middle of the mountains, knew about the MacDonald hotel chain. It was the apex of luxury for travelers worldwide.

"Hate to tell you this," I said, "but we can't choose our families. I know you're not really the spoiled, pesky, beggar-girl I first saw down there"—I pointed over the wall at the Riverwalk—"two weeks ago."

She tried to fight off a grin, but failed. "I'm not pesky."

"Have you met you?"

A middle-aged woman with salt-and-pepper hair tied up in a loose-but-tidy bun, black pants, and white blouse came out onto the balcony.

"Miss Dara," she said with a warm smile, "I didn't know you were home. And you have company." If my cut-off jeans shorts and tunic bothered her, she didn't show it. Then again, she was used to Dara with her army-grunge wardrobe and semi-dreads.

"Elena, this is my friend Desiree. She works at Rita's Kitchen. Desiree, Elena is our," she paused and made a face.

"I'm the butler," Elena said with a slight bow.

A female butler? Righteous!

"I don't like that term," Dara said. "A butler is a servant. You're family." She turned to me. "Elena runs this house. My parents count on her for everything. So do I."

I got the feeling that Elena was more of a mother to Dara than Ms. MacDonald was. The closeness between them was obvious. It made me sad that her own mother hadn't been that for her, but happy that she had someone to fill the role.

"I've heard about you," Elena said, taking my hand in both of hers. "It's a pleasure to meet you."

I didn't realize Dara talked about me.

Elena turned back to Dara. "Shall I ask Andres to bring out a tray?"

"That would be nice. Nothing fancy though." She held up her hands and wiggled her fingers. "Finger foods will be great."

"I'll leave you girls to talk," Elena said with a grin that said she was thrilled Dara had a friend over. "Let me know if there's anything you need."

"Thanks, Elena."

"Who's Andres?" I asked, taking a seat at a bar stool next to the glass balcony wall. I'd already adjusted to the feeling that nothing was there to stop us from plunging to our deaths. The Riverwalk was absolutely magical from this view with the twinkling lights in the trees and plants.

"Andres is our cook and housekeeper. He's also Elena's husband." She let out a scoffing laugh. "It's ridiculous. Most of the time they're here by themselves. Elena has plenty to keep her busy, but what is there for Andres to do? It's not like the place gets dirty with just the two of them and I doubt he prepares gourmet meals every night."

"Have you ever asked him?" I loved that the traditional butler and housekeeper roles were reversed.

"No," Dara admitted.

"Maybe you should."

A few minutes later Andres—dressed in black pants, a white chef's coat, and a simple black hat that resembled a skull cap—came out pushing a small cart filled with drinks and snacks. The coat made me think of Mandy again and her dream of becoming a chef. I wished she could see all of this. Especially that kitchen I passed by on the way out here. Maybe she'd work someplace like this someday, preparing gourmet meals for the rich and famous.

"Here you go, Miss Dara." Andres gave her the same warm smile his wife had. He set plates, silverware, and glasses on the table in front of each of us and handed us each a cloth napkin. "How does this look?"

In only twenty minutes, Andres had whipped up little toasts topped with what looked like hummus and bits of red bell peppers, small sandwiches filled with a variety of meats and cheeses, and a plate of fresh berries with a cup of whipped cream at the center that I was going to dunk my finger in as soon as he walked away. To drink there were pitchers of what looked like iced tea and lemonade.

"This looks great," Dara said, eyeing the serving cart happily. "Oh, Andres, this is my friend Desiree."

Andres gave me a little bow. "Elena told me you were here. It is our pleasure to meet you."

Once again, I felt happy and sad at the same time. I knew she missed her parents, any kid would, but if Elena filled in as Dara's mom, Andres was clearly the father figure. Dara's friends may be on the other side of the planet, but she still had people who loved her at home.

"Dara's right," I said. "This looks delicious. Thank you."

"Summon me if there is anything else you require," he said and went back inside. I immediately scanned the serving tray for a Zen stone, then felt like an idiot. Not that kind of summoning.

We ate and talked and stood by the balcony watching people on the Riverwalk below. It was a warm night but the humidity wasn't that bad. Or maybe I was just getting used to it.

Dara's phone rang. She looked at the screen and let out a little squeal as she punched a button.

"Ohmigosh, I'm so glad you called. Hang on one sec." She turned to me. "Friend from school. I haven't talked to her in forever." She jerked a thumb toward the far end of the balcony. "I'm going to go over there and talk to her."

As she walked away she started talking about Wyatt in a true girlfriend way. At ease, partial-speak, like the girl at the other end was filling in the blanks and completing Dara's thoughts. So different from the stiff, new-friend way she talked to me. And she surely didn't need to hide her MacDonald self from the girl on the phone or her other school friends.

Dara, despite her claim of being so bored and lonely, had plenty of people in her life. She had Elena and Andres and whoever that was on the phone. She didn't *need* me like I thought she did. She didn't need to be set on a new path, as I assumed everyone I came across did. She just needed to get back to school and her friends there.

Except for a few minutes here and there talking to charges or Kaf or maybe one of the other Guides, I'd spent the last forty-five years totally alone. Now I had people all around me and even though I'd been sure I'd found my new path, I couldn't remember ever feeling lonelier or more invisible.

I pulled out the phone that Dara had given me. It had exactly three phone numbers saved in it. Hers, Rita's, and the Kitchen's. I knew there was a way to find Mandy's and Crissy's numbers, but I didn't know how.

"I wish I had their numbers."

The phone buzzed. Mandy's phone number was cued up, ready to be dialed. I immediately wanted to summon Kaf and throw my arms around him in gratitude. But he was only acting as my Guide, supplying me with something my wish needed. So I simply whispered, "Thanks."

I pushed send and immediately my spirits soared. But with each unanswered ring, I deflated a little. I was about to hang up when, "Hello?"

"Mandy?" I could barely speak. My throat constricted and my eyes stung.

"Who is—Desiree? Oh my god! Is that you?"

I blinked and tried to pull myself together. "Yeah, it's me."

"I've been so worried about you. Is everything okay? Where are you?"

"I'm in San Antonio."

"Did you find your sister?"

As much as I'd missed Marsha and Glenn and my parents over the years, I'd been missing Mandy, and Crissy, just as much. I hadn't realized that until hearing her voice.

I lay on a lounge chair, stared up at the stars, and told Mandy everything that had happened from the minute I left the Haven right up to Andres bringing me food. The longer we talked, the more whole I started to feel. I never should have left them. I had to go back.

Chapter Twenty-Three

The phone call with Mandy energized me for days. Now that I had their numbers, the three of us texted all the time and Mandy set up group calls so we could talk every night. It was almost as good as being there with them. Almost.

"Every time I see you you're smiling," Rita said Saturday after lunch.

"I got back in touch with some friends," I said.

She grinned. "I can hear you outside on the phone, giggling and chatting up a storm."

"I don't giggle." I'd never been a giggler.

"I'll record you tonight." She put on her sunglasses and took her keys from her bag. "I've got some appointments to take care of. I should be back in a couple of hours. Do you think you can handle dinner prep?"

"Sure," I said. "Burger Fest tonight, right?" Regular burgers, turkey burgers, and even veggie burgers.

"Yep and seasoned fries," she said, already halfway to the door. "I think we have enough sweet potatoes to make sweet potato fries, too. Call me if anything comes up."

About an hour after she left, a woman with two little kids came in. She looked really familiar to me, really familiar, but I had no idea why.

"Sorry," I said, "we're not serving dinner until five."

"Oh, we're not here to eat, darlin'." Her voice sent tingles through me, as familiar to me as her face was. Slow and easy, like the words had all time in the world to get from her mouth to my ears. It was whisper soft, more breath than voice, and came out in the sweetest Southern accent I'd heard in years. She smiled at me like she knew me, too. Probably from the news. "Is Rita Morales here?"

This was really bugging me. I knew this woman. How?

"No, Rita's out right now," I said. "Can I help you with something?"

She held out her hand to me. "My name is Janice Hardy."

And for a second, the world stopped turning.

Janice? My mind went to the picture of me and my girlfriends hanging on the visor in my bus. I tried to connect that face with this woman's and wondered, she couldn't be *my* Janice, could she?

"You're Desiree," she said. "I saw you on the TV. This is going to sound crazy, but you look exactly like one of my very best friends from when I was a kid."

It was her. A dry laugh, as breathless as her voice was full of breath, came out of me. "That's funny. I was just thinking that you look like a friend of mine."

"Oh, honey," she said with a little *pshaw* swat, "I'm old enough to be your grandmother."

I shrugged. If only I could tell her.

"My friend's name was Gloria," she said.

My eyes stung, tears threatening at the mention of my given name. I made my sister believe. I could probably do the same with Janice.

She stared at me for a long, long moment. She knew, but she couldn't admit that. The possibility that a high school classmate looked exactly, *exactly* the same as she had forty-five years earlier was just too much to accept. She shook her head, dismissing the thought.

"Anyway," Janice said, "I saw you on the TV and was inspired by the story of Rita's Kitchen. I'd like to help. My friend, Gloria, she was the most independent girl in our school. She used to tell everyone that women could be anything they wanted and didn't need to let society decide what our futures would be."

My heart swelled with a thousand memories of Janice and school and the excitement of the change we knew we could make. It got so full, I don't know why it didn't burst open.

"You talk like you don't see her anymore." It was cruel, but I needed to know what she thought of my disappearance.

"Gloria died," she said, blinking fast. "She went on a road trip with some of our friends just before our senior year and died in a car crash. If only she could know how much she inspired me."

My breath caught. "Inspired you?"

"Because of Gloria," Janice said, shaking her head as if to shake away her threatening tears, "I decided to do more with my life than be simply a housewife."

The softest imaginable puff of a breeze could've knocked me over. Janice was the most domestic person I'd ever known.

"Oh, I still got married and had babies," she said. She placed her hands on the heads of the two kids with her. "I had three children and these beauties are two of my ten grandchildren."

Grandchildren. If I hadn't gone on that road trip, I could have grandchildren right now.

"Nice to meet you both," I said, smiling down at them. I

looked up at Janice. “What else did you do?”

“Have you heard of Auntie Jan’s Cookies?” she asked.

“Of course. Who hasn't?”

I only came out of the mountain valley, or wherever Gypsy V had been parked, when a wish began or I'd been summoned by a charge. Still, even with those few exposures to the real world, I'd heard about Auntie Jan's. A charge would have one of the distinctive red-and-white checkerboard bags sitting on a counter or a magazine would be open to an ad. Once, to Kaf's express displeasure, I desperately needed to be around people so I wandered around a mall. The glass cases with the checkerboard design that resembled a picnic tablecloth and trays and trays of cookies beckoned me. I conjured a twenty and bought a mixed bag. And a large milk, the only beverage Auntie Jan's provided. It was "a cookie's best friend" the menu board read.

“I’m Auntie Jan,” Janice said and laughed when my mouth dropped open. “When Gloria died I was only seventeen, but that taught me how short life could be. If I died tomorrow, I thought, what would I leave behind? I decided I was a good person, most people liked me and I liked most people. I'd probably be a good mother, but I could hear Gloria's voice in my head. ‘What do you want for you?’”

“So you decided to create a cookie empire?”

Never, not in a million lifetimes, would I have guessed this. I mean, this was *Janice*. The girl used to break out in hives at the mere thought of going against the flow. I'd jokingly suggested she go braless one time and she had to lay down for an hour to recover from the image it had put in her head.

“Eventually,” Janice said of her empire. “I got married right out of high school. Had my first baby a year and a half later. Like all good mommas at the time, I made cookies for the school bake sales. Mine always sold out immediately. I made cookies for our church raffles. Mine always brought in the most money. I started to wonder if I could make money for myself. My husband supported the idea. Especially because there would be cookies in the house all the time. So we gave it a go and…success!"

"Far out," I said, nodding my head.

Janice froze at the phrase. I knew what she was thinking. Same face, same voice. She wasn't willing to accept the truth though. Not sure I could have either if the situation was reversed.

"Anyway," Janice said, her poise off a little now, "I came to offer a donation to Rita's Kitchen."

"Oh, that's great," I said. The donations had picked up again after Dara's public apology, but only a little. "We've gotten so much help from so many people. What donation would you like to give?"

"Cookies and cash," Janice said with an enthusiastic nod of her head. "I'll have three hundred cookies delivered every other Wednesday." She took a checkbook out of her purse. "And this will be an annual donation."

I was already stunned by the offer of that many cookies twice a month. When she handed me a check for fifty-thousand dollars, I couldn't speak.

"I'm having a special wrapper designed," Janice said. "The cookies baked every year on August first will be in packages with inspirational messages about being true to yourself and giving to those in need. If there was anyone who was true to herself, it was Gloria." She blinked rapidly, six or eight times. "Not only is August first the anniversary of this lovely place, but it's also the day Gloria and my other friend Marsha left on that trip with their boyfriends. Neither came back."

My hands were shaking so hard I worried I'd tear the check. I had really made that much of a difference in Janice's life? All I'd done was speak the truth. Well, my version of the truth. I said what I believed and never let anyone convince me I was wrong.

Janice stood there, studying me for a long time. She started to speak a few times but stopped herself. Finally she said, "Gloria would love this place. She always believed it was her duty to help those who couldn't help themselves. I saw the interviews with the people who eat here. Y'all are truly helping them. It's just wonderful." She studied me again and shook her head. "You look so much like her."

"I'm honored." And then I couldn't resist adding, "She sounds like she was one groovy chick."

Janice narrowed her eyes at me once again before turning to her grandchildren. "We should let *Desiree* get back to work. She has a lot of good to do and that means lots of hard work. We'll see you again, I'm sure." She handed me her red and white checkerboard business card. "Give that to Rita, please, so she can get in touch with me if she ever needs anything."

"I will. Thanks, Janice." It took all my willpower to not throw my arms around her and make her believe I was who she was suspecting I might be. Instead I flashed her a peace sign when she stopped at the door to look back at me.

☮☮☮

Later that night Rita and I had dinner outside on her patio and had discussed all of the donations that had come in. Auntie's Jan's Cookies posted the news of their donation on all of their social media sites along with a plea for everyone to help wherever and however possible. Word spread and by the end of the day a local dairy called in with a bi-weekly donation of three hundred pints of milk, one for each of Auntie Jan's cookies.

"I was worried," Rita said, "that the donations would die to a trickle. Auntie Jan really gave us a boost. I just can't believe how much attention we've gotten."

"Not to mention the understanding raised about why our guests come to us." Rita had the feeding people part down.

My goal was to educate.

"Problem is, the more I do, the more I want to do," Rita said. "San Antonio is a big city. There are hungry people in every corner of it. Even if every one of them knew about us, it's not possible for all of them to get to us. And even if they could, this location can't possibly serve that many people."

"So open another location." I joked.

She nodded and popped a new fuel can into the fire bowl. "I lay awake at night thinking that someone's kid is out there, hungry and alone. If only she had somewhere to go for a meal." She meant Soledad, I assumed. "I have a total for the donations we've received so far."

"And?" I asked.

"It's impressive." Her eyes sparkled in the fire light.

"Quit teasing me," I said, settling further into my chair. "How much?"

"Enough that we can hire a chef. I enjoy the cooking but there are other aspects of this business that need my attention. Also, we can open another location."

"Seriously?" I held my hand up for a high-five. "That's great. How will you run two locations though?"

"Well," she said, "you're with us now."

She gave me a look that sent a shiver up my back. But whether a shiver of excitement or unease I wasn't sure.

"Funny," I said, laughing to make light of the topic, "that almost sounds like you want to hire me."

"Ideally we'll have Rita's Kitchens scattered across the metro area," she said, like I hadn't spoken. "Even in the more upscale areas of town, there are people living paycheck to paycheck." She laughed. "Or as one guest told me, 'paycheck to four days before paycheck.' If they have someplace to go now and then, when money is tight, it could make a difference."

"You keep saying we and us," I said. "What do I have to do with this?"

"You're a natural," Rita said. "You understand the

guests. You care about their situation."

"You want me to run the second location?"

"What? Oh, no." She patted my knee. "Sorry, didn't mean to lead you there. It's possible you could one day, but you have a lot more to learn first. Faith is going to run the second location. I do need someone to take over her shifts when she moves over there though."

She yawned big. Even though she wasn't sick anymore, Rita got really tired by the end of the day.

"You should go to bed," I said before she could start talking again. It was groovy that she had this vision and I was happy she could do it. It was also cool that she trusted me to help. But I'd already decided where my path was headed. Straight back to Mandy and Crissy.

"Think about it." She yawned again and stood. "See you in the morning."

I snagged a beer from Rita's refrigerator and as I sat there, staring up at the stars, Janice's words came back to me.

Gloria would love this place. She always believed it was her duty to help those who couldn't help themselves. I saw the interviews with the people who eat here. Y'all are truly helping them.

No, I wasn't fighting for women's rights or using my voice to speak for minorities, but I was helping people. That's what I'd always wanted to do. Well, what Gloria had wanted to do. Did Desiree want the same thing?

Just when I'd made up my mind, my path ran smack into another fork.

Chapter Twenty-Four

The thing about life paths is, they're never straight. Sometimes they bend a little. Sometimes they take a ninety-degree turn. Sometimes they twist all the way back around on themselves.

Dara's path had become a strange place filled with rainbows and trolls. (That was what Marsha had seen during one particularly memorable acid trip. "Don't you see the rainbows?" she'd asked. "They're so bright and beautiful." Two minutes later she'd screamed "Troll!" and hid behind me.) Wyatt had not only kept his promise to come to the Kitchen on the weekends, he came every day. He didn't have a driver's license, but he'd found a friend to drive him.

This completely undid Dara. She was still so love struck she could barely function, but was freaking out at the same time over him being around all the time. Rainbows and trolls.

"What's the problem?" I asked when she nearly hyperventilated after receiving a text saying he was five minutes away. "I thought you liked him."

"I do," Dara said, twirling one of her dreads.

"If you keep doing that it's going to stick that way," I said.

She released the dread and shrugged. "He's just so different."

"What do you mean?"

"From the guys at my school." Like this should be obvious to me.

"How?

"I don't know," she said, avoiding eye-contact with me. "Wyatt's such an ordinary guy. He's nice. Really *nice*."

"So the guys at your school," I said, handing her an empty salt shaker from the tray between us so she could help me fill, "they're not nice?"

She made a face at me. "That's not what I meant."

"I agree, Wyatt is different," I said. "He's not rich like the guys you're used to being around. He doesn't jet off to another country to go to school. He doesn't live in a mansion or a penthouse. He's earthy and…normal."

Actually, if he grew his hair out and went back in time forty-five years, he'd fit in perfectly with my crowd.

"Are you calling me a snob?" Dara asked.

"I was talking about Wyatt and the other guys you know. I didn't say anything about you."

She chewed on her top lip, doing a fine chimpanzee impersonation. "Fine. You want me to say it? I'll say it. I'm not sure my friends would understand me going out with him."

"Why are they a factor?" I asked. "This isn't *West Side Story*."

"What?"

Seriously? Even if she hadn't seen the movie, I figured everyone knew the play. "The Sharks and the Jets? Two people from opposite sides who fall in love with each other?"

She just scowled and shook her head.

I tried a different comparison. "It's not like you're a member of some royal family and you're only allowed to stay within your social circle."

Was that Kaf's problem? Did he look at himself as the king and I was a mere lowly servant? Or was I only seeing what I wanted to see and he didn't actually have any feelings for me?

"I'm not even sure people in actual royal families care about that anymore," I said, more to Kaf than Dara. I knew he was listening. "What's important here? Our feelings or what the other Guides think? You and your stupid rules."

Dara's eyebrows practically touched with confusion. "Who? What are you talking about? What rules?"

"Your friends," I said, ignoring the heat spreading across my face. "Is what your friends think more important or being with a guy who's willing to hunt down a ride every day just so he can see you for an hour?"

Kaf wasn't my boss anymore. As soon as my wish completed he wouldn't be my Guide. We'd be free, finally, to be together. That had to be what had been holding him back all this time.

"Do you like him?" I asked Dara.

She nodded. "I really do."

"Then quit with the rainbows and trolls." I held my hand up before she could ask. "Never mind. You have to head back to Scotland in a few weeks. Just have fun with him. If it turns into more, groovy. If not, you've got a couple of weeks to have a summer romance to tell your friends about."

"Groovy?" she asked.

"What? It's a word."

Almost as if waiting for us to be finished talking about him, Wyatt walked through the front door. Dara squealed and ran over to throw herself in his arms.

"You're in a good mood," he said.

"Did a little soul searching," she said, giving me a wink over his shoulder.

"You can tell me all about it," he said. "I'm staying until after the dinner service today." He jerked a thumb toward the street. "My friend's got stuff to do so he won't be back 'til later."

"It's so sweet that you come all this way just to see me," Dara said, walking with him to the back room so he could check in with Rita and get an apron.

Dara and Wyatt never got farther than three feet from each other that day. He followed her into the back to get more napkins. She followed him around the dining room, wiping off tables. They laughed, a little too loudly at times, took pictures of each other, and watched funny videos on each other's phones.

Honestly, I was a little jealous. It had been so long since I'd been with Glenn, I didn't remember what it felt like to have someone be in love with me.

In the back of the dining room, Leo also noticed Dara and Wyatt. He watched until he couldn't sit still any longer, then he started following them. At one point he even followed them into the kitchen.

"Out," I told him. "You're not allowed back here, remember? Only employees and volunteers."

He shoved his hands in his pockets and shuffled his toes back to the line of the doorway. "It's not fair that he can go in there and I can't."

"Leo," I said and pinched the bridge of my nose. He was exhausting sometimes. "It *is* fair. Wyatt is a volunteer."

He stomped over to his standard seat, dropped into his chair, and glowered at Wyatt whenever he was in the dining room.

The fact that Wyatt stayed all afternoon made it a very long day. If his friend hadn't shown up to take him home when he did, I was going to have to make either him or Leo leave because Leo looked ready to blow. As if things weren't bad enough, Dara went outside with Wyatt and gave him a long, involved goodbye hug and kiss. Right in front of the windows. When she came back inside, half the dining room whistled and cheered for her.

"Is Wyatt your boyfriend?" Leo asked, charging her. He stopped one step over the kitchen line this time.

"Leo," I said, pointing at his feet. "Seriously, dude. Last warning."

"He is my friend," Dara said with a renewed level of sappiness. "And he is a boy."

"Wyatt is her friend," I told Leo and shot Dara a glare that hopefully reminded her to tread carefully.

"Right," Dara said. "He's my friend."

But she had the same look on her face that Marsha had the day Stan finally, after months of waiting, asked her out. Double rainbows with nary a troll to be seen.

At seven-thirty, when dinner was officially over, I called out, "Time's up, gang. We'll see you tomorrow."

While I restocked the hand washing station with soap and paper towels, Dara stood outside and held the door. Leo was the last one to leave.

"Goodnight, Dara."

"Bye, Leo."

"Dara? Am I your friend?"

Dara laughed. "Of course you're my friend, Leo."

Just that fast, Leo grabbed Dara by the shoulders and kissed her. When she tried to push him away, he wrapped his arms around her.

I rushed over and tried to pull him off. "Leo, stop. Let go."

The more she fought, the tighter he held on. He pulled her into him and slid his hands to her butt, like Wyatt had done during their goodbye. Dara turned her face toward me and Leo buried his face in her neck. Also as Wyatt had done.

"Desiree, do something," she begged, her eyes wide.

I tried again, but Leo was too strong. Not knowing what else to do, I tried grabbing him by the ear like my grandmother used to do to my cousins when they got rowdy.

“Leo,” I said pinching and pulling hard. “Let go of Dara right now. You know the rules. No touching.”

I had just wormed my hand between him and Dara and literally hung on his arm when Rita appeared in the doorway.

“What in the hell is going on?” she asked.

My weight on his arm loosened his grip enough that Dara could get free. She stood behind Rita, breathing hard and wiping her mouth, face, and neck where Leo had slobbered on her.

“God, Leo,” Dara said, disgusted and scared, her eyes welling with tears. “Why did you do that?”

“I was saying goodnight.” Leo looked genuinely confused. “That’s what Wyatt did when he said goodnight to you. I saw him. You said I am your friend. Just like Wyatt is.”

I looked at Dara. “I think he set us up.”

“Leo!” Rita snapped and pointed to the curb, indicating Leo should sit.

“Let me talk to him,” I told her.

Rita took a moment to decide. “Deal with him properly this time. If you’d enforced the rules with his outburst the other day maybe this wouldn’t have happened.”

I’d screwed up too many times. I had to get it right this time. “Yes, ma’am.”

Leo was sitting on the curb with his chin on his knees. I crouched down in front of him.

“What is the number one rule we talked about a few days ago?”

“No touching.” Leo stared at the street. “But Wyatt touched her.”

Rita looked questioningly at Dara.

“He gave me a goodbye hug and kiss,” Dara said. “We were out here, not inside. We respected your rules.”

“I was outside too,” Leo said and pointed to where he’d been standing. “Right by the door. Just like Wyatt was.”

I sighed. “You’re right. You were outside. The thing is,

if someone doesn't want you to touch them, it doesn't matter where you are, brother. You have to stop."

"Another rule?" He asked this like a toddler who couldn't believe the number of rules he had to remember.

I nodded. "Another rule. What if you had hurt her?"

"Hurt Dara?" Leo stared at me in total confusion. "I would never hurt Dara. I love Dara. I would never ever, never ever hurt her."

"Not on purpose," Rita said, her arm around Dara's shoulders. "But you don't understand how strong you are, Leo."

"Right," I said. "We know you would never *want* to hurt her, or anyone, on purpose. But you might by accident. That's why we have rules. So an accident doesn't happen. Do you understand?"

"Are you going to make me stay away?" Leo asked as he stared at his hands and played with his fingers.

I felt awful. Why was it so damn hard for me to do this now when it had been so easy to be hard on my charges? I had already discussed the consequences with Leo. He said he understood and then broke the same rule again. Leo's brain may work a little more slowly than others', but he was smart enough to manipulate details to get what he wanted. No matter how hard it was for me, sometimes I had to be the heavy and let people learn lessons the hard way.

"That's what we agreed would happen. We agreed that if you broke another rule, you had to stay away for one whole day."

"But I was outside."

"Leo," I said as firmly as my emotional voice would allow, "you need to go. You can come for breakfast in two days."

Would he get to eat at all tomorrow?

"I'm sorry, Dara," Leo said, pleading.

"It's not okay to kiss someone unless they say it is," Dara said, wiping her neck again. "And friends don't kiss each other like that."

"But Wyatt—"

"Leo," Dara snapped, closed her eyes, and took a breath. "Things are different with Wyatt. He's not my boyfriend right now, but I would like him to be. I'm sorry if that makes you feel bad but it's the truth."

"I'm sorry, Dara," Leo said again, panic in his voice now. "I will not do it again. Don't be mad at me. I love you, Dara."

Dara shook her head and moved even closer to Rita.

"You heard Desiree, Leo," Rita said, backing me up. "Go on now."

He turned and walked away, staring at his feet as he did.

I moved over next to Rita and she put her free arm around me. "You did the right thing, darlin'."

If only I felt as confident about that as she did.

Chapter Twenty-Five

The morning of August tenth, Rita drove us to work, pulled to a stop in front of the building, and handed me the list of donations that had been pledged to Dara and I the day before.

"Will you do the pickup run please?"

Running little errands for her was something I did often, but I hadn't picked up donations yet. She liked the face time with the restaurant managers.

"Sure," I said. "No problem."

We'd done well again. Our regular contributors hadn't let Dara's lie influence them. Although many of them did make comments to her about learning her lesson. And Auntie Jan's offer continued to encourage others to do more. The donations filled every square inch of the van.

I got back to the Kitchen about forty-five minutes before lunch was to start and found Rita, Dara, and the rest of the volunteers huddled in a circle in the reading corner. Rita straightened when she saw me come in.

"All right, everyone back to work," she said and clapped her hands once. To me she asked, "Did you get everything?"

What had they been talking about? The only time we did a team huddle before a meal was if the volunteers were new. The volunteers today were our regular group of devoted folks. Guess whatever they'd been talking about didn't involve me.

"Yep," I said, slipping into business-mode and brushing away the feelings of being left out. "No problems."

She mumbled her thanks but wouldn't meet my eyes. Neither would Dara. They were up to something. In fact, the entire crew was either purposely not looking at me or obviously staring and then turning away. Things got better as the day went on, but the strange vibe hung in the air.

That night on the way home Rita told me, "You can take tomorrow off if you want to."

"Why would I do that? Don't you need my help?" Maybe I'd screwed up too many times with Leo. Not to mention bringing Dara's lies to the Kitchen. Was I was being punished?

"Tomorrow is your birthday. Don't you want to do something fun? I thought maybe you and Dara would—"

But I didn't hear any more. My entire body went numb.

My birthday? Was it really? Was I really going to turn nineteen?

I looked up. Rita was staring at me, waiting for a response.

"Yeah. That sounds good."

I could barely wait for Rita to go to bed. I almost didn't. I almost summoned Kaf with her sitting right there outside my bus. As soon as she went in her house, I darted for the Zen stone.

"Is it true?" I asked the moment he appeared, two feet away from me. I checked the time. It was after midnight. "Is it really my birthday?"

"It is August eleventh," he confirmed. "August eleventh is your birthday."

"You know what I mean. Do I really get to turn nineteen?"

He nodded once, slowly. "You do indeed. That was our agreement. Once you had completed your contract with me, you would be able to move forward with your life."

He had an attitude. Well, Kaf always had an attitude. This one was different. Envy? Was Kaf jealous that I was turning a year older?

"How old are you, Kaf?" I asked. "How many years has it been since you got older?"

"Nearly two hundred. I am twenty-five until my contract is fulfilled."

Two hundred years? "And when is your contract fulfilled?"

His face darkened. "When I find a suitable replacement, I am free to move on with my life."

"Two hundred years is a long time. Are there others like you? Someone who could, I don't know, fill in if you need a sick day?"

"There is no being above me," Kaf said. "My powers come from the universe, bestowed to me by Regina, the person who held the post before me."

"So you have no one to ask questions." Did he have any friends? That made me feel sad for him. "You fly or fall on your own."

He lifted one bulky shoulder. "I do have my compendium to refer to. It contains all of the answers I require."

"And have you found anyone yet? To replace you, I mean." I hoped he had. We would both be free of our contracts and then, maybe, we could…no, I wasn't supposed to be thinking that way anymore.

"I may have found someone," he said.

"That's great," I said with too much enthusiasm. "When

will you know?"

He wouldn't look at me. "Soon, I think."

As he stood before me, I thought back six months to the night Mandy had made her wish. It was her birthday and she had gone to a party. Ethan, the boy of her dreams, was there and all she had wanted was a kiss from him. As I let my gaze travel down Kaf's bare chest and back up to his eyes, I wanted the same thing. A birthday kiss from the man of my dreams. It had been years since I'd been held for a reason other than 'thanks for the wish' gratitude. And even longer since I'd been kissed.

Kaf's sweet-and-spicy, bitter-and-sour scent enveloped me and every nerve in my body twitched with wanting to feel our bodies pressed together. He stared down at me. Neither of us moved as we absorbed each other's auras. The he placed a finger under my chin and tilted my face up towards his.

"I knew it was you."

I spun to find Rita standing on the stairs of my bus.

She was staring at Kaf with an ear-to-ear grin. What had she said? She knew it was him? What did that mean?

"I thought I saw you out here the other night," Rita said, coming all the way in, her attention fully on Kaf. "At first I thought Desiree had a date over and I didn't want to barge in. But my gut started telling me it might be you."

"But it's okay to barge in tonight?" I asked. "What the hell is going on? You two know each—"

And then I understood. I spun on Kaf whose expression was somewhere between seen-a-ghost and caught-stealing-a-cookie.

"It *was* you," I said. "You granted her wish."

"Ah-ha," Rita said, pointing at me. "I had a feeling you knew about the wishes. Why didn't you tell me?"

I sat hard in my chair, my head spinning, and mumbled, "I couldn't take the chance. You would've thought I was crazy if you hadn't received a wish."

Rita nodded and crouched down next to me. “I knew there was something special about you, girlie. So tell me, what’s your wish?”

It took me a second to realize she didn’t know the full truth yet.

“No, that’s not it,” I said. “I didn’t get a wish. Well, I did, but I’ve been working for him,”—I nodded toward Kaf—“for many years.”

“You’re a genie!” Rita said and pointed at me like she’d known it all along.

“She was a Guide,” Kaf said. He hated the term genie even more than I did. “She is no longer in my services.”

“You!” I jumped to my feet. “You’ve known all along that she would understand everything. She wouldn’t think I was crazy. I could have confided in her instead of feeling like such a liar.”

“I prevented nothing,” Kaf said. “Yet another of your self-imposed rules. You have been free to tell your truth to whomever you choose.”

Damn it. I hated it when he was right.

“O-kay,” Rita said while backing toward the door. “You two clearly have a thing to work out. Desiree, honey? You go ahead and take the day off tomorrow like we said. I’ll see you later and we’ll have a good long talk about,”—she looked at Kaf and I and gave me a little wink—“a lot of stuff. Good to see you again, Kaf. Thank you for everything. My wish has come true and then some.”

Kaf placed his palms together and bowed his head to Rita.

“I can’t believe you did this,” I said as soon as she was gone.

“What exactly is it that I have done?” Kaf asked.

“You knew how important it was to me to be able to tell her the truth. I even asked you directly if you’d granted a wish for her. How could you lie to me like that?”

“If I told you nothing, how could it be a lie?”

I spun away from him and he grabbed me gently by the arm to turn me back.

"You made a wish," he said, trailing a finger down my temple to tuck my hair behind my ear. "I have provided all that you require to bring your wish to a satisfying conclusion."

"It's not fair to use my words against me like that," I said, resting my forehead on his chest. I absorbed his warmth, as comforting as a crackling fire on a cold winter night, letting it soothe away every shiver. "Am I almost done?"

"With the wish? I believe you are very close." He turned my face up to his and I saw turmoil there, like he was trying to make a hard decision. "I have an offer for you that may help bring your wish to its conclusion faster."

"What?" I asked immediately, ready to move on to whatever was next.

He turned his back to me as he spoke. "I have always found it ironic that you labeled yourself the Wish Mistress. My own title has always been Wish Master."

All these years and I'd never heard him use a title. I always assumed he was Leader of the Guides or something like that. Wish Master. That was ironic. In a soul mate kind of way.

"As I mentioned," Kaf continued, "my term ends when I find a suitable replacement. I believe that person to be you."

Me? He wanted me to return to the magical world. As the ruler?

In my mind, a new fork appeared next to the other two on my path. As soon as it did, Mandy, Crissy, Rita, Dara, and even Kaf appeared standing at their respective junctions. Which of them would I walk with? Who would I leave behind? And how the hell was I supposed to decide?

"Kaf—"

He held up a hand. "I do not want an answer now. This is not the moment for you to choose. That moment will come soon, however, and you will know when it is here. At that point, I would like you to consider this option along with the others."

He turned back to me and I could see the conflict on his face. In forty-five years I'd never seen him conflicted about anything. Was he doubting that I should be his replacement? If so, why did he even offer it to me? Or was it something else entirely?

He stepped closer until we were barely an inch apart and placed the softest possible kiss on my forehead. "Happy birthday, Desiree."

And he vanished.

☮☮☮

I slept late the next morning. Mostly because I could. For the first time in as long as I could remember, I had nothing to get up for. I didn't have to report for duty, to either a job or a wish. For twenty-four hours I wasn't responsible for anything or to anyone but myself. That should have made me feel as free as a butterfly. Instead, I felt empty and unneeded.

And now Kaf had thrown this flaming curveball at me. Me, no longer a Guide who called herself a Wish Mistress, but *the* Wish Mistress? The ruler supreme who reported to no one. Well, except for the cosmos.

I would definitely be needed again. And I'd be able to do good again. But was returning to the magical world, giving up my life for possibly two hundred years, the way I wanted to achieve those things?

My phone rang. Dara's name showed on the screen. I wiped my eyes—why had I been crying?—and took a deep breath.

"Good morning," I said.

"I was waiting for you to call," Dara said.

"Was I supposed to?" I didn't remember saying I would.

"I thought we'd spend the day together."

"Rita told you to entertain me today, didn't she?"

"What?" Dara asked in obviously feigned shock. "Why? What's today?"

"Very funny."

"Happy birthday," she said with total sincerity. "What would you like to do? Oh, I know. I'll take you shopping. You seriously need some new clothes."

I glanced at the tunics and bell-bottom pants and mini-dresses hanging in the make-shift closet near my bed. Those were the clothes I'd left home with in 1969. It seemed they remained in an ageless state for forty-five years as I had, because now they were looking old and threadbare in spots. Like time had finally caught up with them.

"You know what?" I asked. "I'm going to let you do that. It's been a long time since I've gotten new clothes."

"Cool. I'll take you to lunch after. Get dressed. I'll pick you up in half an hour."

Thirty minutes later, I stepped out of my bus to find the same stretch limo and chauffeur from a few days earlier standing by the back door waiting for us.

"This is Stefano," Dara said. "Stefano is Elena and Andres' son. Stefano, this is my friend Desiree."

"Nice to meet you," I said and held my hand out to him. Instead of shaking it like I'd expected, he held it gently in both of his hands and gave me a little bow. I should have noticed the resemblance. He had the same beautifully bronzed skin as both of his parents and his dad's long, curly eyelashes.

"You still want to go to the mall first, Miss Dara?" he asked, holding my gaze for a few seconds longer than seemed professional. While his parents' 'Miss Dara' came out respectful, Stefano's sounded more teasing.

"Yep," Dara said and got in the back of the limo.

With my hand still in his, he gave me another little bow. "Happy birthday, Miss Desiree."

I smiled stupidly at him. His flirting, mild as it was, flustered me. I nodded and stepped into the car. Dara laughed at me as I got settled.

"He loves doing that to my girlfriends," she said, teasing me, too. "I brought a friend home for winter break last year and he flirted with her so hard she lost the ability to speak around him."

We went to Dara's favorite store at the mall, where she'd called ahead to have a personal shopper waiting for us. The woman, Kimberly, took my measurements and questioned me about my style. Fortunately hippie, which Kimberly referred to as boho, was popular so there were plenty of free-flowing, organic items for me to choose from.

There were three outfits I really liked. Despite my protests, Dara insisted on buying all of them for me. Plus a blue, tunic-style dress that I liked but had no idea where I'd wear it.

"We'll alter these items right away," Kimberly said. "While you're waiting, you are welcome to have lunch at our restaurant."

"They make the best little quiches," Dara said as Kimberly escorted us to a private elevator and used her passkey to deliver us to the rooftop restaurant. "Don't tell Andres, but they're even better than his."

We sat by the windows overlooking the Riverwalk and ate quiches and fresh fruit and drank iced tea. Dara ordered a salmon and artichoke quiche, but I couldn't decide on only one flavor so ordered three: pear and Roquefort cheese, ricotta and asparagus, and a classic quiche Lorraine. When Dara told them it was my birthday, our server brought me a fruit tart with a chocolate cookie crust that was amazing. I wished Mandy could have been there to try it all with me.

"How do I send a picture?" I asked Dara. I'd figured out how to take pictures with my phone, but sending them anywhere was still beyond my ability.

After a quick lesson, I sent a text and a picture of the tart to Mandy and Crissy…at the same time. I felt so techie. *It's my birthday. Look how I'm celebrating.*

Mandy: *Birthday? Really? You're 19?*

Me: *Yeah. How cool is that?*

Mandy: *Far out!!! That tart looks amazing. Might have to replicate. Happy birthday, D.*

Two minutes later came a reply from Crissy: *We should be celebrating with you. Too bad you can't wiggle your nose or blink your eyes or whatever genies do and bring us there.*

Me: *That would make this day perfect.*

I missed them so much it hurt. I couldn't wait to get back to them.

By the time we were done with lunch, my clothes were ready. All of the pants had needed to be shortened as did the shirt sleeves. They even nipped in the waist of the dress so it wasn't quite so tent-like.

"Wear that," Dara said of the dress. "It looks like something you could party in."

"Am I going to be partying?" I was joking, but her lack of response made me wonder where else she planned to take me.

At Dara's order, Stefano drove us to the Alamo next. I'd been there during an elementary school field trip in fifth grade, but that was so long ago the only thing I remembered was that there had been a battle there. After that we spent an hour strolling around a beautiful botanical garden.

"Who knew being on vacation could be so tiring," I told Dara when we got in the limo after the garden. "This has been a blast. Seriously, thanks for everything today."

"You're welcome. Are you ready for dinner?"

I was starving. And grateful for the day of distraction. I'd barely thought of the offer Kaf had made me the night before. He said I'd know when it was time to make my choice. I wanted to forget about it all until that time. But whenever Dara wasn't chattering at me, mostly about Wyatt, it was the first thing that popped into my head.

Instead of going to a restaurant for dinner, Dara took me to her hotel.

"Andres and Elena have a little surprise for you," Dara said. "I told them today was your birthday."

Apparently she'd told every one of the hotel employees, too. As we walked through the lobby, random employees would pop in front of me, hand me a white rose, and say, "Happy birthday, Miss Desiree."

"White roses signify friendship," Dara said. "Thank you for being a good friend. I'd still be out on the Riverwalk begging if it wasn't for you. And you were right, I probably would've ended up in a situation I didn't want to be in."

I couldn't speak. No one had ever done anything like this for me. Well, the surprise birthday cake at the campsite Marsha had arranged came close. As the elevator doors closed, I wrapped one arm around her—the other filled with roses—and pulled her in for a hug.

"You've become like a little sister to me," I told her. "I could never let anything happen to you."

When the elevator came to a stop and the doors opened, I was completely unprepared for what I saw there.

Chapter Twenty-Six

A chorus of people shouted, "Surprise!"

Rita, Faith, all of the volunteers including half of the Boy Scout troop, and many of the Kitchen's regular guests were there, crowded into the entryway. They weren't all there for my birthday, were they? Maybe they'd heard there was going to be a party in the penthouse of the finest hotel on the Riverwalk and couldn't pass it up.

After I'd gotten so many hugs my arms were getting sore, Rita locked me in a hug I wasn't sure I'd ever get out of. When she pulled away, her eyes were shiny and her smile huge.

"Happy birthday, darling girl. I have something for you. Hold out your hand."

I did and she dropped a key into my palm.

"What's this for?" I asked.

"I signed the papers today," Rita said. "I found the perfect building. We can start setting up the new location tomorrow."

"Far out! It's really going to happen. But why are you giving me a key? You said Faith was running the second location."

"Come," she said and took my hand. She led me to the far side of the enormous great room where we sat by the fireplace. She acted excited and nervous at the same time. I'd never once, even for a minute, seen Rita nervous. It sort of freaked me out.

"Rita, what's going on?"

"I wanted to know if you gave any more thought to what we talked about."

"Me taking over for Faith?"

She nodded and before I could say anything, she said, "That key is symbolic of what you could be doing in a few years. We agreed that this isn't something you're ready for right now. If you want to learn though, there is a fine business school in the area that can help you with that. That's my birthday gift to you."

"What is?"

"When Soledad was born," Rita said, blinking hard, "we set up a college fund for her. It's not enough for Harvard or anyplace like that, but it would've put her through a decent local school. I've never touched the account. Never took even a penny from it for the Kitchen because my gut said there would be a purpose for it one day. I want you to use that money. I want you to go to college and get a degree and then you can run the third location."

"No, Rita, it's too—"

"Desiree," she patted my hand that was still in hers and locked eyes with me, "yes."

College? Really? I'd be able to finally get the degree I'd always wanted? In a few years I could be running a soup kitchen. I'd actually be helping people in need like I'd always dreamt of doing. As I stood there, the fork that led to Rita grew wider and longer. It didn't just lead to a job anymore, but college and a career.

The one that led back to Mandy and Crissy glowed bright and shiny though. And the third one leading back to the magic realm was still there, too. Ruler of the magical world. That was no small thing.

"You look shell-shocked," Rita said. "Talk to me. What's bouncing around in your brain?"

After a minute I said, "I thought I knew what I was going to do."

"And what was that?"

I could barely look at her. "I thought I would go back to Minnesota. My friends, Mandy and Crissy, live there and I really, *really* miss them."

Rita nodded and twisted her mouth around in a way that said she wasn't so sure about that plan. But like any good, supportive mom she said, "Tell me about them."

I spent the next half-hour telling her first about Mandy and then Crissy. I even included the wish-related details and a twenty-second recap of my life since Kaf kept me from dying.

"We'll talk more about the wish-granting thing in a bit," Rita said with a grin and a wink. "Mandy and Crissy do sound like good friends. If you go back to them, what will you do when they go off to college next year?"

"I, um," I hadn't thought through the details. "Go with them?"

"I'm not trying to discourage you." Rita put her hands up in surrender. "I'm just saying it sounds like they've got plans for their futures. Yours are kind of up in the air. If you accept my offer and stay here, you could always go visit them or they could come here."

I couldn't argue.

"Take my gift as a loan if that makes you more comfortable," she said. "I look at it as an investment in the Rita's Kitchen Collective. You can pay me back someday."

"This is so generous, Rita." This woman, who I'd only

known for a few weeks, just offered me a college degree and a future.

"About a month ago you showed up in my kitchen," Rita said, her eyes misting again. "No one is more surprised than I am to say that in that time I have come to love you like a daughter. Not only are you a great addition to my work life, you make me feel like I have a family again."

My heart clenched. A future and a family?

We're hippies, Marsha had told me once. Now I heard her voice as clearly as if she was there beside me. *We bend with the wind that blows through our lives.*

Marsha was right. When an opportunity presented itself, we always took it. Go on a road trip? Sure. Go to Woodstock? You bet. Go live on a commune? Well, maybe we shouldn't have done that one.

What I knew was that if I was going to become the independent woman I wanted to be, I had to give myself a fighting chance. Kaf said I'd know when the moment was here. This had to be it.

"Okay," I said.

Rita inhaled. "Okay what?"

"I accept your offer of college and the job of running one of your locations once you decide I'm ready."

She wrapped her arms around me and her body shook with silent sobs. Just that fast, I knew I'd made the right choice. Rita was right, Mandy and Crissy would always be in my life. It would be selfish of me to go and possibly interfere with their plans. We'd have plenty of opportunities to see each other.

As for Kaf's offer? I'd done my time as a genie. It was time for me to move forward. No more going back.

When Rita released me, I gestured at the party going on around us. "You planned all this, didn't you?"

The penthouse looked amazing. They'd done it up in a hippie theme. Anything that could be was tie-dyed—napkins, tablecloths, even the pillows on the sofa and chairs—and there were peace signs and flowers all about. I choked back a sob, missing Glenn, when I realized the music playing in the background was the music from Woodstock.

"Dara and I decided on the theme," Rita said. "Elena and Andres took care of the details."

"They're good at that," Dara said, coming up behind us. "They can throw together a dinner party for fifty with three hours' notice."

Andres had gone all out. Well, as far as I could tell after only one of his meals. The dining table was loaded with hundreds of hors d'oeuvres, a huge beef roast, chicken, shrimp, salads, vegetable and fruit trays, and on and on. Two girls dressed in bell-bottomed hip-huggers, cropped prairie blouses, and skinny hippie headbands circulated around the room with trays filled with a bit of everything. Two other girls passed out drinks.

If that wasn't enough, Andres wheeled out a birthday cake that was an exact replica of Gypsy V.

"You did this?" I asked, my voice thick with emotion.

"I did," he said with a nod.

"How?"

"Rita," Andres said. "She gave me many, many pictures. Quite an interesting paint design you have given your home."

"I've had a lot of time to play with it."

Everyone sang "Happy Birthday" and Andres gave me the first slice of cake. It was chocolate and vanilla marble filled with something creamy and chocolaty called ganache, and fresh raspberries. I took one bite and could've died a happy, happy, happy girl.

"Oh man, Andres." I closed my eyes and savored every flavor. "This is out of sight. Thank you."

"You are very welcome, Miss Desiree." Pleased, he returned to cutting slices for everyone else.

"I have to have another piece," I told Dara once I'd finished every crumb. I gave her a little shoulder bump. "Thank you for all of this."

She waved off my compliment. "You already thanked me."

Andres helped Elena slide away some floor-to-ceiling panels in the window wall and opened the party up to the balcony. The pool had been covered and converted into a dance floor and a DJ played songs from the 60s and 70s.

"Does the birthday girl have a request?" he asked over the speakers.

"'Into the Mystic'," I said. "Oh, and 'Landslide'. I dedicate that one to an old friend of mine named Kaf."

"Nice choice," Rita said and slipped her arm into mine. "We have a lot to talk about, don't we?"

"Probably," I said, swaying to Van Morrison.

Dara and Wyatt dragged me out onto the dance floor before we could say more. Rita raised her glass of punch to me and mouthed, "We'll talk later."

I nodded and danced like I hadn't danced since Woodstock. When a slow, mellow song came on, I stood back and watched Dara and Wyatt, locked in each other's arms. She had fallen for him hard.

"Would you like to dance?"

I looked up, hoping, ridiculously, to see Kaf standing there. Instead it was Stefano. He held his hand out to me like he had at the car earlier that day.

"Aren't you working?" I asked, but he'd changed from his chauffeur uniform into a pair of shorts, a short-sleeved button-down shirt, and sandals.

"I'm off duty," he said.

We danced and talked about nothing important. He wanted to know how I'd liked The Alamo and the botanical gardens. I asked him what he did while we were having fun.

"Studied," he said.

Not the answer I expected. "Studied what?"

"Psychology," he said. "I'm in the graduate program at Trinity. One of the local universities. This chauffeur gig is only helping me get through school."

I laughed. "I was going to study sociology."

"What do you mean you were going to?" he asked. "You must've just graduated from high school. Aren't you planning to go on to college?"

"I am," I said, still hardly believing Rita's gift, "but I'm going to study business instead."

Stefano and I danced and ate cake and talked for hours. It was one of the best nights I'd had in a really, *really* long time. The party wound down around two. The guests had left, even Rita. I was going to get pampered further by staying in Dara's guest suite. I could already feel the warm bubble bath.

Stefano and I stood at the balcony, staring down at the Riverwalk, exchanged phone numbers, and made plans to see each other again in a day or two.

"We could go out for dinner," he said. "Maybe go for a walk along the river?"

I smiled and stood on tiptoe to give him a kiss on the cheek. "I'd like that."

He tilted my face up to his and placed a single, perfect kiss on my lips. "I'll call you."

"I'll answer."

"Dang, girl!" Dara moved in next to me once Stefano had left. "Hittin' on the help."

I couldn't stop the smile on my face. "He's your help. I can hit on him all I want."

"My friend just called," Wyatt said. "He's waiting over there." He pointed to a parking lot on the street level across the Riverwalk from the hotel. "I wanted to say goodnight and happy birthday."

"Thanks," I said. "Looks like you two had fun."

Their fingers seemed permanently intertwined and they gave each other that super-sappy, fresh-love look. Dara wasn't likely to spend any of her school breaks anywhere but here from now on.

"Why is he parked over there?" I asked.

"He said the valet gave him a nasty look when he pulled

up in his rusty pickup," Wyatt said. "So he parked in the lot. If you stand right here I can wave goodbye one last time."

"I won't move from this spot," Dara said and gave him another kiss.

Wyatt hadn't been gone thirty seconds when Dara realized he'd forgotten his hoodie.

"I'm going to run this down to him," she said sending him a text to wait.

"I won't move from this spot," I vowed. "I'll watch the two of you say goodnight one last time."

"Shut up. Be right back."

A few seconds later I saw Wyatt appear on the sidewalk below. The Riverwalk was quiet, the restaurants all closed for the night. There were still a few people down there, but only a few. He looked up and held his hands out in a questioning *where is she* pose.

"Stay right there!" I called. "She's coming down."

She found him immediately. I watched as they walked over the bridge a few yards from the hotel and up the stairway that led to the street. They kissed and Wyatt got in the pickup.

Dara stood there until they pulled away, and then she turned and went back down the stairs. As she emerged at the bottom, a figure came out of the shadows. He, I assumed it was a he because the figure was large, stopped in front of her. She stood there, like she knew him, and talked to him. After a few seconds she started to walk away. He grabbed her by the arms. She tried to push him away. I could hear her voice but not her words. She struggled, trying to get free as he pulled her in closer. She needed help and there was no one around to give it to her.

"Dara!" I screamed, trying to scare the guy away.

I was about to go down to help her when the guy turned and ran.

And Dara collapsed to the ground.

Chapter Twenty-Seven

I had no idea where Elena and Andres were, but I couldn't take time to look for them. I had to get to Dara. As I left the penthouse, I called that Dara was hurt and that they should send an ambulance to the Riverwalk. The elevator took forever, even though it didn't stop on any other floor. I ran through the empty lobby, out the back door, and over the bridge to her. When I got there I found her lying on her back, a pool of blood slowly expanding around her.

I froze and tried to swallow the sob threatening to burst out of me. I dropped to my knees so I could be face-to-face with her.

"Dara? Sweetie, open your eyes."

Slowly, her eyes fluttered open. "Desiree?"

"Hey. Everything's okay," I said. "Elena is calling for an ambulance. The hospital is just a few blocks away. You're going to be fine."

She pointed off to the side. "Leo stabbed me."

Leo? I turned to look where she had pointed. The knife he had shown me that first day we met, the nasty-looking five-inch serrated one, lay on the ground about ten feet away. Rita had placed it on a shelf over the prep table in the kitchen. She said it was perfect for cutting through hard things like chicken bones.

He must have grabbed it the day he followed Dara and Wyatt into the kitchen. He hadn't actually planned this, had he?

"He," Dara started and let out a moan of pain.

"Don't talk." I held my hand to the ugly, jagged wound in her stomach, trying to stop the blood.

"Why?" she asked. "He promised he'd never hurt me."

I raised my head to blink away tears. When I did, I saw the river a few feet away. Except the river became the stream near the commune. Next to it, Marsha lay where someone had left her to die from a heroin overdose. I blinked again, a few tears burst free as I did, and the plants surrounding the river became the garden where Crissy lay, her body broken and bloodied from the beating Brad had given her.

"Desiree," Dara said, her voice getting weaker with every breath.

"Sweetie, don't talk," I said. "Save your strength."

"Desiree, please." She pulled on my arm, wanted to tell me something.

I placed my ear close to her mouth. "Tell me."

"Tell my mom and dad that I love them. Wyatt too."

Oh god. She was dying. Right here in my arms. People thought about what was truly important when they were about to die. The ambulance would never get to her in time.

"Kaf!" I screamed. "I know you're watching. I don't have the stone. Kaf!"

And he appeared.

"Save her," I demanded, my face drenched with tears. "Whatever it takes. You have to save her."

Dara stared at him blankly. If his appearance surprised

her at all, she didn't show it.

"Save her," I repeated, my voice losing its intensity and turning desperate.

"She hasn't made a wish," he said.

"Dara." I turned to her and put my hand on her cheek. "Listen to me. Sweetie, you have to make a wish to live."

She was growing weaker by the second.

I shook her by the shoulders with more force than I'd intended. "Do you want to live? Kaf can make it happen if you do. But you have to wish it. You have to want it more than anything you've ever wanted before."

She stared, blinked, and said, "I want to live."

"You have to wish it." Her eyes closed. I was going to lose her. If I could have killed Kaf at that moment I would have. I glared at him. "Just save her, you selfish bastard."

Dara let out a weak moan.

"Dara, please." My voice was so choked I don't know how she could have understood me. "Say 'I wish to live'."

In a voice that was barely a whisper she said, "I wish to live."

I looked up at Kaf. "You heard her. She said it. Save her."

"I can only make it grantable," he said. "A Guide must make it happen."

"Don't bullshit me right now," I said. "Enough of your damned rules. You saved me. You can save her. Do it!"

He pushed his shoulders back and lifted his chin. "There are conditions."

"Conditions?" Now I was too angry to cry. "If she dies I will *never* forgive you. How's that for a condition?"

As though an electric charge had passed through her, Dara sat straight up and slumped back down to the sidewalk.

"She is alive," Kaf said before I could accuse him of killing her. "She will live. If she agrees."

The reality of what he was saying finally hit me. Like in the gulley the day he 'saved' me, he healed my body so he could explain the conditions. When I first said no, he re-broke every bone in my body, then when I ultimately agreed he healed me again.

"What does she have to agree to?" I asked, dreading the answer.

"She must agree to serve. A fifty year term."

I had never hated anyone as much as I hated Kaf at that moment. He could just save her and be done with it. He didn't need to do it this way. But after four decades, I knew him. I knew he would never back down from these self-defined, petty rules he imposed on people.

"Dara?" I asked.

Her eyes fluttered and she sat up. "What happened?" It all seemed to come back to her then. "Leo." She placed her hands over her stomach. Her shirt was still soaked with her blood, but when she lifted her shirt, there was no wound. Her skin was unmarked.

"This is going to seem impossible to believe," I said and pointed to Kaf. "He has the ability to save you. You made a wish to live and he can make that happen, but you have to agree to some conditions first."

"What do you mean?" She stood up and jumped up and down. "I am alive. I'm fine. I've already been saved."

Kaf flicked his fingers at her and she doubled over. He hadn't reinstated the wound, but he did give her back the pain.

"I can revoke the wish as fast as I have granted it," Kaf said, losing patience. "Explain the terms to her."

"You're serious?" Dara looked confused and angry at the same time. I had felt the same way as I lay broken and dying in that roadside gulley. "Who puts conditions on saving a life?"

"He does," I told her. "You have to agree to work for him for the next fifty years."

"Not me," Kaf said.

I could barely speak. "You cannot be serious. I thought

you said becoming your replacement was an option."

"It is," he said. "You are free to say no."

It felt like all the blood in my body had drained out onto the sidewalk next to Dara's. Just as my fingertips were brushing up against everything I'd wanted, he was ripping it all away from me. Rita wouldn't be my mother. I wouldn't go to college. I'd have to disappear from society again. How could I say no and let Dara die though?

Everything became clear to me.

"You set this all up," I said.

He stood there mute, with his arms crossed over his chest.

"You allowed Rita to win that lottery because you knew what she would do with that money. You put me on her path just as she was about to become successful enough that she would need more help. You allowed Mandy's and Crissy's wishes to come true because you knew that guiding them would force me to this very point. And you couldn't find a girl more like Marsha than Dara. This has all been about forcing me to become your replacement."

"Believe it or not," Kaf said, "I only provided Rita. The universe placed you and Dara together. And I am not forcing you. I am simply providing you with choices."

I did believe him. This was exactly what I'd done to Mandy and Crissy. I presented them with the possibility of exactly what they wanted and then threatened to take it away from them. Guess my karma finally caught up with me.

"For how long?" I asked.

"Until you find a suitable replacement," Kaf said.

I would be the Wish Mistress. That meant I would make the rules. I'd decide which wishes would be granted. I'd decide where I lived and who I saw. I could also decide the rules that governed my Guides' lives.

I turned back to Dara. "What do you want to do?"

"What are my options?" she asked, clearly not feeling any pain right then if the sass in her voice was any indicator.

"You agree to guide wishes and make people's lives better."

"For how long?" Dara asked.

"Fifty years."

"Fifty years?" she said. "I'll be practically dead."

"You can stay fifteen for the entire time." I shot Kaf a look that warned him not to argue that point.

Understanding spread across Dara's face like a sunrise. "That's what happened to you. You really are a hippie. You used to be a—"

"I was a Guide," I told her. "Kaf decided what wishes would come true. My job was to guide people through their wishes because sometimes,"—I paused until I was sure she was listening, this part was important—"things don't always go so well. That's what you would do. Guide people to a successful conclusion."

"Yes or no?" Kaf asked. He flicked his fingers and Dara dropped to the ground. The wound and the flowing blood had returned this time and she truly was moments away from dying.

"You didn't have to do that," I said and knelt down to take her hand.

"She understands the conditions now," Kaf said, crossing his arms over his chest. "She either agrees and lives or does not and dies."

"Can I still see my mom?" she whispered.

"Really?" I asked. A little spot in me warmed at the request.

"We were going to try and fix things," she said. "I want to do that. And I want to see Wyatt."

I groaned a little at that one.

"I love him, Desiree."

"You agree to the conditions?" I asked.

"Fifteen for fifty," she whispered, "if I can still see my parents and Wyatt. If I can't, what does it matter if I die?"

She really was good at getting what she wanted. Had I

known how awful it would be, I would have negotiated for time with my parents, too. If it meant that she would live, I would make sure she could see anyone she wanted.

"She agreed," I told Kaf. "Save her."

"And what about you?" Kaf asked me. The look on his face was an emotional mix of anticipation and pain. "What is your decision?"

The truth I had figured out just before my powers had been taken from me, was that I had been doing exactly what I'd always wanted all along. I'd been helping people by making their deepest wishes come true. Sometimes it took a while to work out the kinks, but every one of my charges ended up with a life that was better than before they'd made the wish. As the one in charge, I would be able to decide which wishes were granted. I'd be able to help even more people. And I'd make the rules.

I stared at Dara, waiting for the moment the magic entered her when I said, "Yes, Kaf, I agree to be your replacement."

For a few seconds, she and I glowed with a warm, golden light. She sat up again. The wound gone, her shirt no longer bloody. She was alive and whole again.

I turned to him, but Kaf had already disappeared.

Chapter Twenty-Eight

I stood in front of Carol's house, my body shaking in anticipation of what I had to tell her. I was always disappointing my sister. Hopefully this time she'd understand.

"Gloria?" Carol came out the front door and her gaze skimmed past me to Gypsy V. "One of my ncighbors just called to let me know a traveling crack house was parked in front of my house. I knew right away it had to be you. I thought we agreed you'd come to dinner on Saturday."

"I need to talk with you," I said. "Something's happened."

The color drained from behind her tan. "I have a tennis game in half an hour."

"It's important."

Her shoulders slumped and she sighed. "Come on in. I'll call and reschedule it."

She didn't question the magic this time but she still had a

hard time believing. That was understandable. Other than looking the same as I had forty-five years ago, I hadn't offered her solid proof. So I manifested a tray of tea and shortbread cookies, and a huge bouquet of her favorite flowers, right in front of her. Then I placed my hand on her shoulder and transported us to the front yard of the house we grew up in and back to hers. She was fully on board.

"You grant wishes," she said. I'd just gotten done telling her about Mandy and Crissy and some of my other recent charges.

"I know, it's a little hard to believe."

"That's what you always wanted, isn't it? To help people in need. I wasn't at all surprised to see that you were working at the soup kitchen."

That was the first time she'd ever acknowledged my ambitions. She'd always been so wrapped up in herself as a kid, I wasn't sure she'd ever known anything about me. Other than that I wore weird clothes.

I nodded. "It's really satisfying."

"I'm sure you're a good…genie," she stumbled on the word.

"I prefer Wish Mistress."

She looked down at her hands. "You're leaving me again."

"No," I insisted and knelt next to her in her flowered chair. "I make the rules now. I won't be here, in San Antonio, but it's like any other job. Better even. We'll be able to see each other anytime we want." I reached into my fringed, brown-suede bag and pulled out a Zen stone. I'd altered the etching on it to be part Zen circle, part peace sign. New leadership, new logo.

"What is this?" she asked.

I couldn't help but smile as I said, "Think of it as a mystical paging device. Anytime you want me, place your thumb on the peace sign and I will come."

She studied the stone, her head bobbing up and down as

she did. "Okay."

"Carol," I said and waited until I had her attention. "I'm not leaving you again. If you need me, if you need anything, summon me."

We talked for another two hours about what our lives had been since 1969 and then she walked me to my bus.

"You live in this thing?" she asked.

"You bet I do. Do you want to see inside?" I can only imagine the look on Ritchie's face, or whomever had my stuff, when it all disappeared before their eyes. Gypsy V was once again my Victorian gypsy wonderland.

Carol approved and then we held each other for a long time before I left. No hug, not one in the last forty-five years, had felt so good.

☮☮☮

"I knew it had to be something like this," Rita said as we settled into the chairs on her back porch. "Elena is frantic. She's called everywhere trying to find Dara and you."

"Dara's giving her and Andres the details right now," I said. I refused to do to her family what Kaf made me do to mine. "If she can't convince them, I'll transport them all to Dara's mother's side in…whatever country she's in. That oughta do it."

We sat quietly, neither of us wanting to talk about the other side of this. The side that meant I would not be staying with Rita. I wouldn't be going to college. I wouldn't be running location three.

Finally, after ten minutes of silence, Rita said, her voice breaking, "You're sure?"

"It's not like I have a choice now," I said, plugging my granny glasses on my face.

"But are you happy with your choice?"

"Me? Everything's fine and groovy in my world. I get to help the masses. It'll be a real gas."

"Why don't I believe you?"

I held my hands palms up. "Don't know. Why don't you believe me?"

"Because you're transforming into a hippie before my eyes."

"What's wrong with hippies?" I asked. "Hippies are cool."

"Desiree—"

"Rita," I sat up and took my glasses off. "I would've loved to work with you. If I have a regret, it's not that I'll be doing a different job."

"What is it then?"

"I regret that I won't get to see you every day. It's been a long time since I've had a mom and I was sort of hoping you'd be that for me."

Rita blinked then slapped her hands on her thighs. "Who says I can't be? You want a mom, you've got a mom. I expect you to call and check in with me. Come to dinner now and then."

I put my glasses on again to hide the tears now standing in my eyes. "You got it."

"I expect you to do good job with this new position of yours."

"Yes, ma'am."

"Be choosey with the wishes you grant. Make sure they'll truly make a difference."

"I will."

"And think twice about whatever this thing is that's going on between you and Kaf."

"What thing?" I asked.

☮☮☮

I transported to the mountaintop and stood before the entrance to Kaf's cave. Regardless of everything that had happened, I was still in love with him. And I couldn't get that look on his face out of my mind. The one he wore while waiting for me to make my decision. The one that told me he was as conflicted over the way things turned out as I was. Maybe it really had been the employer/employee thing all these years. That had to be why he never touched me or indicated that he wanted to be with me. He did though. I knew it.

I crossed the cave's threshold and followed its narrow pathway. It wound between the thick, twisted stalagmites and stalactites of luminescent green and purple and beige. It took me past rock formations that resembled giant mushrooms and through sunbeams streaming from small holes in the cave walls.

My heart rate increased with every step. If I was right, if that was the reason he'd kept us apart all these years, we could finally be together now. He was no longer my employer and he wasn't my Guide. There was nothing stopping us.

But at the very back of the cave, instead of the enormous Japanese man I'd expected would be there, I found a woman. She had long, corkscrew-curly black hair and skin the color of cocoa powder.

"Indira?" She was sitting on Kaf's cloud throne. No one sat on Kaf's cloud.

"Hello, Desiree."

"What are you doing here?" I asked.

"I'm here to help you learn your new job," she said as though this should have been obvious. "You know how to be a Guide, but your responsibilities are far greater now."

"Where's Kaf?" I thought he would teach me. That there'd be an apprenticeship period or something.

Indira gave me a smile that told me I wasn't going to like the answer. "He's gone, Desiree."

"Gone? He's coming back though, right?"

She shook her head, her elaborate gypsy earrings jangling. "I don't know where he is."

This couldn't be right. He wouldn't just leave, not after all this time, without at least a goodbye. Would he?

"He left me in charge of the universe with no guidance?" My laugh held an edge of hysteria. "Did he leave a pamphlet, at least? Where's his compendium? There must be instructions in there. What about all the Guides? There must be things I need to know about them."

"He left me," Indira said, holding her hands out. "I have been the behind-the-scenes second in command, I guess you could say, for a long time."

"Then why am I here?" I couldn't believe he'd left me. Again! "If you're second in command, why aren't you his replacement?"

"That's not what I agreed to," she said. "I don't…didn't work for Kaf. Remember? I serve those who ask for my services."

She was talking about him like he was dead.

"I've been a sort of consultant to Kaf," Indira said. "Everyone needs to bounce ideas around now and then. Even someone who has the power to do pretty much exactly as they choose. You're not alone. I have learned how things work over the years and I'll help you if you would like me to."

The power to do exactly what I chose?

"Well then," I said, pushing my shoulders back, "things are going to change. Gather the Guides. Tell them we're moving to this bitchin' valley I know of in Colorado."

Visit www.shawn-mcguire.com to sign up for my email list and be the first to know when my new releases are published.

I hope you had a good time with Desiree. If you have a moment, it would be far out, groovy, and totally bitchin' if you would help others find my books by leaving a review with the vendor where you purchased this book and/or Goodreads. Telling, texting, Facebooking, Tweeting, Instagramming, or any other way you have of telling your friends about it is cool, too.

I love to hear from readers! You can find mc on the web at Facebook.com/ShawnMcGuireAuthor and Pinterest.com/shawnmcguire1/ where you can see images of how I envision Desiree's world.

Peace, love, and good wishes!
Shawn

Acknowledgements

The deeper I go into The Wish Makers' world, the more I rely on my tribe to make sure I'm doing it right! Thanks to Eva Apelqvist, Sue Berk Koch, Amy Laundrie, and Donna O'Keefe for your critiques that always, always make me a better writer. To Rachael Dahl and Corinne O'Flynn, thank you over and over again for the brainstorming and support. I swear there are times you two seem as invested in Desiree's world as I am.

To Bree Ervin for her stellar editing. Thank you for making this book so much stronger!

Special thanks to Doris Orman and Maria Pease for telling me what to do when I haven't got a clue. I know, that's a big job!

Finally to Paul. You never stop believing in me. I love you, always and forever!

About the Author

Shawn McGuire is the author of young adult, coming-of-age novels that blend contemporary settings with a touch of fantasy and magic. She started writing after seeing the first Star Wars movie (that's episode IV) as a kid: she couldn't wait for the next one so wrote her own episodes. Sadly, those notebooks are long lost, but her desire to write is as strong now as it was then. She grew up in the beautiful Mississippi River town of Winona, Minnesota, the small town that inspired the setting for *Sticks and Stones* and *Break My Bones*. The Milwaukee area of Wisconsin (Go Pack Go!) was her home for many years and now she lives in Colorado with her family where she loves to read, cook and bake, craft, decorate her house, and spend time hiking and camping in the spectacular Rocky Mountains.